EVERY DOG
HAS
HIS DAY

T0284317

GONE
to the
DOGS
Mysteries

BOOK 5

EVERY DOG
HAS
HIS DAY

JANICE THOMPSON

BARBOUR
PUBLISHING

Every Dog Has His Day ©2023 by Janice Thompson

Print ISBN 978-1-63609-587-5
Adobe Digital Edition (.epub) 978-1-63609-588-2

All rights reserved. No part of this publication may be reproduced or transmitted in any form or by any means without written permission of the publisher. Reproduced text may not be used on the World Wide Web.

Scripture quotations are taken from the New Life Version copyright © 1969 and 2003 by Barbour Publishing, Inc., Uhrichsville, Ohio 44683. All rights reserved.

This book is a work of fiction. Names, characters, places, and incidents are either products of the author's imagination or used fictitiously. Any similarity to actual people, organizations, and/or events is purely coincidental.

Cover Illustration by Victor McLindon

Published by Barbour Publishing, Inc., 1810 Barbour Drive, Uhrichsville, Ohio 44683, www.barbourbooks.com

Our mission is to inspire the world with the life-changing message of the Bible.

 Member of the
Evangelical Christian
Publishers Association

Printed in the United States of America.

DEDICATION

To Maddy. Thank you for giving the real Ginger such a spacious place in your heart. You've saved her from her past and given her a beautiful future with a precious owner who adores her.

CHAPTER ONE

Monday, September 11

Y ou have got to be the cutest little thing I've ever seen in my life!" I adjusted the leash on the wriggly red dachshund and did my best to hold her in place so I could clip her nails.

In true doxie style, the little dog wailed as if I were killing her. Dachshunds were nothing if not predictable.

"Silly girl." I had to laugh at the little drama queen. "You've just been saved from a life on the streets, and you're whining about a pedicure? Really? Do you know how many dogs would love to be in your shoes right now?" I gave her an empathetic look. "Okay, okay. . .*paws*. Not shoes."

She settled down as I finished the clip and carried her to the bathing area. Little Miss relaxed against me as I lifted her into the bubbly water, but she rejected the idea of the bath quickly, offering almost as many yelps over the tepid water as she had the nail clippers.

"You're something else." I laughed as her little legs took to paddling in the shallow water. "Maybe I should call you Drama Queen."

"Hey, Isabel, how's she doing?" my coworker said as she popped her head in the door.

I glanced over my shoulder at Marigold and shrugged. "She's a dachshund. How do you think she's doing?"

Mari entered the grooming area and took a few quick steps my way. "She's certainly feeling better now than when we brought her in last night.

She was in rough shape at the time, poor thing. Do you need help holding her down?"

"Maybe. She's small but slippery." I turned my attention back to the dog, who was now crawling up my arm, leaving scratch marks with the newly clipped nails. "Man."

Mari slid into the spot beside me and reclipped the leash to its holder above.

"Where did you say you found her?" I asked as I lathered the pup with my favorite floral-scented dog shampoo.

"In a really expensive neighborhood in Houston called River Oaks." Mari held tightly to the leash while I worked. "Parker and I were in Houston already, at a ministry event, when the call came in from a Houston-area rescue asking for help. This slippery little weasel had evaded them for a couple of days."

"And she's not chipped?" I asked.

"Nope." The pup twisted, and Mari ended up getting wet.

The microchip part struck me as odd. Pedigree pups were usually chipped and well cared for. This poor baby was muddy and a little on the thin side.

"She has bite marks on her." I pointed to a spot just above her tail and another near her neck.

"Yeah, Dr. Kristin examined her last night and pointed those out. No telling how long this poor little girl had to survive on the streets, but it's obvious she took a beating while out there."

That made me love her all the more.

The pooch wriggled once again, causing a splash of water to wash up and cover Mari's scrubs.

"Ugh." My friend took a giant step back.

"Told you she was slippery!" I adjusted my position as I worked the shampoo into a luxurious lather and lightly massaged it into her fur.

Mari swiped her hands on her shirt. "When we first got to the location to look for her, she wanted nothing to do with us. It took several minutes to coax her to us, but food did the trick. She was so emaciated and dehydrated that Kristin ended up giving her fluids. Would you believe she came up to the clinic at ten last night to do that?"

I did believe it and said so. Our vets were remarkable and completely supportive of Mari's rescue pups.

"Between that and the bite marks, she was in really rough shape." Mari turned her attention to the sweet little dog. "Weren't you, girl? But you look better now."

"That's awful. But you're right, she's so thin I can see her ribs. Poor baby. Are you absolutely sure she's not microchipped?"

Mari nodded. "Parker checked right away, and I checked again after we got back to the clinic last night."

"But she's a purebred miniature dachshund," I argued, giving the dog a second look. "It's very rare to find a dog like this running the streets."

Mari shook her head and reached for the leash once again to still the tiny dog. "Not as rare as you might think. She's my third doxie in six months. They're runners. And let's be honest: little dogs can be a handful. Some owners don't come looking for them after the fact."

"That's horrible." I paused to scratch the dog behind her ears, and she calmed completely. "Someone is bound to be missing her."

Mari gave the pup a sympathetic look. "The rescue in Houston was completely swamped, so I offered to take her, but they're posting on their website, social media pages, and even in the local papers. Maybe an owner will turn up."

"I can't believe you're already back to doing ministry events and rescuing dogs this quickly after just getting back from your vacation. How was Hawaii, by the way?"

Her face lit into a lovely smile. "Amazing! It was so great to have the whole family together for a full week. And you know Aunt Trina. She wouldn't let any of us pay our share. She treated us to the whole trip."

I knew her aunt Trina, all right. The legendary country music star was definitely in a position to treat the family to a Hawaiian vacation after her latest hit single. And the one before that and the one before that.

"I'm sure your grandmother was beside herself," I said.

"Grandma Peach came up with a dozen new ideas for dog costumes while we were at the beach." Mari gave me a knowing look. "Think hula and muumuu."

I couldn't help but laugh. "What's next, a roasted pig with an apple in its mouth?"

"Please don't give her any more ideas. She'll whip one up as a Halloween costume for Beau Jangles."

"No doubt." Though Mari's spaniel, Beau Jangles, would look rather cute in a Hawaiian-themed costume this Halloween. He had become something of an office mascot over the past year or so, since the night Mari rescued him from a drainpipe. He and Dr. Tyler's cat, Aggie, were ever present at the clinic, and our clients loved them. No doubt they would adore Beau Jangles in any kind of a costume.

"Grandma also rediscovered a love for pineapple while we were there," Mari explained. "She's planning all sorts of baked goods with pineapple as the key ingredient."

"I'm in. I love pineapple." I rinsed the bubbles off of the dachshund.

Mari smiled. "We had a great time, and I have a lot to tell you, including a really fun story you're going to love. I'll wait till we wind down for the day. Let me know when you're done with this little one's groom. Dr. Kristin wants to run more labs on her to compare against the ones from last night. Before I take her out to the rescue, I want to make sure she's well enough."

"Sure." I gave the pup a closer look. "Hey, did you happen to notice she has a white spot on her left front paw?" I lifted the paw to show off the dime-sized spot. "It's a distinguishing feature. Most solid-colored dachshunds don't have any markings at all."

"Yeah, we saw that. The rescue in Houston is listing that, along with her weight and where she was found. And Cassidy is going to list her on our wall of fame, just in case anyone in Brenham knows who she belongs to."

I smiled as she mentioned our office manager's name. Cassidy was one of the hardest workers I knew, though she had been a little distracted these past few months over her new beau, Jason. I didn't blame her. He was Washington County's hunkiest game warden.

"Maybe someone in River Oaks lost her?" I suggested, doing my best to focus. "Or maybe she was one of those dogs who went home at night but played on the streets during the day?"

"That's a crazy busy neighborhood, though." Mari reached for a towel. "The cross streets are dangerous too. The neighborhood is just outside downtown, and the traffic is nuts over there, especially late in the afternoon, which is when we found this little girl. No responsible owner would let a dog run loose on purpose there. It's kind of shocking to me that she didn't get hit by a car."

"Well then." I rinsed the pup off and reached to scoop her into my arms as Mari slipped the towel around her. I spoke directly to the wriggly little thing: "If your owner deliberately let you run those busy streets, he—or she—doesn't deserve you."

"Agreed." Mari grabbed some paper towels to wipe her hands. "But the rescue posted multiple times about this dog, and no owner came forward, so I'm thinking we'll never see one."

"She won't have any trouble finding a home." I set her on the grooming table and removed the towel. The pup started that crazy shake-off-the-water thing, and before long I was nearly soaked.

"I hope you're right," Mari said. She'd backed away and somehow managed to stay dry. "I'm so preoccupied planning my wedding right now that I don't have as much time to devote to the rescues."

"It's going to be amazing. I can't wait."

"Same." Her smile faded a little bit. "Now, if I can just get Aunt Trina to calm down. Her new album is debuting this week. She's a nervous wreck."

"Why?"

"She wrote a song about my grandmother. She's been pretty hush-hush about it, but she's hoping it's going to take off like that last one did."

"Another one? Wasn't 'Don't Mess with Mama' about your grandma?"

"Yeah. But this one is about falling in love later in life. It's a tribute to Grandma and Reverend Nelson getting married during their golden years. She said it's funny but really sweet."

"I can't wait to hear it."

"Me too. Well, I've got to get back to a patient. Just wanted to check in. Parker was asking for an update."

"Does she have a name?" I called out as my friend slipped through the open door.

"Nope," she called out as the door swung between us. "Call her whatever you like."

I settled on Sasha, the same name my grandma Lita had given her tiny dachshund when I was a child. This little imp was similar in many ways to Grandma's dog, if not a little more dramatic.

It didn't take long for little Sasha to win pieces of my heart. I had fostered for Mari's rescue in the past but didn't currently have any dogs at my place, so I took it upon myself to offer my services, news I shared in front of all my fellow employees as we closed up shop later that evening.

"Isabel, thank you!" Mari's eyes reflected her joy at this news. "She's been through so much already. I could take her out to the rescue with the others, but I think she'll do so much better in a home. Poor little thing just needs some sense of stability in her life, and you're just the one to give it to her."

"As long as she doesn't try to run away." I gave the precious little girl a closer look. "I'm going to need a collar. And a harness, since she's such a wiggle worm."

"I have both in every size and color." Mari returned a few minutes later with an adorable pink collar with a pink-and-white polka-dot bow, which she fastened around Sasha's neck. Then she helped me fasten on the matching pink harness.

"There you are." Mari beamed. "Hey, I just realized you're wearing pink and white too, Izzy. You're a matched set."

"Am I?" I glanced down at my filthy green scrubs.

"Your earrings." She pointed to my ears, and I fingered the earrings, smiling when I realized they were my pink-and-white hearts.

"Oh, you're right."

"It's meant to be." She gave me a knowing look.

I didn't respond to that. Didn't want to encourage her.

"She'd better be a football fan," I said after offering to foster her. "There's a game tonight."

"Oh, that's right." Mari flashed a broad smile. "You're quite the football fan, as I recall."

"Fan isn't a strong enough word." Brianna laughed and then wriggled her index finger in my direction. "You don't want to get in Isabel's way when the Texans are playing."

"What's the deal with you and football, anyway?" Parker asked.

"Yeah, I think you like that sport more than any of us," Dr. Tyler added.

"Hey, don't blame me," I countered. "I get it from my grandmother. She was the biggest football fan of all time. When she and my grandpa first got married, he worked for the Houston Oilers."

"The Houston Oilers?" Cassidy looked perplexed.

"They were Houston's professional football team before the Texans came along. Sold to Memphis in '96 then moved to Nashville after that. You know them as the Titans."

"Honestly?" Cassidy said. "I don't know them. . .at all."

"That must've been before my day." Mari shrugged. "Your grandpa worked for them?"

"Not as a player. He was a water boy. He was on the field for every single game and managed to get passes for Grandma Lita to go to most of them. So, she spent most of her twenties watching the games up close and personal."

"That's so cool," Parker said. "I'm sure she had great memories."

This, of course, led us down a rabbit trail where we spent several minutes online looking at photos of the various games the Oilers had played.

"My grandpa died when I was little bitty," I explained. "I barely remember him, but he was the stuff legends were made of. Grandma Lita talked about him all the time. He developed a love of the game in her and she shared that with me."

"You're the only granddaughter, right?"

"Yeah." I laughed. "That's the crazy thing. She had all these grandsons, but none of them played football. Everyone in the family is crazy about baseball. Don't even get me started on the Astros. Folks in my family live, eat, and breathe the Astros."

"Mine too." Kristin laughed. "My brother Waylon was at Minute Maid Park when they won the World Series."

"Jealous." Tyler sighed.

"Well, I like baseball too," I said. "But when Little Lita was around, we only ever talked about football. She revered the sport. And now that she's gone, I watch most of the games with Carmela."

"Carmela?" Mari's nose wrinkled. "Another name I don't know."

"Grandma's next-door neighbor. They were best friends. She's eighty-seven years old and sharp as a tack. She has a rock-solid memory of every player, and trust me when I say she knows her game. She and Lita used to get into it all the time over who was the better player. They each had their opinions."

"I think it's sweet that you spend so much time with your elderly neighbor, Isabel." Mari gave me a warm smile.

"After that big falling-out with my ex, I needed some stability in my life. Lita had just passed away, then Matt caused all that trouble."

"It's kind of you to refer to your ex by his name," Cassidy said. "I might've given him some other names."

"Right." I paused. No point in going down that rabbit trail. "Anyway, it might sound weird, but I was just drawn to Carmela. She felt like home to me."

I had parents in Houston, of course. Mama was crazy busy with her cooking, and my dad was working to renovate their forty-year-old house.

Cassidy gave me a compassionate look. "I guess we never really spent much time talking about how you landed in Brenham."

That was a story for another day. Right now I needed to get home for the big game. And this little dachshund was coming with me, whether she liked football or not.

CHAPTER TWO

I scooped up the adorable pup and carried her out to my car, then began the drive to my tiny house.

It wasn't really a tiny house in the cool, contemporary sense. It was just. . .a tiny house. Nine hundred square feet of space that had once belonged to my grandma Lita and now belonged to me, her favorite granddaughter.

Okay, her only granddaughter. All my cousins were of the male persuasion, and none of them had been terribly close to her.

But inheriting this precious house was a blessing and the reason behind my move to Brenham a couple of years back.

My parents and cousins—especially Luis, the eldest—were shocked that our abuelita left the house to me, but I wasn't. We were soul sisters until her final breath, Grandma Lita and I.

And now, the tiny house that reminded me of every moment with her was an ever-present reminder of all I used to have and all I had lost. I hadn't changed much of the home's decor. Only the bedding and towels were different. Maybe one day I'd make the place my own, but for now it seemed sacrilegious to change anything.

A few minutes later I pulled into my narrow driveway. After I parked the car in the garage, I reached for my phone, which I'd placed in the car's charger. Only then did I notice I'd missed a call.

From Matt.

Ugh.

I'd been through the wringer over the past couple years. My ex— a phrase I hated to use—had really done a number on me during his drug-and-drinking years. Sure, he was clean and sober now, even doing some sort of inner-city ministry in the Houston area, but I had firmly turned away from any prospects of a renewed relationship with him.

I knew that God could change a person—I'd seen it in my own life over the past couple years—but heading back to Egypt, as my pastor liked to call it, wasn't something that interested me. Not when the Promised Land was in sight.

I decided to listen to the message before going into the house. Might as well get it over with.

"Hey, Izzy. It's Matt."

Just the sound of his voice gave me the shivers.

"I don't blame you for not wanting to talk to me. But I wanted you to know that I'm doing great. I ran into a guy at the outreach the other day—Parker something or other. I think he works with you? Anyway, I just wanted to reach out to say I'm doing better. A lot better. I'm still in the program. I won't quit this time." His voice faded away. "Anyway...that's it. Just thinking about you."

The wildest mixture of emotions ran over me. I'd dumped this guy a couple years ago when his threats and other erratic behaviors became scary. And yes, I'd forgiven him for all that. I was even proud of him for joining a program to get clean and sober. But the sound of his voice—especially so chipper and fun—was almost too much to take. I knew this side of him, the happy, healthy side.

But I also knew the other side...and it scared me to death.

I did my best to push this out of my mind. I climbed out of the car and waved at Carmela, who was watering the azaleas in her front garden next door.

I reached to grab the little pup and my purse. Sasha tried to wriggle out of my arms, but I managed to hang on to her. Carmela turned back to her garden and missed the whole thing. I'd have to fill her in on the dog story later.

I settled in at the house with Sasha, then showered and slipped into clean, comfy clothes. Afterward, my thoughts shifted to tonight's big game. Carmela and I had a routine, and I wouldn't break it for anything. A person would have to be crazy to interrupt Carmela Rodriguez's schedule, especially if there was food involved. The woman could cook. She'd picked up where my grandmother left off, filling my heart and my belly.

But first, I needed to find a crate. I pulled down the stairs leading to the attic, then climbed them to search for it. It was über-hot up there—we struggled through some serious heat waves in September in the Brenham area—but I eventually found the crate and brought it down. I also located a dog bed.

And that's when I noticed a little piddle spot on my carpet and an even ickier surprise in the middle of the bathroom floor.

"Looks like I got the crate just in time."

I tried putting Sasha in it, and she flipped out on me. Turned out, this was one street dog who had a significant problem with being crated. She howled so loudly that Carmela texted to ask if I was okay.

Fostering a dachshund, I wrote back.

To which she responded, Ah.

God bless my sweet elderly neighbor. Carmela rarely complained about the fosters that came and went from my house. Hopefully, this one would settle down quickly.

You still coming over to watch the game tonight?

Did she even have to ask? Had I ever missed a Texans game, even during the preseason? I was particularly keen on tonight's game, as a new player would be playing his first game. I'd seen pictures of the handsome quarterback, Corey Wallis, online.

Carmela must have Corey fever too.

That new quarterback is starting tonight. I don't want to miss a minute. All the women are swooning over Corey Wallis. I might as well join the club.

Me too.

Everyone was buzzing over our new talent. Fresh off the plane from Pittsburgh, Corey had only linked arms with my beloved Texans a week ago. Tonight he would prove himself on the field for the first time.

Or not.

I'll be there, I texted. Can I bring the dog?

Sure thing. See you in half an hour.

I settled onto the sofa and kicked my feet up. Sasha curled up next to me. I decided to shut my eyes for a few minutes and felt myself drifting off.

I wasn't sure when or how it happened, but Sasha managed to chew a hole in my love seat while I was dozing. Or should I say Little Lita's love seat, since the small sofa originally belonged to her. My heart sank to my toes when I saw the spot. I quickly covered it up with a throw. I'd have to deal with it later. Right now I had a football game to watch.

I clipped Sasha to a leash and headed next door to Carmela's with a tin of six-month-old Girl Scout cookies in hand. I knew she would scold me. I also knew the cookies would probably go uneaten, as she had likely stirred up a batch of tres leches cake or her infamous flan. But I still felt the need to offer something.

I went to Carmela's back door, of course. She would fuss at me if I arrived at the front door. A Back Door Guests Are Best plaque hung in her kitchen, just over the back door. And she meant it.

I tapped on Carmela's door, and she answered a couple of minutes later.

"Hey, sweetie!" Her gaze at once traveled to the pup in my arms, who took to wriggling like she wanted to jump in Carmela's direction.

"Oh, this one's precious!" She held out her arms. "Come to Carmela, baby!"

The pup scrambled into her arms, and she ushered us inside. The luscious smell of home-cooked foods greeted me, as always. I set the cookies down on the table, and Carmela moved them to the counter.

"Are you ready for the game?" she asked.

"Am I ever!" I pulled out my Texans cap and plopped it onto my head.

Sasha took that moment to start barking. She went into an absolute panic at my cap, nearly bounding from Carmela's arms, so I removed it and stuck it back in my waistband.

"I think she's scared of it." Carmela laughed. She leaned down and spoke in mock sternness. "Well, you're just gonna have to get over that, little girl. We love our Texans here. If you want to fit in, you have to join the team."

She put Sasha down and got busy in the kitchen working on some queso blanco. Yum.

I knew our routine, of course. We would nibble during the first half of the game and eat dinner in our seats during halftime using TV trays that dated back to the 1980s. This was just how we did things on game night.

We eventually made our way into the living room for the pregame chatter. I took a seat on the sofa, and Sasha curled up next to me.

"Is this okay?" I pointed to the dog.

"Oh, sure. Your abuelita used to bring her little doxie over all the time. I miss those days." Her eyes misted with tears.

I missed my days with Grandma Lita too. But nights like this really helped.

Carmela pulled down a small quilt and tossed it onto her recliner. "I'm so excited about our new quarterback. Have you seen him, honey?"

"I saw pictures in the paper. Pittsburgh trade?"

"Yes. He's got a great story and seems like a wonderful man." Her eyes twinkled.

"Well, I guess we'll see," I countered. I didn't fall for just every quarterback that came along, after all. Grandma Lita had taught me to hold my applause until preseason games were behind us. Anyone who got paid that kind of money needed to earn my praise.

Carmela went into the kitchen and came out with a big bowl, which she'd filled with the queso blanco, my favorite. She returned a few minutes later with a huge bag of tortilla chips.

"Let the games begin!"

And they did. The game got underway, and we had a chance to see Corey Wallis in action. He was a little taller than our favorite quarterback but ran with admirable speed. And he managed to get the fans worked up, so I had to give him points for that.

Speaking of points, the Texans were up by seven when the halftime show began. Carmela and I usually muted the TV to talk and eat dinner during the halftime show—she was a bit put off by all the music and choreography and such—but this time an unexpected phone call distracted me. I reached for my phone from my purse and smiled when I saw Mari's name on the screen.

"Let me get this, Carmela," I said. "Coworker."

"Sure, honey. I made tacos. I'll go get them."

She headed to the kitchen, and I answered the phone with a quick, "Hey there."

"Isabel, are you sitting down?" Mari's voice had an urgent ring to it.

"Um, no." I stared at the TV with its muted halftime show carrying on without me. "I'm at Carmela's watching the game. I don't think I'll be sitting for a while at my place. Sasha just ate the sofa. And by the way, why didn't you tell me you ran into my ex at that outreach the other day?"

Long pause.

"I didn't, actually. He talked to Parker, not me. I didn't want to bring up anything weird, so I decided not to mention it."

"You should have."

"Okay." She paused. "Maybe I should have, but my heart was in the right place. Parker says he's doing well, by the way."

"Yeah. That's good."

"Well, that's not the reason I'm calling. I'm not sure you're going to believe me when I tell you this, but I just got a call from the rescue in Houston and they think they found Sasha's owner."

My heart did that weird flip-flop thing, and I plopped down onto the sofa. "Oh no."

"I thought you would be happy, especially since she ate your sofa."

"It's not a very big hole." The pup jumped into my lap for a cuddle. My heart twisted inside of me as I nuzzled her close. Of all the pups I'd fostered, none had won me over as quickly as this one, torn love seat or not. Piddle spots or not. "But how can this person prove ownership if the dog isn't chipped?" I asked.

"He gave a great description, right down to the white spot on her paw."

"Ugh." Still, that didn't prove anything.

"It's who he is that startled me," she said. "And that's why I asked if you were sitting down."

I eased my way down onto the sofa. "Why? Who does she belong to—the mayor or something?"

"No. Even better than that. Corey Wallis, the new star quarterback of your favorite football team, the Houston Texans!"

CHAPTER THREE

Wait. . .what?" My heart did that weird twisting thing. "The new guy? The Steelers trade?"

"Yep." I could almost hear the laughter in her voice. "You know him?"

"I'm watching him in action right now."

But. . .my little Sasha belonged to Corey Wallis? How was that even possible?

"Girl, I FaceTimed with him just before the game. Let's just say he's every bit as handsome in person as he is on TV. Maybe more so."

"I heard that!" Parker's voice rang out in the distance.

Sweet Parker had nothing to worry about. He and Mari were up to their eyeballs in wedding prep, after all. She wouldn't trade him in for anything—or anyone—in the world.

"You know I would never swap you out for a quarterback, sweetie. I'm not even into football. Now, if we were talking baseball. . ." Mari giggled and her voice faded off. She returned a moment later. "Anyway, we've established that he's handsome."

"And a decent quarterback," I threw in. "A great addition to the team."

"I'll take your word for it. But Corey's also our little runaway's owner. He explained that the movers left the door open and she got out."

"He's been in town a week," I said. "She's been on the loose that long?"

"I guess so. Poor little thing didn't know her way around his new neighborhood. River Oaks is pretty big."

"But that doesn't explain why she's not chipped."

"No idea about that," she said. "But anyway, I'm going to send you a link to a TV station in Houston. There's a recent news story that explains everything. Watch it and then we'll talk. Anyway, I have to go. Parker and I are supposed to be meeting with Reverend Nelson tonight to talk through the ceremony, and I'm distracted by dogs."

"She's always distracted by dogs," Parker's voice rang out.

"Guilty as charged." Mari offered a little sigh. "But I wanted you to know that you won't have her long, Izzy. Corey's coming to the clinic to get her, so bring her back in the morning, okay? We'll pass her off there. And if we're lucky, we'll get an autograph or a picture."

"Okay." Crazy, that I would be meeting the Texans' new quarterback one day after watching him in action on the television.

I turned my attention back to the pup, who had taken to chewing on the edge of Carmela's coffee table leg. The weirdest feelings washed over me as the precocious pup looked my way with those big brown eyes. She was a little doll. A naughty doll, but a doll, nonetheless.

After I ended the call, I took a seat on the sofa just as Carmela walked back in the room with the most beautiful tacos I'd ever seen. Sasha immediately jumped into my arms and curled up in my lap.

"Sure, now you want to cuddle." I patted her with one hand while using the other to manage the phone. I pulled up the video Mari had sent from a Houston-based news network. Seconds later, Corey's handsome face came on the screen.

He stood in the center of NRG Stadium, backdrop for most of the Texans' games. Off in the distance, I saw some of my other favorite players warming up on the field. But Corey's voice held me spellbound as he poured out his heart about this dog.

"My mama passed away five weeks ago, just before I got the offer from the Texans. A couple months before she passed, I gave her a little dachshund puppy as a gift, hoping it would turn my mama's cancer situation around, give her something to look forward to, but. . ." He paused and drew in a deep breath.

"Oh no!" I said. My gaze shot to the dog, who didn't seem at all interested in the video.

"What are you watching over there, honey?" Carmela asked.

I paused the video and explained.

"Whoa." She stared at me, wide-eyed. "This is Corey Wallis' dog?"

"Apparently." But you couldn't tell it by me. The little doll was sound asleep in my lap at the moment.

"And he's coming to the clinic tomorrow?"

"At ten thirty."

"Can I come? I'll think of some excuse why I need to be there. Maybe to buy some dog shampoo?"

I laughed. "That might be too obvious since you don't own a dog."

"I know!" Her eyes lit up. "Bring Sasha to my house before you leave for work. I'll watch her until ten and bring her then. You can call me the dog sitter. I think they'll buy that story."

I wasn't sure how I felt about that, but told her I would think about it.

"Turn that video back on, honey," she said. "I want to hear what else Corey had to say about the dog."

I turned it on, and his face once again lit my phone's screen.

"I bought the dog from a reputable breeder in Pittsburgh a couple months ago," he said. "And gave her to my mom, who was battling breast cancer."

He paused, and I could see the emotion in his eyes.

Carmela must've picked up on it too. "That's so sad about his mama." She put a couple of tacos on a plate, then passed it my way.

Corey continued, "I was just getting settled in my new place in Houston when the movers accidentally left my front door open, and Ginger got out."

The moment he said the word *Ginger*, the pup's ears perked up.

"She's a red dachshund with a white spot on her front paw." He paused and appeared to be battling his emotions. "Mama said that white patch was where an angel kissed her."

"Oh my goodness." Carmela took a serving of tacos and settled into the recliner, plopping the quilt over her knees.

"An angel, eh?" I said as the pup took to chewing the sleeve of my blouse.

"I like this young man already!" Carmela said exuberantly. "He loved his mama!"

"If you have any information about Ginger, please call the 1-800 number on the screen," Corey continued. "There's a reward. A handsome one."

The reward wasn't the only thing handsome consuming my thoughts right now. This guy was broad-shouldered, blond, and had eyes such a delicious shade of blue that I could get lost in them.

If I were so inclined. Ordinarily, I went for the tall, dark, and handsome guys—with rich brown hair and eyes. But I might be willing to rethink my preferences for this guy.

He wrapped up the interview, and the reporter went on to ask viewers to be on the lookout for the little red dachshund.

I released a slow breath as I reached to give the pup a closer look. I felt really bad for the guy, but if this pup wasn't chipped, how could he prove it was the same dog?

That was a question I was thinking about again the following morning at the clinic. I wrapped up bathing an overly energetic Great Dane who had managed to soak me in the process. And I'd forgotten to bring an extra set of scrubs. Ugh. I'd call and ask Carmela to grab some from my place before she brought Sasha up to the clinic.

She arrived at ten, arms loaded with a feisty pup but no scrubs.

"I'm so sorry, honey," Carmela explained, "but I couldn't find the key to your place."

"No worries." Still, I hated to face our new star quarterback looking like something the dog dragged in. Literally.

Carmela followed on my heels as I made my way out to the lobby with Sasha in my arms. I found Mari behind the reception desk, chatting with Brianna, our receptionist.

I quickly introduced Carmela, who blurted out, "Oh my! I totally forgot the flan! It's in the car. You all like flan, right?"

Dr. Tyler came out of his office with Dr. Kristin behind him just as Carmela bounded toward the door.

"Who was that?" Kristin asked.

"My neighbor. She made flan."

Tyler's eyes bugged. "I love flan."

"Me too," Cassidy interjected.

So we all ate flan with Carmela while I tried to figure out what to do about the fact that I wasn't quite ready to give up this adorable little dachshund just yet. Not that I really had a choice, of course. She wasn't my dog.

Such were the woes of fostering.

"You're absolutely sure Sasha belongs to him?" I asked Mari as I snuggled the tiny doxie. She wiggled and licked me on the cheek.

Mari shrugged. "Well, there's the issue of the white spot on the front paw. That's an anomaly for a dachshund who's only one color, to have a little patch like that."

"But not impossible." I began to pace the lobby, holding tight to the tiny dog. "I tell you what...I'm willing to let him come and visit her to see how she does with him. If she's really his dog, Sasha will go right to him."

"You're still calling her Sasha? Did you try calling her Ginger to see what happened?"

The minute she spoke the word *Ginger,* the pup stopped licking my cheek and turned to face Mari.

"Oh my!" Carmela giggled. "Well, she knows her name! That's sure and certain."

"See?" Mari said. "It's a sign."

"Not necessarily." I felt heat rise to my cheeks. "Well, I mean. . ." I released a slow breath. "She's taken right to me, Mari. And you know I've put off adopting a dog all this time, thinking my life was too crazy. But I really love her." The little pooch squirmed in my arms and went on to lick me on the cheek. "See? She loves me too."

"We have to at least let him see her. And we're talking about someone pretty famous here, so we don't want to upset him."

"Very famous," Carmela said. "And he played a great game last night, Isabel. And you heard all that stuff he said about his mama dying. Poor guy is hurting right now."

"True." I chewed my lip.

"He's bringing a team of reporters with him," Tyler said. "I got a call from KBRT in Houston that they have a team on the way."

"Reporters?" I glanced down at my messy attire and groaned. Well, great.

Cassidy, our office manager, nodded. "All the major news stations in Houston are coming and a couple from Austin. We'll have a local reporter here from the paper too. You remember Mollie Kensington, right?"

"Right." I shifted Sasha to my other arm, and she settled down at once. Then I turned my attention to Mari. "Mollie did the big write-up on you when you first started the rescue. She works for the Brenham newspaper."

"Yes. And trust me when I say she's more than a little excited to meet Corey Wallis in person."

"Who wouldn't be?" Carmela giggled. "This is going down as one of the top days in my life, second only to the day I married my Humberto."

I sighed. . .then stared down at my scrubs, covered in dog hair and grimy water. "I didn't pick a very good day to bathe a Great Dane." I pointed to my filthy attire. On the other hand, I probably wouldn't end up on camera anyway. That would be Mari, speaking for the rescue. I breathed a sigh of relief.

"Corey's going to arrive at ten thirty. Just thought you'd want to know. I know what a football nut you are."

She would have to use the word *nut*.

I tried to prepare myself—mentally, anyway—before the building filled with people at ten thirty.

Unfortunately, they arrived just as I wrapped up bathing a filthy Alaskan malamute. My scrubs were covered in mud, soapy water, and dog hair. Not that the reporters seemed to notice or care. They only had one thing on their minds as they crammed their way into our lobby—seeing that adorable little dachshund. I passed off the extra-large malamute to his owner, then went to grab Sasha from the crate in the boarding area. I carried her in my arms to the lobby.

Cassidy, our office manager, was already there, working her magic with the reporters, cameramen, and other folks now crammed into our lobby. I felt a little sorry for our clients, who seemed mesmerized but confused by all the chaos.

I stopped to ask Cassidy about the plan of action, and she shrugged. "I'm just trying to look professional."

"Well, you're doing a great job," I said.

"Hardly. Our parking lot is jammed full of media vehicles, taking spaces away from our clients."

A middle-aged man with thinning red hair walked over to us. I was a little distracted by the splattering of freckles across the bridge of his nose and the oversized glasses that didn't suit his face.

"Ray Haas." The man extended his hand in my direction. "I'm Corey's manager. He'll be here any minute."

"Right." I timidly shook his hand, doing my best not to drop Sasha. Then I pulled back and adjusted the pup in my arms.

"We're here to get Corey's dog back." He reached to pet Sasha, but she snapped at him. "Whoa."

Was this pup reactionary, or did she sense something wrong with this guy?

"I've never been much for dogs," Ray mumbled. "Don't know how you folks do it, to be honest. I'm definitely not an animal person, myself."

I did my best not to take his words personally. He came across as one of those guys who simply didn't see others or give much thought to their opinion.

Cassidy faced him. "What did you say your name was again?"

"Ray Haas."

"Ah." She stuck out her hand. "Cassidy Carter. We spoke on the phone earlier."

"Right. You're the office manager."

A reporter shoved his way to the front of the line. The tall, handsome fellow stationed himself front and center, as if he had every right to be there. Others in the room grumbled but allowed him to take charge.

This guy came across as one who wouldn't take no for an answer. After dealing with my ex, I knew better than to cross this guy. Instead, I took a giant step backward and did my best to avoid him.

"Sorry about the media circus." Ray's words interrupted my train of thought. "It's hard to get used to, especially that guy." He gestured to the reporter who'd taken center stage. "Lance Henderson. Lance the Legend. That's what he calls himself, anyway. Works for one of the bigger news stations in Houston and likes to flaunt it."

"Oh, right." I recognized him now. Lance was a well-known newscaster from the Houston area, one with quite a following. He seemed a little preoccupied, checking his appearance in a small mirror. With a broad fake smile, he checked his teeth. Then he reached into his pocket for a comb to run through his hair. To his right, a cameraman—a kid who looked to be in his mid-twenties—set up his camera.

I couldn't figure out why the cameraman was wearing a mask and cap in this heat. I caught his eye, but he quickly turned the other way. Weird.

At that moment the door swung wide, and Corey Wallis entered the lobby of Lone Star Veterinary Clinic. I heard a collective gasp go up from the female clients in the room. Even the malamute owner seemed duly impressed to have someone of Corey's fame in our midst.

A tiny pocket poodle started yapping, and the woman holding on to her leash accidentally lost control of her. The micro-pup headed straight for Corey. Thank goodness Corey caught the poodle, scooping her into his arms.

"He really is a hero." Carmela's words were laced with admiration.

"Oh no, ma'am." Corey flashed her a broad smile and tipped his cap. "Just a dog lover who happened to be in the right place at the right time."

A dog lover who hadn't bothered to microchip his dachshund. Should I mention that?

No, I was too distracted by his shocking good looks. With the light streaming in through the plate-glass windows, Corey had that glow you often saw on old church paintings—saintly glow, Mama would call it. He loomed tall—maybe six-foot-four"? And those shoulders. Mamma

Mia. Was it just my imagination or did they fill the whole expanse of the doorway as he stood directly in front of me?

The man moved with confident strides, but as his gaze darted my way—*Heavens! Does anyone have eyes that shade of cobalt blue?*—I thought I picked up on a hesitancy in his expression.

"Please pinch me."

Those words came from Carmela, who looked absolutely giddy.

The click of cameras began at once, and I watched as a couple of the reporters pressed their way to the front of the crowd to get a better picture. Looked like I was going to be on the evening news, whether I wanted to or not.

CHAPTER FOUR

Tuesday, September 12

I 'd seen a lot of things at Lone Star Veterinary Clinic, but I'd never seen the national media swarm the place like they did on Tuesday morning when Corey Wallis arrived to be reunited with the dog that might—or might not—be his.

Dr. Tyler, owner of Lone Star Veterinary Clinic, came out of his office to greet him. Our only female veterinarian happened into the room at that very moment. Kristin looked a bit overwhelmed by it all and hovered in the background.

I got it. I hated being front and center, especially in my dirty scrubs. But what could I do about it at this point?

The cameras were pointed my direction, but the real attention wasn't on me—or even the dog in my arms. It was on the tall, handsome, broad-shouldered football player gazing down at the pup.

As the noise level in the room increased, Sasha buried her nose in my armpit and began to tremble. Clearly, she was terrified of all the noise coming with the barrage of questions that suddenly went up from the reporters. My heart went out to her as the whimpering began.

Before Corey could answer any of the questions, his manager stepped up to say a few words.

"I'm Ray Haas. Corey's manager. That's Haas—H double A S."

Cameras clicked.

"I'm sure you can imagine that Corey is very relieved to be getting his dog back. It's been a difficult week, thinking he would never see her again. We're going to take about five minutes for questions, and then Corey and Ginger are going to be reunited."

Carmela leaned in close, eyes bugged. "Am I dreaming this, or is Corey Wallis really standing ten feet away from me?"

She wasn't dreaming and neither was I.

Corey glanced my way with a broad smile on his face as his gaze traveled down to the pup in my arms, the one with her face pressed against me. I didn't blame her. I wanted to hide my face too, especially with the KBRT cameraman angling his camera right toward me. His mask slipped down, and he juggled the camera with one hand while he adjusted it.

Mari shot him an odd look, as if she recognized him. So did Parker, though neither of them said a word to the man. They didn't have time.

The pushy reporter called out to the group from his position at the front of the line, his booming voice commanding the attention of the room. "Lance the Legend, KBRT News at five. Can you give us a little backstory on the dog, Corey? Where did you get her? How long have you had her?"

"Sure." Corey cleared his throat. "I bought her a couple months back just before my mama passed away from cancer. I thought Ginger might be just the ticket to help her heal after her last surgery. Unfortunately, that didn't happen. My mom passed away about a month later."

"So you brought her to Houston with you?" Lance nudged himself in front of the other reporters.

"I did." Corey's eyes scanned the room and landed on mine as I shifted the pup's position in my arms. "And now I'm here to take her back to my place in Houston, where she belongs. The two of us are going to do our best to get over the loss of a woman who—frankly—was the best mother and dog owner in the world."

Well, that certainly twisted my heart.

Corey looked my way and extended his hand as he took steps toward me. "Are you Mari? The one who found Ginger? If so, I want to offer you the reward."

"Oh no." I held tight to the pup, who didn't seem at all interested in him, in spite of his claims of ownership.

"This is Isabel Fuentes, honey," Carmela spoke up from the spot next to me. "She's fostering that sweet little dog of yours. She's a good girl, our Isabel."

"Thank you for taking such good care of my dog," he said. "I'm grateful to you for fostering her."

"You're welcome."

"Tell us what you do for a living, Isabel." Lance's words rang out, startling me. I shifted the dog to a different position in my arms.

"I'm a professional dog groomer here at Lone Star. I've been fostering Sasha for the past day or so."

"Who's Sasha?" Lance asked.

I gestured to the dog in my arms. "Sorry. I've been calling her that in memory of my grandmother's little dachshund who passed away years ago. We didn't know her real name, of course."

And it was a little weird that she seemed to respond just fine to Sasha.

"Thank you so much for taking care of her. I know my mom would be so relieved to know she's been in good hands." I could read the sense of genuine relief in Corey's voice as he continued to gaze directly into my eyes.

I found myself a little lost in those beautiful eyes for a moment.

Until Carmela nudged me.

"We watched the game last night, Corey," she said. "I'm a Texans superfan! Will you sign my coffee mug?" She reached into her bag and came out with a tall Texans mug along with a marker.

"Sure." He grinned and signed her mug.

Cameras began to click madly as he signed and passed the mug back to her and she threw her arms around him.

Well, tried to throw her arms around him. Carmela was only five-foot-one after all, and nearly as round as she was tall. This didn't stop her from trying to embrace the six-foot-four quarterback.

The frightened little dog continued to shove her face into my armpit as if to hide from the chaos. I didn't blame her. The click of cameras, the overlapping of voices. . .it was all a lot to take in.

"Ginger!" Corey's voice rang out above the din. "Come to me, sweet girl!"

Only, she wouldn't even look at him.

I finally eased her around so that the sweet little pooch was face-to-face with the man who claimed to be her owner.

Still, she did not respond to him.

There was no tail wag, no perked ears. . .nothing that indicated this dog belonged to Corey Wallis.

He reached for her and scooped the little dog into his arms. She immediately leapt from his hands back into mine.

Alrighty then.

The cameras kept clicking.

"Like I said, she was my mama's dog," he explained. "We've hardly had any time together, what with the move and all. But she'll get to know me soon. As soon as I get her back home, we'll have some quality time together."

He tried to take her once again, but she wasn't budging from my arms.

"Oh my." These words came from Carmela. "This is problematic, I'd say."

It was problematic, all right. Something about this whole thing just felt. . .off.

Or maybe that was just the icky smell coming from my muddy scrubs.

"Did you bring the paperwork I asked for?" Mari asked as she took several steps in our direction. "Medical records? Adoption papers from the breeder?"

"Well, that's the thing." His brow wrinkled. "All those papers are at my mom's place in Pittsburgh, which we're in the middle of selling right now. I can contact my sister, who is a Realtor in Pittsburgh, to see if she can text photos of what you'll need. Or maybe I can contact the vet up there."

"But you didn't bring any proof of ownership with you?" Fine lines formed on Mari's brow.

"Well, no, but. . ."

"Sasha doesn't really seem to know you, so before we let her go. . ."

The little pup's ears perked up, and she nuzzled against my face. "See how she responds to her name?" I said. "I think Sasha suits her."

"Gotcha, but she's really Ginger. My mom named her, and she would say that name suited her." Corey reached to take her from me once again, but the little dog refused to be handed over. She fought his touch as if she was scared of him.

"Sorry." I shrugged. "Not sure what to make of that, but it doesn't look like she wants to go with you."

Mari cleared her throat. "Without proof that she belongs to you, I don't know how we can let her go," she explained. "If you can get that paperwork to me, it will be helpful, especially lab work from the vet in Pittsburgh. Something to prove her blood type would work. We can compare it with the labs we ran a couple of nights back."

"She came to us in really bad shape," Dr. Kristin interjected from her spot against the wall. "I had to give her fluids. And I definitely did lab work, so we have her blood type to match the records against."

"I'll pay whatever price is needed for all of her vet care," he said. "Thank you for taking such great care of my mom's dog."

Kristin nodded but didn't say anything.

"What's your name, ma'am?" Lance called out.

"Kristin Keller. Veterinarian."

I could tell that Corey was starting to get upset. "All I have are photos of Ginger with my mom from two months ago. They'll prove it's the same dog."

He whipped out his phone and showed off pictures of a tiny red dachshund puppy.

"She was just twelve weeks old when I got her," he explained.

"That's not possible." Kristin took several decisive steps toward us. "If you're saying you bought her two months ago and she was twelve weeks old at the time?"

"That's what I was told." His downcast expression shared his concerns.

"This dog is closer to a year old," Kristin explained. "I examined her teeth to determine that. Either you were lied to by the breeder, or this is a completely different dog."

Which would explain why she didn't seem even remotely interested in going to him.

"But. . ." He shot a frantic look my way. "She's got the same mark on her paw."

"We're not saying she's not your dog," Mari explained. "But obviously we can't let her go until we know for sure. If you can get that paperwork from her vet up in Pittsburgh, we'll get things squared away."

"So. . .I can't take her?" Corey's disappointment was obvious. "I drove all this way and you're not going to let me have my dog back?"

The cameras started going crazy at this point.

"Yeah, well. . .just wait until the lawsuit hits." These words came from his manager. "Then you'll see how serious we are about Houston's new star quarterback not getting his dog back."

"Lawsuit?" Kristin, Tyler, Mari, and I spoke this word in unison.

The cameras began to click in rapid succession, which served to upset the dog even more. She began to tremble in my arms.

Ray Haas' face turned almost as red as his thinning hair. "I don't know how you do things here in the hick town of Brenham, but in the big city we still believe that taking someone else's possessions is called stealing."

"We didn't steal his dog," I countered. "Mari found his dog, Dr. Kristin offered critical medical intervention, I bathed her, and Dr. Tyler—the owner of this fine establishment—allowed all that to happen on his dime because he's a great guy like that."

"Like I said, I'll pay whatever it costs for her medical care." Corey looked back and forth between us. "That's not a problem."

"Don't say anything we can't take back in court, Corey," Ray said. "I'm calling my attorney the minute we get in the car."

The cameras went crazy now, clicking in rapid succession. The videographers all tilted their video cameras in his direction. I'm sure the expression on my face was going to come back to haunt me, but I couldn't help myself. This was all so awful.

"I really don't think that's necessary." Corey looked sad. "Let's not overreact, folks. We'll get this figured out, and I'll get Ginger back. This story will end well."

And for a moment, I felt sure it would.

Until the front door swung open and my gaze shot to a familiar duo—Mari's aunt Trina and her fiancé, Wyatt Chastain.

The news crew must have recognized Trina. She was one of the nation's top country-western singers, after all. Her hit single, "Don't Mess with Mama," was all the rage last year. And now that she'd bought a lovely piece of property in her hometown of Brenham, the local news media couldn't get enough of her.

All the cameras turned in unison as Trina—who seemed pretty oblivious to the chaos going on—rushed our way, left hand extended, and squealed, "We did it, y'all! Did Mari tell you? Wyatt and I got married in Hawaii!"

CHAPTER FIVE

C haos unfolded as the cameras turned all their attention away from Corey and toward Trina and Wyatt.

I had to get over the shock that Trina was married, before I could somehow make sense of the paparazzi-style ambush taking place in front of me. The reporters pressed in around her. I could tell from the look on Trina's face that she wanted to back out the door and disappear. I didn't blame her. That sounded like a good idea, in fact.

Corey moved in my direction, leaned my way, and whispered, "Am I supposed to know these people?"

"Trina Potter, country music star," I offered.

Those compelling blue eyes widened in amazement. "Wait, the one who sings that song about her mama?"

"That's the one."

"Whoa. My mother loved that song."

"Number one on the country charts for weeks. Maybe months."

"So, she's married to that guy?" He pointed at Wyatt as the reporter continued to hound the happy couple with questions.

"Looks like it. Kind of a surprise to me. Don't know why Mari didn't tell me. I'm always the last to hear everything."

"Me too." He sighed. "Wait, who's Mari?"

"The one who found your dog. Er, this dog." I lifted Sasha up, and she sniffed him then stuck her nose back under my armpit. "Marigold runs the rescue. She's Trina's niece. The rescue is actually on Trina's property." I gestured to Mari, who was busy talking to Trina.

"Oh, right. I remember now. Sorry, all the names are confusing to me. Did I mention I'm new in town?"

"Yeah." And what a welcome.

Lance Henderson, in full-out TV reporter mode, switched gears and started interviewing Trina and Wyatt, as if they'd planned this whole thing just for them.

I couldn't get over how shocked Trina looked. And poor Wyatt. He stumbled through some of his answers, his gaze on the cameras and reporters.

And Corey.

Wyatt seemed to recognize Corey Wallis, but that recognition was coupled with what appeared to be confusion over what he'd inadvertently stumbled into here at the Lone Star Veterinary Clinic.

"I feel for that guy," Corey said. "I guess that's what it's like to be married to a superstar."

"I guess. I'll never know." I shifted the dog to my other arm. Tiny as she was, she was getting heavy.

Corey took her, but she jumped straight back into my arms again. The little dog simply didn't want to be with him.

We looked at each other and shrugged.

I decided this was a great time to crate her, to get her away from all the chaos. I slipped into the back room, and Corey followed on my heels.

"Hey, where are you going with her?" he asked.

"Back to our boarding area. You're not supposed to be back here. This is an employees-only area." I pushed through the door to the boarding area then located an empty crate. I placed the little pup inside and closed the door. At once, Sasha started to whimper and scratch her front paws against the wire door.

"You're really going to keep her? I don't get to take Ginger home with me?" Corey looked mortally wounded.

"Mari's the one to make that decision, not me. Just send her the paperwork from the vet in Pittsburgh, and she'll probably connect with you then."

"But. . ." His words faded, and he gazed directly into my eyes.

So. Totally. Unfair. How could I go on questioning anything about a man with eyes as beautiful as this?

He released a lingering sigh as the pup took to whining in dramatic fashion. "I don't think she likes it in that kennel. She was never very good being crated."

"Which is why she managed to run off the day your movers left the door open," I countered. "You probably should've left her in the crate that day when your house was full of strangers. Believe it or not, dogs really do acclimate to being crated."

He stared at me as if not quite believing what I'd just said. Okay, so I'd come on a little strong, but my words were true.

Corey reached into his pocket and came out with his wallet. Was he going to try to bribe me with money? Surely not.

Nope. He handed me a business card. "That's my number. Please call me as soon as I'm able to come and get her. It means a lot to me. She's one of the last living, breathing pieces of my mom I have, and I miss her."

"O-okay."

He offered a little shrug then headed back out to the lobby.

I turned my attention to the pup, who continued whimpering in the cage. "Sorry, girl," I said. "It's crazy out there. We're safer back here."

I headed back to the grooming area and resumed my work on a tangled Lhasa Apso, who seemed more than a little feisty as I fought to clip her.

Several minutes later, Mari appeared beside me. "I don't blame you for escaping."

"Yeah, crazy. All of it." I adjusted the leash and continued taking my concerns out on the plethora of tangles.

"Even crazier right now. Your neighbor has managed to latch on to Corey. She followed him to the parking lot. I think she's telling him her life story."

"Oh dear." Poor Corey. Carmela was quite the talker. My thoughts shifted back to the situation with the dog. "Mari, are we doing the right thing, hanging on to Sasha?"

Worry lines creased my friend's brow. "Until he produces the paperwork, you bet. It's the right thing to do, cameras or no cameras. I can't tell you how many times I've had people claim to own dogs when they really didn't. It's not safe to release them until we know for sure. I've heard horror stories, trust me."

"He seems genuine enough, but Sasha's not having it. She refuses to go to him. That's not a good sign."

"Yep." Mari nodded.

"It's obvious she hasn't bonded with him."

"Exactly." Mari gave me a compassionate look. "He can get me the paperwork from the vet in Pittsburgh, and we'll go from there. You just hang on to her for me in the meantime, okay?"

"Gladly. Oh, and Mari. . ." My words hung in the air between us as she headed out of the back door leading to the hallway. "Why in the world didn't you tell me that Trina and Wyatt got married?"

Her face lit into a smile. "Oh, trust me, I was going to. I was just waiting for them to give me the okay. I didn't want to break the news and have it backfire."

"Um, yeah." I laughed. "Well, I'd say they walked into the biggest backfire in the history of, well, ever."

"No kidding." Mari laughed. "Leave it to Trina to land on the national news without even trying."

"Is she still here?" I asked.

"Nope. She and Wyatt just skedaddled out to Grandma Peach's place. Apparently, they're all headed out to lunch."

"Are the reporters still here?"

"Yep." Mari shrugged. "But Cassidy told them they had to go out to the parking lot. Our clients were starting to get confused."

"And nervous, I'm sure. That's a lot to handle in the lobby of a vet's office."

"It's a lot to handle anywhere." Mari's nose wrinkled. "But I think the reporters are pleased as punch to be in the parking lot, because Carmela's enthusiasm is giving them material to film."

"Lovely."

Mari shrugged and then grew quiet for a moment. "I am really sorry I couldn't tell you about the wedding," she said at last.

"Which took place in Hawaii?"

"On the beach. Kind of a random, impulsive decision on their part. They didn't tell us until we got there, but apparently, they had the whole thing planned out from start to finish."

"Wow."

"Yeah, Trina and Wyatt had every detail mapped out, so there wasn't much for us to do except go along with them."

"I'm sure you were startled." I reached for another set of clippers, hoping to have better luck with the tangles.

"And overjoyed. And a little confused." She smiled. "But in the end, it couldn't have been any better. We loved every second."

"I'm so glad. So, did anything else happen I need to know about?" I stopped fussing with the tangles and decided to go ahead and start bathing the Lhasa Apso. I turned on the water and waited until it got warm before turning it onto the pup, who relaxed right away.

"Well, let's see. . ." Mari seemed to lose herself to her thoughts. "I shared a room with Trina until the night she got married. Then, because of some mix-up with the reservations, I somehow got stuck in the room with Grandma Peach and Reverend Nelson."

"Ew. You roomed with the elderly newlyweds?"

"Yes, but Grandma insisted on sleeping with me and leaving the poor reverend in the bed by himself next to us. It was the most awkward night of my life."

I couldn't help but laugh at that image.

"And don't get me started on how the snoring kept me up all night."

"Reverend Nelson?"

"Grandma Peach! I had no idea she snored like that." Mari paused and her lips curled up in a smile. "Anyway, the wedding was obviously the big story. It was a simple ceremony on the beach with the reverend presiding."

"Sounds great."

"Yeah, and a lot simpler than what Parker and I are planning." She laughed. "I heard a lot about that from Grandma, trust me. She thinks we're going a little over-the-top with our plans, but I love them."

"Girl, I can't wait for your wedding. It's going to be glorious." I really meant that too. Not every bridesmaid looked forward to the upcoming wedding, but I sure did. Mari and Parker deserved the best that life had to offer. I finished soaking the pup and reached for the shampoo.

"Very country. Not at all beachy."

"To each his own," I said. "I wouldn't want to get married on a beach. Too much sand." I lathered up the dog, who seemed to enjoy the process. I was grateful for that.

"Oh, there was sand all right," Mari said. "And an incoming storm that almost shut the whole thing down. But the good reverend managed to get the deed done just before dark clouds rolled in. Then we headed back to the hotel for a luau reception. The whole thing was pretty divine."

"Sounds like it." I used my fingertips to massage the shampoo into the dog's fur and felt some of the tangles releasing.

"All in all, we had a wonderful time, and it was great to get away with the family." Her eyes took on a faraway look. "But I really missed Parker while I was gone. I'm such a sap. I can't be away from him for more than a day or two without feeling lost."

"He missed you too," I said. "None of us have ever seen him looking so. . ." What was the word? "Forlorn. He was like a lost puppy without you, Mari."

She sighed. "We're hopeless."

"Just promise the two of you won't run off and elope between now and your wedding day."

"After all the work we've put into our wedding?" She rested her hand on her heart. "You think I would do that?"

"Well, no. Not when you put it like that. And besides, I'm looking forward to being a bridesmaid."

"I would never take that from you." The edges of her lips tipped up in a smile. "But I'm dying to tell you all about Hawaii. I'll give you the inside scoop about how Trina and Wyatt let us know about their plans on the day we arrived in Maui if you promise not to take the info to the papers."

I laughed. Little chance of that. And honestly? By now the paparazzi probably knew all the details anyway.

"Maybe we could grab dinner after work?" she suggested.

"Sure," I countered. "Triple B's? I'm dying for a burger."

"Perfect. Just don't tell my grandma Peach. She's back on one of her health kicks and would have a conniption if she heard I was eating beef."

"This is Texas. We all eat beef."

"I know, right?" A grin tipped up the edges of her lips. "You okay if I bring Parker along to our dinner?"

"Of course."

"Feel free to bring a date of your own." She gave me a knowing look. "Want me to see if Cameron is free tonight? He loves burgers too."

"Mari!" I clucked my tongue at her. Would she ever stop trying to pair me up with Cameron Saye? Okay, so our part-time vet was easy on the eyes. And yes, he was single. But he wasn't my type. Not even close. Besides, our receptionist had her eye on him. Brianna couldn't think straight when Cameron was in the room.

He was incredibly handsome. I'd give him that. But definitely not my type. My type was. . .

Honestly, I wasn't so sure anymore. For a while I thought Matt Foster was my type. But my ex-boyfriend ended up being more the narcissistic abusive type, and I never planned to move in that direction again.

A shiver ran down my spine as I remembered all he'd put me through less than a year ago.

For whatever reason, my thoughts traveled back to Corey Wallis. Okay, I'd given him more than a passing glance. A girl would have to be blind not to notice a man like that.

I tried to picture myself sitting at dinner with him beside me.

With cameras in my face and lights flashing all around me and reporters tossing out a thousand questions for the two of us to answer.

Nope. I couldn't live that life. I was way too introverted for all that. I was perfectly happy in my tiny house with my tiny life and my not-so-tiny passion for football.

"Have I lost you?" Mari looked my way, concern etched on her brow.

"Oh no. Just thinking."

"Me too. Thinking Tyler's going to kill me for bringing this much trouble to the clinic. He and Kristin have been so good to me, opening up the clinic's doors to so many of my rescue dogs. But after today. . ." She shivered. "He might be giving me the boot."

"Seriously?" I laughed. "Tyler couldn't run this place without you and Parker. You have permanent job security."

"You too," she said. "But you might want to change into some clean scrubs."

"Well, a girl has to look good for the cameras." I laughed. "What are the chances I'd end up on television wearing filthy scrubs?"

"A hundred percent?"

I laughed. "Yep. All I can do is laugh to keep from crying." I glanced toward the lobby. "I guess I should go out there and see if Carmela has proposed to Corey yet."

"I think he was headed out with his manager. Stop fretting over all of that, girl. We'll figure it out. And hopefully all still keep our jobs in the process."

"Yep."

Her eyes sparkled. "We'll talk more at dinner tonight. We're going to have a blast, I promise. We're long overdue."

"Okay. But don't you dare try to fix me up with you-know-who. He's not really my type, you know."

"Tall, blond, and handsome isn't your type?"

My thoughts shot back to Corey Wallis. He was all those things she'd just described, after all.

Stop it, Izzy. I scolded myself for allowing my thoughts to even travel in that direction for a moment.

She giggled. "I won't say another word about Cameron, I promise. But I'm worried about you, Izzy. You've only been on a couple of dates since you broke up with Matt and—"

I put my hand up. "I thought we agreed not to bring up Matt's name?" My ex wasn't exactly high on anyone's list, mine especially.

"Right." She chewed her lip. "I'm not bringing him up. Only, you've been shy on guys ever since all of that happened."

"I'm ready to get back out there," I said. "But it's all in God's hands, not mine. All I can do is pray that He brings the right guy at the right time."

"He did it for me and Parker," she said.

"And He did it for Trina and Wyatt," I added.

"And Tyler and Kristin."

"And Cassidy and Jason." I paused after naming our office manager's new love interest.

Somehow this conversation was just making me depressed. Was I the only single lady in town?

No. Brianna was still blissfully single too. And I would make sure she received an invitation to dinner so that I wouldn't feel like the odd man out.

I followed Mari back out to the lobby. She took off toward the exam rooms, which left me alone with the remaining clients.

I was happy to see the reporters and camera folks were gone. My gaze shot to the reception desk, where I noticed Carmela was hovering. From the looks of things, she was keeping Brianna entertained with her over-the-top reaction to Corey Wallis.

My elderly friend seemed completely giddy over the whole experience and all the more as I approached. She turned my way, all smiles. "I got his autograph, honey. And he promised to come back to Brenham soon. I think I talked him into visiting the Blue Bell factory for a tour. We should go with him. It's the neighborly thing to do, don't you think?"

"Carmela, I really don't think he—"

"You'll have to give the man his dog, honey." Her nose wrinkled. "Sooner or later. Though I do see your side of things. And it might be kind of fun to drag it out if it means he'll have to show up more often. That might be our best strategy. Do you think?"

"Well, it's not really my decision. I—"

"Your friend Mari runs the rescue? She's the one he needs to talk to, not you. He can't blame an innocent bystander like you for any of this. You just happen to be caught in the middle."

"Yes." Yes, I was. And it didn't look like I was getting uncaught anytime soon.

CHAPTER SIX

Carmela eventually left the clinic, taking her flan dish with her, and we somehow got back to work. I was relieved to know we were no longer surrounded by media types, but it also bothered me a little to know that Corey was going back to Houston without his dog.

Our clients had a lot of questions about all that had just transpired. Their comments ran the gamut—everything from "You should keep that dog, honey" to "Do you think you could get Corey's number for me?" One fellow—the owner of a rottweiler with dental issues—claimed that Texas would be better off if that guy went back to Pittsburgh.

Why? What did he have against Corey Wallis?

The whole experience felt rather surreal to me. I was walking around with Corey's number in my pocket. How many girls could say that?

Oh, the star quarterback of the Houston Texans? Sure, I have his number. He gave it to me personally.

Only, I couldn't tell a soul.

Still, I pulled it out of my pocket more than a few times as the day carried on, making sure I didn't lose it. By the time I wrapped up for the day, I'd shoved it into my wallet behind my driver's license.

Just in case I needed it.

After we closed up shop for the day, I took Sasha home. We went for a little walk, I fed her dinner, then I crated her so that I could go to dinner with Mari, Cassidy, Parker, and Brianna. There had been some sort of disagreement about Triple B's. Apparently, Cassidy and Brianna wanted to have dinner at Simply Eat, a farm-to-table restaurant owned by Cassidy's friend Nora. I didn't mind. I could always get my burger fix later.

Turned out Parker wasn't able to join us until later, so it was just the Lone Star Ladies for the first hour or so.

Well, the Lone Star Ladies and Trina, who showed up just as we got seated in the booth. I was tickled to see her but incredibly confused.

"Leaving poor Wyatt so soon?" Cassidy asked.

Trina laughed. "Trust me when I say the man is at home decompressing. That whole paparazzi thing today was a little too much for him. He doesn't do big crowds like that."

"I couldn't do it on a regular basis," I said. "All that publicity and stuff. I just couldn't."

"Yeah, he's more like you in that regard," Trina said. "But I'll be honest... if I'd known what we were going to walk into, I would've planned to come a different day. What are the chances we'd walk in on a press conference?"

"Not exactly a press conference, Trina," Mari said. "Corey just came to get his dog, and the reporters were there to capture the moment."

"From what I gathered, he left without her." Trina gave her a knowing look. "Where's the dog now?"

"Crated at my house," I said. "She's worn out too."

"Don't blame her." Trina shifted gears. She spent the next several minutes sharing the story of their wedding.

"We had it all planned out for weeks," she explained. "We'd set up everything with the hotel in advance."

"Tell a person!" Mari said. "You let me show up with nothing to wear to your wedding."

"We took care of that, didn't we?" Trina smiled.

"She had the most beautiful dress for me to wear," Mari explained. "It was divine, actually. And the perfect fit."

"Why do you think I made such a big deal out of shopping with you for your wedding dress several weeks ago?" Trina said. "I was secretly memorizing sizes, measurements, your design preferences...everything."

"Well, you did an amazing job." Mari gave her an admiring look.

Trina pulled up pictures on her phone, and I gasped as I saw Mari all decked out in the beautiful tea-length dress in a lovely shade of soft teal.

"You look gorgeous, girl," Cassidy said.

"Like a dream," Brianna added.

"That color is divine," I threw in. "Almost the color of the water behind you."

"That was the point," Trina said. "We wanted the whole thing to have a very beachy feel."

"Grandma Peach was thrilled." Mari laughed. "And yes, I'm being sarcastic."

"Apparently, Mama's not a big fan of sand," Trina said. "Who knew?"

We continued oohing and aahing over the pictures of Mari, and she finally had enough. "All eyes on the bride, please," she said.

"No, I love that your friends are noticing you first," Trina said. "I get way too much attention anyway. And your big day is coming up soon, Mari. That's one reason Wyatt and I wanted to go ahead and have our ceremony, so the focus could stay on you once we all got home from our vacation."

The conversation eventually shifted to Mari's upcoming wedding, and before I knew it, I was lost in my thoughts. I must've been in my own head a little too long because Cassidy finally glanced my way, a concerned look on her face. "You okay, Isabel?"

"What?" I snapped out of my daydream. "Oh. Yes. Yes, I am. I'm so excited about the wedding!"

I still couldn't get over the fact that Mari had asked me to be a brides-maid. Then again, she had pretty much asked every female employee to be a bridesmaid, with her aunt Trina as matron of honor.

"I still can't believe you're getting married outdoors," Cassidy said. "What if it rains?"

"Then we'll move inside the barn," Mari explained. "I'm not worried either way." She gestured to her aunt. "I've been dying to get married on Trina's property all along. It's breathtaking out there, especially at sundown. You'll see. We've picked the perfect spot."

"Trust me when I say we've been working on the area, getting it cleared and smooth so everyone can maneuver it safely," Trina said. "Wyatt's been working his tail off out there since we got back from Hawaii."

"And the guests are really sitting on bales of hay?" Brianna quirked a brow. "Because I may or may not have heard a certain person's grandmother grumbling about this decision."

"We'll have a special place for Grandma Peach to sit," Mari explained. "She'll be fine, I promise."

"Okay, okay."

Before long Nora brought our drinks and took our food orders, and then the chatter picked back up again. I sat back in the booth and looked out at the friends God had given me. I adored these ladies, every last one of them. They were as different as could be, but He had somehow bonded all of us together. They'd seen me through the worst season of my life, and I had a feeling we'd all be together for years to come.

If all the upcoming nuptials didn't cause us to drift apart.

Nah, that would never happen. We worked together, after all.

Well, all but Trina. But she seemed to be a colorful thread in our fabric these days, and I sure enjoyed having her around.

Eventually the conversation turned back to her wedding and the details following that big day.

"What are you going to do about your last name?" Cassidy asked.

"I'm Trina Chastain."

"But all your fans know you as Trina Potter," I said.

"Yeah, my manager says I should keep Potter, at least for this upcoming album. I guess we'll decide after that. It's kind of hard to ask people to acclimate."

"You could always ask Wyatt to take your name," Brianna suggested.

"Heavens to Betsy. Never in a million years!" Trina looked duly mortified by this idea.

"So, where are you guys living?" Cassidy asked.

"At Wyatt's place."

"Yes, and are you ready for this piece of news?" Mari's eyes widened. "She's giving us her house, y'all."

"What?" Cassidy, Brianna and I spoke in unison.

"I was shocked."

"Don't be," Trina said. "I'm absolutely sure about this. I'll get a great tax write-off by donating it to the rescue."

"She said I'm not supposed to feel one bit bad about it, but I'm just to accept it as a gift." Mari shook her head. "I'm still processing this news. She just told me today."

"It is a gift, honey," Trina said. "I love that ranch. But I love Wyatt even more."

Trina had passed "smitten" and gone right on into happily-ever-after mode.

"I'm so happy for you, Mari!" Cassidy seemed giddy. "This is the best news ever."

"I was happy with the little guest house, to be honest," Mari said. "I never dreamed I'd own the big house one day."

"If anyone deserves it, you do." Trina slipped an arm around her niece's shoulder and gave her a warm hug. "It's truly a win-win for all of us."

Before long, our food arrived. As we settled in to eat some of the most delicious food imaginable, I found my mind drifting back to my recent call from Matt.

"Tell me more about that inner-city ministry in the city," I said. "What do you guys do there?"

"It's mostly twenty-somethings who live on the street in the Montrose area. We feed them, and then there's always some sort of service. Worship music. Someone shares a testimony. That sort of thing."

"Sounds great," Trina said.

"Yeah, I don't get to go with Parker very often," Mari said. "But I especially love the prayer time at the end. Lots of those kids—I call them kids—go up for prayer. So many of them are lost—and I don't just mean spiritually. They've fallen away from their families, their friends."

"Sad," I countered.

"That's why Parker's late for dinner tonight. He has a meeting with the team about this coming weekend."

"I love that he does that." Trina took a nibble of her salad, a contented look on her face.

"He's been a part of this ministry for the past couple years. He goes down there every month or so to help with outreach. They minister to the homeless community."

"That Parker's a great guy." Trina offered Mari an encouraging smile.

"He sure is." Mari's eyes took on a dreamy look. "I'm blessed to have him."

"And he's blessed to have you too, Mari," I said. "Truly."

A smile lit her face, and she used her fingertips to brush a loose blond hair from her face. "Oh, pshaw."

"You really are from the South." I laughed. "Pshaw?"

"That's Grandma Peach's phrase. She always says pshaw. Guess I picked it up from her. Now, if only I had picked up her affinity for baking."

"Don't look at me," Trina said. "I'm not really much of a baker either."

"My neighbor sure is." I sighed as I thought about that flan she'd made.

"No kidding!" Cassidy dove into an excited conversation about how Carmela's flan was even better than her grandmother's.

Parker came in just as Nora returned to fill our drink glasses. He quickly ordered a sandwich and a soda, then settled into the spot next to Mari.

"How did it go?" Mari asked.

"Good." He shrugged. "We're doing a lot more work with that program I told you about before. The one that. . ." His words drifted off and he looked my way.

"It's okay," I said. "You can say Matt's name."

"The one that Matt is at," Parker said. "They seem to be having a lot of success getting people off of drugs and alcohol, and we're excited to link arms with them." His gaze traveled back to me. "I don't know if Matt told you, but he's graduated from the program now and is a volunteer."

"That's good." And I meant it. I was happy for him.

"Matt is leading worship this weekend," Parker said.

Okay, I had to admit. . .that surprised me. Still, I was ready to change the direction of this conversation. I turned in Trina's direction. "Hey, speaking of songs, Mari told me you've got a new song coming out. Another one dedicated to your mama and Reverend Nelson?"

"Yep." Trina chuckled and set her fork down. "And it's high time I shared the title so you're mentally prepared for it. It's going live in the morning, so brace yourselves."

"Oh?" I took a bite of my salad and leaned back against the seat, curious to know what she meant by that."

"It's called 'The Cat Can Stay.' "

I nearly spit out my lettuce. " 'The Cat Can Stay'?"

"Yeah, it's dedicated to Hector, Mama's ornery cat."

Hector. A name we all knew well. A shiver ran down my spine at the mention of Peach's demon-possessed cat.

"When the good reverend proposed to my mother, he knew it was a package deal," Trina explained. "If he took Mama, he had to also take the cat—for better for worse, for richer for poorer."

"Trust me when I say they're a lot poorer, thanks to Hector," Mari chimed in. "Grandma buys that cat everything. His catio is finer than most of our houses, and don't even get me started on his toys and clothes."

"He's a good man, that Reverend Nelson," I observed.

"Right?" Trina laughed. "Mama struck gold when she found him. But the whole thing gave me the idea for the song. When you marry someone who's been living alone for so long, you're taking on their quirks, their habits, and their—"

"Demon-possessed pets?" I offered.

At this, Parker started choking on his soda. Mari slapped him on the back until he finally got control of himself.

Still, none of us could deny it. Hector. . .well, he was a handful.

CHAPTER SEVEN

I t's true," Mari said. "Hector is a royal pain. Which reminds me. . ." She turned to face Parker. "Are you ready for Beau Jangles and his many quirks?"

"If you're ready for my dog and his many quirks."

"We'll start our marriage with two feisty children, used to ruling the roost." She flashed a playful smile.

He quirked a brow as she mentioned the word *children*. I couldn't help but laugh.

"At least these kids don't require cribs, playpens, and toddler gates," Parker responded.

"Wrong about the toddler gate," Mari countered. "If I leave Beau alone in the house, I always have to use the toddler gate to keep him in my room. There was that one time. . ." She shivered. "Let's just say I came home to an ocean of white after he chewed up an entire roll of toilet paper."

"And I thought Sasha was a handful!" I said.

"She is." Mari gave me a knowing look. "Remember? She ate your sofa?"

"Ate your sofa?" Parker seemed more than a little confused by this comment as he reached for the menu.

"Yeah, but it's not a very big hole," I explained. "I'm prone to exaggeration."

Parker turned his attention to Trina. "For what it's worth, I think it was very brave of you to write that song about Hector." He shifted his gaze to Mari. "And in case I haven't told you, Mari, I'm writing a sequel."

"Oh?" Mari gave him an inquisitive look. "You're writing songs now?"

"Yep." He leaned back in the chair, a quirky smile on his face. "My version is called 'The Pea-Green Sofa Can Stay.' "

She slugged him on the arm. "Really? I thought you loved my sofa. And it's mint green, not pea green."

He quirked a brow. "When you love someone—really love them—their home decor choices are part of the package. But as for the true color, I think we're going to have to agree to disagree on that one."

This led to a lengthy conversation about home decor, a very animated one at times. When the chatter finally calmed, Mari and Parker looked at each other then to us.

"So, we have to ask a favor," she said.

"What's that?" Cassidy asked.

She gestured to her aunt. "Trina and Wyatt have been moving her stuff out of the house over the past few days," Mari explained.

"We've had professional help," Trina was quick to point out. "I'm not exactly the furniture-moving kind of girl."

"But she's left quite a bit in the main house for me to keep," Mari explained. "A lot, in fact."

"I still can't get over the fact that you gave her a house, Trina," Cassidy said. "I think that's the most generous thing I've ever heard of."

"It was the right thing to do," Trina countered. "That place has her name written on it—from the rescue to the layout of the house. One day there will be little mini Maris and Parkers running around, and they'll have all the room they need, inside and out."

Mari's cheeks flushed the prettiest shade of pink as she said all of this. Parker, on the other hand, looked like he wanted to climb under the table.

"Well, I think you're a real blessing." These words came from Brianna. "I don't know what I'd ever do if my parents left me a whole house."

I understood the kind of bond that would cause someone to pass down the family home. After all, my grandmother had left me her house. When you loved someone, you did everything you could to bless them. That's what Lita had done, and that's what Trina was doing now.

"What's the favor, Mari?" I asked.

She set down her drink and reached for her napkin. "I need help moving my stuff from the guest house into the main house."

"I'm going to get the guys to help with the bigger stuff," Parker explained.

"But that leaves all the smaller items and the dishes and decor and stuff." Mari shrugged. "I want to use as much of my own stuff as I can in the main house to make it my own."

"Our own," Parker corrected her.

She grinned. "Right. Though I'm quickly learning that Parker's such an easygoing guy that he doesn't really care what we do or don't possess. You should have seen him when we were filling out our wedding registry."

Parker laughed. "I'm totally cool with the stuff I have at my house right now. Don't need another thing."

"Speaking of your house..." I turned to face him. "What are you doing with your house, Parker?"

"I'm renting it out. Decided it would be a good investment income for us. And I think I'm going to rent it furnished, which will make my move to the ranch much easier."

"Perfect," Trina said. "Having a rental house is a great idea, especially in this current economy. And your house is in great shape."

He smiled. "Thanks. I've already got some interest in it, so I think it will work out."

"So, you both need help moving," Brianna interjected. "Is that what you're saying?"

"Yes. And setting up for the wedding too," Mari said. "It won't take long to move my stuff from the guest house. We'll let the guys handle the big items, like Parker said. But I was thinking it would be a good day to look over the space where we're holding the wedding and show you the plan for the layout of the land for the big day. I'm going to need help with that too."

"So, basically, a workday?" Cassidy asked.

Mari nodded. "If you don't mind. I would be so grateful."

Not only did we not mind, the whole thing sounded like fun. Helping the new bride and groom set up and prep for the wedding as well? Perfect.

We finished our food, conversation rolling along, but my mind kept slipping back to my tiny house.

You seem lost in your thoughts over there, Isabel," Parker said. "You okay?"

I looked up from my near-empty salad bowl. "Yes. I'm actually thinking about my little house. Have you guys ever been there?"

"I have," Mari reminded me. "Remember that time I came to drop off that little foster, the one who chewed up your fence?"

"The Lab mix," I said. "I remember."

"And I've seen it," Brianna said.

Cassidy hadn't and neither had Parker. So, I described the house to them.

"It's tiny. Wood-framed. Built in the 1950s, I think. My grandma Lita left it to me. In so many ways, what Trina is doing for the two of you is bringing back memories—in a good way—of what Grandma Lita did for me."

"I love what you told us about how you bonded over football," Mari said.

"Yes, and she really would've flipped over meeting Corey Wallis, even though he's what she would call green."

"Because he's new?" Mari asked.

I nodded. "Yeah. He's not a tried-and-true Texan—in any sense of the word."

"Yeah, but the fans seem to love him," Parker said.

"Can you blame them?" Mari's lips tipped up in a smile. "I mean, have you taken a good, close look at the guy? What's not to love?"

Parker cleared his throat and grabbed another chip from his plate.

"Anyway, my house is stuffed full of memorabilia that prove what a superfan Grandma Lita was."

"That's so cool." Kristin turned to Cassidy. "Are you a fan too?"

"Me?" Cassidy paused and appeared to be thinking through her answer. "Can I be perfectly honest?"

We all nodded.

"I don't really care for pro football. I mean, why would you pay millions of dollars to a bunch of guys to wear tight clothes and chase each other around a field with only a pigskin as the prize? We'd have more luck at a family BBQ."

Trina laughed so hard she snorted.

When we finally calmed down, Nora brought our checks and we prepped to leave.

Mari glanced at her watch. "Oh, man. I totally forgot. I meant to go by Bubba's before they closed tonight. They're having a sale, and I need to pick up some things."

"Oh?" Bubba's Weed & Feed was a top hangout in Brenham.

"Yep. Mane and Tail shampoo," Mari explained. "Buy three get one free. Want me to pick up a bottle for you?"

"Um, no thanks," I managed.

"You don't know what you're missing, girl," Cassidy added. "These shiny locks of mine haven't been the same since Mari recommended Mane and Tail."

"Same here," Trina said. "I didn't believe Mama when she first told me, but now I don't use anything else."

Mari took on a dramatic flair as she said, "Please welcome our own local country-western sensation, Trina Potter, singing her great new single, 'Mane and Tail.'"

Trina laughed. And then stopped and appeared to be thinking it through. "Not a bad idea, Mari. Want to help me come up with the lyrics?"

I fought the temptation to offer a whinny as they carried on about the benefits of Mane and Tail. Instead, I turned my attention to Brianna. "What about you? Are you hooked on horse shampoo too?"

"Um, no. I get my shampoo at Walmart like every normal person I know."

"Me too," I responded, then turned my attention back to the other ladies, who continued to sing the praises of their shampoo of choice.

We paid our checks and parted ways a few minutes later. As I climbed into my car, my thoughts gravitated back to Parker and Mari's wedding. And to Cassidy and her boyfriend, Jason. And to Trina and Wyatt.

They all had their significant others. And me? Well, I had a dog who would have to be returned to her rightful owner this coming weekend.

An exaggerated sigh followed as I thought this through.

My phone rang, and I reached down to my purse to grab it. My hand started trembling the moment I saw the name come through on my screen.

Matt Foster.

My ex. Again. Should I take the call or ignore it?

I took it. No doubt I would regret that decision later, but if I ignored him, he would just keep calling.

"Hey, Izzy. Thanks for picking up."

"You're welcome." *Should I add, "I didn't feel like it"?* Nah, I'd let it lie there.

"So, I know it's none of my business," Matt said, "but what's the deal with you and that football player?"

My heart rate quickened. Really? He'd called to talk about Corey Wallis? "There's no deal."

"You have his dog or something?"

"We don't know for sure it's his dog."

"Right." Matt paused. "Only, I read a whole article about it in the paper. The city of Houston is rallying. They want their favorite quarterback to get his dog back. Don't you think you should. . ." His words trailed off.

"There's an article in the paper?"

"Yeah. A big one. And something about a lawsuit. I even saw a story on the five o'clock news. You know that reporter, Lance the—"

"Legend. Look, I—I have to let you go, Matt. I'll figure it out."

And when I did, he would be the last to know.

I ended the call and tossed my phone into my purse then scrambled to find my car keys. A few seconds later, the engine roared to life, and I backed out of the parking space. I pointed my car in the direction of my house.

Matt's words stung. And what was up with that lawsuit comment? Was Corey really going to take action if we didn't give the dog back?

Tears flooded my eyes as I thought about having to let Sasha go. What could I do if the whole city of Houston turned on me? Hopefully, I wouldn't have to find out.

CHAPTER EIGHT

Wednesday, September 13

On Wednesday morning, Sasha woke up in a playful mood. I felt relieved, after the chaos of yesterday, to have what felt like a normal day.

We had several dogs boarding with us at the clinic, and Sasha was particularly fond of the big Labrador, Romeo. I let them play together in the clinic's fenced-in backyard area, which we'd specifically created for our pets to enjoy.

In the far corner of the yard, Parker had built a doggy condo of sorts— an elaborate contraption with two levels where the dogs could romp and play. Sasha seemed enamored with that space. I couldn't help but laugh as I watched her running in and out of the door at the front. She was really wound up this morning.

I glanced at my watch and realized my first client would be arriving soon. Time to get to work. I'd just made it inside with Sasha and the other pup when Brianna walked my way.

"How did she do last night?" she asked.

"Great." I put Romeo in his crate then turned my attention to Sasha, who had taken to running in circles around the room. I knelt down to catch her, and after a moment, she leapt into my arms.

I cradled the sweet girl close and ran my fingertips along that sweet little forehead. She melted at my touch.

Brianna gave me a knowing look. "You didn't let her sleep with you, did you?"

I pursed my lips and refused to say. Some questions were better left unanswered. Instead, I put Sasha into a crate next to Romeo's and closed the door.

Brianna sighed. "I thought so. You're going to have a hard time shaking your motherly feelings if you let this go on."

"Motherly feelings?"

"Sure." Brianna gave me a compassionate look. "I've seen the way you are with her, Izzy. You've bonded."

"And in such a short time too." I did my best not to release the lingering sigh that threatened to erupt. I had work to do. I needed to focus on that. And besides, this sweet baby girl was going to go home to Houston—probably today, if Corey turned up with that paperwork proving he was her owner.

I turned back toward the grooming room, giving Brianna one last look before I left. "She loves being outside. If you have a few minutes later, could you. . ."

"You bet." Brianna offered me a warm and compassionate smile.

She understood.

They all did.

I bathed my first dog of the day, a timid little schnauzer named Linden. Just as I got him lathered up, the door swung open and Dr. Tyler walked in. It was rare for my boss to come into the grooming room, so it caught me a little off guard.

"Hey." I flashed a smile but kept working on the dog and did my best not to overreact.

"Hey, Isabel. Do you have a minute?"

I could read the concern in his voice. Was I in trouble?

"Sure." I kept Linden leashed and turned to face Tyler, swiping the back of my hand across my forehead to get a loose hair out of my eyes. "What's up?"

"Our phone's been ringing off the wall. Reporters, mostly."

My heart plummeted. "Oh."

"Yeah, I guess some big story broke on the news last night about that dachshund."

"Sasha."

"Well, they're calling her by another name. Ginger."

"Right." I sighed. "Do you think we should give her back?"

"That's technically up to Mari, and I know she's the one who made the decision, not you. I'll be talking to her next. But I wanted to let you know that the news story called us out by name. The practice, I mean. There's talk of some kind of protest. Apparently, some woman said she was going on a hunger strike until Corey got his dog back."

"Good grief. Let's not let her starve on our account."

"I guess she's some kind of Texans superfan." He groaned. "It's ridiculous, but I guess it was headline material, so the papers and news stations are reporting it."

"I guess."

"I heard it's even gone national."

"Are you serious?" This was troubling.

"Yeah." He nodded. "So, we're looking at a bunch of protesters converging on the clinic at some point today. I just wanted to let you know since you're the one who's taking care of the dog. I'm hoping they don't give you a hard time when you're ready to leave for the day."

"Me either."

"I'm thinking we might sneak you out the back door if they're still here at that time."

"Man." I stopped my work and turned to face him. "Has it really come to that?"

"I guess so." He offered a little shrug. "I don't know any of these people, and I can't assume they'll do the right thing, especially if they're worked up. You're my employee and my concern. So I'll make sure you're safe."

"Thank you." I swallowed hard. "Tyler. . .I'm sorry. I guess we should have just relinquished the dog, but she didn't seem to know him."

"And the dog isn't chipped," Tyler said. "That would've made everything easier. As I said, this is really Mari's decision, not yours and not even mine, though this definitely affects all of us."

"Right. Mari told Corey to provide the paperwork from the vet in Pittsburgh, so maybe he'll do that today."

"Right," he said. "If it doesn't happen quickly, I have a feeling we're all about to be thrust into the middle of the story in an even bigger way. I just wanted you to be mentally prepared. But I also wanted you to know I'm on it. I won't let them hurt you."

"Ugh." It was all I could manage under the circumstances, but that little word conveyed my frustration over the situation.

He headed back to the surgery to take care of a dog with a paw issue, but I couldn't stop thinking about what he'd said.

As much as I'd grown attached to Sasha, I couldn't see upsetting Tyler and Kristin. They had worked too hard to build this practice. It made my heart sick that the current publicity was all bad. Tyler certainly didn't need that. On the other hand, it was good of him to be concerned about my well-being.

After grooming Linden, I went in search of Mari. I found her in the lab, running some blood work.

She glanced my way as I entered the room and said, "I guess you've heard."

"Yeah." I plopped down into the chair next to her. "Now what?"

"Corey hasn't called me with any information from the vet in Pittsburgh, so I don't really know what to do."

"Can you call him?" I suggested.

She shrugged. "I don't have his contact information, but the manager guy—what was his name again?—gave me a card."

"Ray Haas," I countered. "And I have Corey's number."

Mari looked my way, eyes wide. "You do?"

"Yeah, he gave me his card yesterday. Do you want it?"

"Sure."

I handed her the card. "He might be pretty busy at practice or something. So, maybe try Ray again first to see if you can speed up the process. I don't want this to cause any trouble for Tyler. If those protesters show up, we're bound to see the media again."

"Right. And I don't want it to cause any trouble for our rescue," she countered. "Second Chance Ranch is a 501(c)3. We don't need any trouble that could have ripple effects for our charity status. You know?"

I hadn't thought about that.

"If our donors hear some sort of slanted story about us, it's liable to curb their generosity." She turned her focus back to her work at the microscope.

"Gosh, I hope not, Mari."

She seemed to lose herself to her thoughts. "Well, don't fret. I'll call his manager right now, and if I can't get him to respond, I'll reach out to Corey directly. Thanks for his card. I'll give it back when I'm done."

"Okay. I've got to get back to a shih tzu who needs a clip. Please keep me posted."

She promised to do that.

About halfway into the shih tzu's bath, a tap sounded at the door. I turned that way as Brianna pushed her way inside. She immediately closed the door behind her and leaned against it.

"Um, Isabel?" Her wide eyes clued me in to trouble.

"Yeah?"

"I was just outside with Sasha and the other dogs and heard a commotion coming from the parking lot. I looked over the fence, and. . .well. . .you might want to come see this."

"I'd rather not, thanks." I didn't mean to speak those words aloud, but there they were.

Still, from the look on Brianna's face. . .I'd better.

I wrapped the shih tzu in a towel and lifted him into my arms, then followed behind Brianna into the lobby.

Through the large plate-glass window, I saw a dozen or more people carrying large signs and marching in a wide circle that encompassed much of our parking lot.

"What in the world?"

I took a couple of steps toward the window and gave the crowd a closer look. Which was exactly the moment I noticed the television crew filming us. My gaze traveled to one of the signs a woman was carrying that read "Let the Dog Go!"

Another one read "Give Corey's dog back!"

At that very moment, the cameraman must've realized who I was. The camera turned toward me.

The little shih tzu chose that very moment to go into a yapping fit. I didn't blame him.

The woman with the "Let the Dog Go!" sign caught a glimpse of me and rushed to the window, which she pounded on. This only served to get the little dog in my arms more worked up than ever. He took a flying leap out of my arms, still slippery from his bath.

I dropped the wet towel but managed to catch him before he hit the ground below.

The whole saga was now caught on film for the whole world to see. Or at least the whole city of Houston. I noticed the KBRT logo on the side of the camera, one of Houston's largest and most-watched networks. Well, perfect.

Off in the distance, I caught a glimpse of the man who had introduced himself earlier as Corey Wallis' manager. What was his name again? In the blur of activity, I couldn't remember.

What's-his-name was talking to the other guy, the reporter. I couldn't remember his name either.

Ray. One of them was named Ray. Oh, right. The manager.

"Oh, man." Brianna released a lingering sigh. "They would have to send Lance the Legend again. Have you ever seen anyone as handsome?"

"Or so egotistical?" Mari muttered under her breath.

"Lance the Legend." I said the words aloud. "That was the other name I couldn't remember in the moment."

"If I looked like that, I'd be egotistical too." Brianna sighed.

"Are you a little infatuated with Lance, Brianna?" Mari asked.

"Who? What? Me?" Her lashes blinked rapidly, and she turned to face the computer. "What makes you say that?"

"Well, let's see. First there was the whole conversation about his handsomeness. Then there was the fluttering of your eyelashes. Please tell me you didn't call him to come back out here."

Brianna glanced Mari's way, looking wounded. "Mari! You know me better than that."

"Right now I don't know anything or anyone." Mari gestured for us to join her behind the reception desk—almost but not quite out of view of the watching eyes.

Brianna took an incoming call. Her words, "Lone Star Veterinary, can you hold, please?" rang out. Then she set the phone down and turned back toward us. "I'm going to take this in Cassidy's office."

"Okay, and let her know what's going on out here," Mari said. "You might want to let Tyler and Kristin know that our guests have arrived, so they're prepared too."

"Some guests." Brianna sighed and headed off in the direction of Cassidy's small office.

I turned back toward the window, my heart in my throat as the roar from the crowd grew louder and louder. This poor little dog in my arms needed to be crated to remain calm. So I headed to the boarding area to do just that.

CHAPTER NINE

After I kenneled the little shih tzu, I went back to the reception area so that Mari wouldn't be alone. She pulled me to the far side of the room, out of sight from the watching crowd. Her eyes flooded with tears as she turned my way.

"This is awful. My wedding is almost here, and most of the city of Houston is mad at me. Don't they see the good work I do with Second Chance Ranch? Why does all the news about me have to be bad?"

"I have no idea, but they're wrong." I shifted my attention out the windows and then back to her. "You do amazing work, and you have a lot to be proud of."

"Tell that to the woman on the hunger strike." She pointed to the woman with the "Let the Dog Go!" sign, the one wearing a burnt orange U.T. hoodie.

"That woman looks like she could go a good week without food and still be fine," I countered.

"Still."

At this point Mollie Kensington bounded through the front door into our lobby with a loud, "Whoa." We knew her well, since she'd done several great write-ups in the local paper on Mari's rescue over the past year.

"Yeah, you can say that twice and mean it," Cassidy interjected.

"Whoa!" Mollie laughed. "But seriously, this is a mess."

"How did you know it was happening?" I asked. "You got here really quick after it started."

"Oh, trust me, I was tipped off." Her eyebrows elevated mischievously.

"By who?" Mari asked.

"Who do you think? Certainly not Lance the Legend. You think he wants any other reporters getting first dibs on his big story?"

"Then who?" Mari asked.

"The manager, Ray something or other. He called me about ten minutes ago to say I was missing the story of the century. So, I came running."

"Well, wasn't that kind of him?" Mari groaned and then leaned her elbows against the reception counter. "I hope you'll cover it from the right angle, Mollie. There are two sides to every story."

"Which is why I'm in here and not out there," Mollie said. "Your side comes first. Always. I would hope you'd know that by now."

"Thank you." Mari filled her in, giving her all the details we knew to be true. Mollie took a ton of notes.

Afterward she turned my way. "Anything you want to add, Isabel?"

"Yeah, please make sure you print that we were just waiting for the proof of ownership to release the dog back to him. No one stole anything from Corey Wallis. In fact, I've been doing him a favor by taking such good care of Sasha until we found the owner. That's what fosters do." My eyes filled with tears. Mollie reached for her phone and snapped a photo of me.

"Wait. . .what are you doing?" I asked.

"You have the believability factor," she said. "It shows in your face."

"Well, of course I do. . .because I'm telling you the truth."

"Can I quote you on that?"

"Of course."

"Just one question. . ." She looked at her notepad and then back up at me. "Why did you call the dog Sasha? I thought her name was Ginger."

"Oh." I couldn't help but smile as I thought about the little imp. "My grandmother had a little dachshund when I was a child. Her name was Sasha. She was red like this little girl. So, I gave her the same name in honor of my grandmother."

"See?" Mollie snapped another photo of me. "What did I say? You have the believability factor."

"Well, it's a true story. It's easy to be believable when you're telling the truth. And the truth is, I didn't take that man's dog. He lost her, and I took care of her until the proper owner could be found."

Okay, so I'd also purchased some toys, treats, and enough dog food for a month. . .but Mollie didn't need to know that.

She asked a few more questions and then headed outside. I saw her approach one of the ladies holding a picket sign. Mollie held up her phone, and I realized she must be recording the woman's response.

From there, we watched as she talked to Ray Haas. He seemed very worked up today. Hopefully, she would snag a picture of his face too. He looked irate and irrational. Surely the public would see the difference between the two photos—the weeping foster and the angry manager.

And Corey. Where was Corey? Was he coming today?

Dr. Cameron happened out into the lobby at that very moment. Our too-hot-to-still-be-single vet ambled our way, his gaze on the chaos outside.

"Whoa."

"Yeah," I responded. "That's the right word."

"All of this is over that runaway dachshund?" he asked.

Mari groaned. "Yes. It's all my fault."

"Hey, I didn't say anything about fault." He shrugged. "I came out here to get a cookie. Brianna baked snickerdoodles."

How did I not know this? Our resident baker, Brianna, often baked sweet treats for the employees. In my current frame of mind, I could eat a whole batch.

Brianna came out of Cassidy's office carrying a tray of cookies. I grabbed one and took a bite. "Mmm."

"Right?" Cameron grabbed another one and then gazed Brianna's way with a grateful smile. "You're the best."

She batted her eyelashes in playful fashion and said, "Why thank you, kind sir. I'll go on baking forever with compliments like that."

"Maybe you should offer some to that manager of Corey's." I pointed out the window at Ray, who was currently engaged in an intense conversation with the woman wearing a burnt orange hoodie.

Cassidy came out of her office on Brianna's heels. She joined us at the reception desk, took one look at the crowd, and sighed. "I was hoping you were kidding, Brianna."

"Nope." Brianna shoved the cookie tray in Cassidy's direction.

"Thanks." Cassidy took two, no doubt to drown her sorrows. "This is going to become a PR disaster for the clinic, I'm afraid."

I didn't blame her for fretting. She was our PR person, after all, heading up all of our social media. How would she spin this story?

Moments later we were all reaching for more cookies. Sugar really hit the spot when I was stressed and, well. . .I was stressed.

"Do we have to give that little dog back to him?" Cassidy asked between bites.

"He still hasn't given me the paperwork to prove ownership," Mari explained. "It's not my fault. That's what we agreed to."

"You might want to tell it to that one lady with the big obnoxious sign." Brianna pointed. "She's stretched out on the sideway and is blocking the front door of the clinic."

We all turned at once and gasped in unison. Sure enough, the woman in orange was spread out on the ground, blocking the door. Mollie was leaning over her, phone extended in the woman's direction, no doubt taking photos and getting whatever information she could for her article. Ray stood off in the distance, talking to someone on the phone.

Corey Wallis, perhaps? Ugh.

Mari grabbed another cookie. "Well, isn't this fun?"

"What should we do?" I asked.

"I have no idea." Mari sighed and reached for another cookie. "It's weirding me out that Ray Haas is out there protesting with the others, because he ignored my call earlier, asking if they had any updates for me. And there's still no word from Corey about the vet in Pittsburgh. I even took the time to call several vets myself, just to see if the story rang any bells. No one knew a dachshund owned by a pro football player."

"Maybe he'll be able to explain all of that," Brianna said as she turned to head out to the play yard.

"Or maybe he won't."

Mari turned her attention to me. "I honestly don't know what to do."

"Go outside and talk to his manager in person," Cassidy suggested. "That's really all you can do at this point, I think."

"Right." Mari squared her shoulders and took a couple of steps toward the front door of the clinic, muttering the words, "Pray for me, y'all. I feel like Daniel, going into the lions' den."

We watched through the window as a rather heated exchange took place between Mari and the manager. He seemed more than a little worked up. So did she, for that matter.

A few minutes later, Mari entered the lobby, looking relieved. "Okay, I haven't seen the paperwork yet, but the manager gave me the name of the vet in Pittsburgh. It's not the one I tried before. Apparently, there are two veterinarians with similar names in that area. After they confirm the dog's identity, we'll hand her back over and this will all be behind us."

I had mixed feelings about this, of course. I would be thrilled to see the protesters go away—we all would—but losing Sasha would leave pain in my heart. That little doll had left a lasting impression on me.

Mari went to Cassidy's office to make the call. The crowd out front was so loud I couldn't think straight, let alone place a call.

I kept a watchful eye on the goings-on outside with Brianna at my side. I couldn't help but notice Lance the Legend deep in conversation with Ray Haas.

Brianna must've noticed it too.

"Is it just my imagination, or do Ray and Lance seem kind of buddy-buddy?" she asked.

I shrugged. "I'm sure they know each other. I mean, Ray is a manager for lots of players, right? I'm sure he arranges press conferences and other events with the media. So, I'm not surprised that he and Lance are friends."

Lance shifted his attention to the woman on the ground. He knelt next to her and appeared to be talking to her. Weird. Did they know each other too?

"Well?" Cassidy asked as Mari came back into the lobby.

She looked relieved as she updated us. "Okay, I reached the vet in Pittsburgh, and they're supposed to be emailing me the paperwork to prove she's his. So, I'll connect with Corey tomorrow to return her."

"Is he coming back to Brenham again?" I dabbed my lips with my napkin. "Inquiring minds want to know."

"I'll bet you do." Brianna laughed. "I got a good look at him, girl, and I don't blame you. He's Hollywood gorgeous."

I felt my cheeks flame with heat as everyone looked my way. "Oh, I didn't mean anything by that."

"Sure you didn't." Mari laughed.

"So, you're giving her back?" I asked.

"Parker and I are going back to Houston this weekend for another ministry event," Mari explained. "Maybe we'll drop her off then."

That made perfect sense, though it made me a little sad that I wouldn't be seeing Corey again. Oh well.

"Where is Sasha now?" Cassidy asked.

"In the outdoor play yard with the boarders," Brianna said. "I was with them until I saw the crowd approaching. Then I rushed back in to give everyone a heads-up. I'm headed back out there now."

"Okay." Cassidy went into office manager mode, her tone suddenly businesslike. "Do me a favor and bring all the dogs inside. Make sure you put them in crates in the boarding area, okay?"

"Sure."

"Put Sasha—Ginger—whoever—in a kennel too," Cassidy said.

We kept a watchful eye on the chaos outside as one of our clients somehow made her way past the crowd and through the front door. She had to step over the prostrate woman to do so but managed to make it inside.

"Whew! What a mess." She stared at us, wide-eyed.

"Tell me about it," Mari countered. She got the woman settled in Exam Room 1.

Brianna came rushing back into the lobby, eyes wide. "Um, guys?"

We all turned her way.

"Houston, we've got a problem."

"This is no time to be cryptic, Brianna," Cassidy said. "What's going on?"

"She's missing, y'all!" Brianna cried out. "The dachshund is missing. . .again!"

CHAPTER TEN

A collective gasp went up from the group.

"Sasha is missing?" I asked. "Are you serious?"

"Yes. I went back out after I got the other dogs kenneled just to make sure she wasn't hiding. She's not there. She just. . .disappeared."

"Oh no." I had that heart-to-the-throat sensation.

"She's got to be hiding in the doggy condo," Mari said.

"No, I looked." Brianna shook her head. "She's gone from the play yard. I went through every square inch of it, hoping to find her or some sign of how she might've escaped, but saw nothing. It's like she just disappeared."

"But that's impossible!" I argued.

"I promise, Isabel." Brianna's eyes filled with tears. "She's not there. And I didn't see any signs of foul play. I brought the other dogs in and crated them so we could focus on her."

"Someone came out here and took her?" Cassidy asked. "How did they get over the fence?"

My eyes instinctively filled with tears. "How could he do this? He's a terrible human!"

"He. . .who?" Brianna asked.

"That stupid football player, that's who. He somehow got in here and took his—my—the—dog."

"But, how?"

"He set us up," I said. "That whole group of picketers out there right now? One of them was sent to nab the dog."

"But that makes no sense, Isabel," Mari said. "Corey couldn't have known she would be out in the yard."

Oh, right.

Still, I couldn't help but think he had something to do with this.

"He probably told his manager not to come back without her," I said. "That's what I'm guessing anyway."

"Now that makes more sense," Mari countered. "And the manager just happened to see her out in the yard?"

"What about the cameras?" Brianna asked. "We have security cameras set up outside."

"Not in the back," Tyler's voice sounded, and we all turned as one to discover he had joined us. "And why do I always feel like I'm walking in on the middle of a conversation?"

"Because you are?" Cassidy said.

"The dachshund is missing?" he asked. When I nodded, he groaned. "Well, that's just awesome. Now we've lost the star quarterback's dog."

"Five minutes ago we weren't sure it was his dog," Kristin reminded him.

"Am I the only one who's noticed the woman on the ground in front of our door?" Tyler asked.

"No, we noticed." Mari began to pace the area behind the reception desk. "Should I call the police?"

Tyler shook his head. "That would really heat things up, wouldn't it?"

"But look..." I pointed as one of our clients pulled into the parking lot and got out of her car with her Akita, a trained service dog. "That's Mrs. Fredericks. She's going to need to get in the front door."

Tyler walked to the door and nudged it open enough to ask the woman on the ground to move. I couldn't make out everything she said, but there was something in there about doing so over her cold dead body.

The owner of the Akita seemed genuinely perplexed. She gently pulled at the dog's leash, and he responded in the way any good service dog would—by shifting all of his attention to the woman on the ground. He stood guard over her, clearly hoping to alert onlookers to her collapse.

The woman finally gave up and moved when the Akita refused to budge.

Mrs. Fredericks entered the lobby and joined us at the reception desk. "What in the world is going on out there? You folks holding someone's dog hostage?"

"No." Brianna did her best to explain, but the poor woman was growing more confused by the moment. She ushered her into Exam Room 2 without waiting.

Afterward, my coworkers kept talking about the play yard, but my thoughts were elsewhere. I had Corey Wallis' number. I would call him right now and make sure he wasn't behind all this.

Well, Mari had his number. I'd given her his card. I asked for it back, and she happily obliged. I disappeared into the grooming area then punched in the number on my cell phone. My hands trembled in anger as I held tight to the phone.

He answered on the third ring, sounding a little breathless. "Corey Wallis."

"Isabel Fuentes," I countered, doing my best to hold in my anger. "We met the other day at the clinic in Brenham."

"I hope you're calling with good news."

"I wish I was, but I think you and I both know what's really going on here."

"Huh?"

"If you wanted Sasha that bad you should have just come to me privately. Why you felt you had to steal her from us, I. . .I. . ." At this point anger got the best of me and erupted in tears.

Well, great. So much for coming across as professional.

"Whoa. Wait a minute. What are you saying? Someone stole Ginger?" The tone of his voice immediately shared his concerns on that matter.

"Yes, she's been stolen. Don't play innocent with me. I know you're behind this. But, why? To make the story even bigger on the evening news?"

"I'm not playing. I honestly don't know what you're talking about. She's really gone missing again?"

"One of our employees took her out to the play yard, and then all those ridiculous protesters showed up with your manager—complete with that awful reporter and his crew—and the next thing you know, Sasha's missing. Again. If you really felt you had a claim to her, you should have just called me. Stealing her was a low blow. I've gotten really close to her over the past few days."

"First of all, I didn't steal her. I didn't know she was missing. Second, this little dog is a big part of my mom's story, so the idea that she's gone missing again is gut wrenching. I can't believe this."

"I. . .I'm sorry." And I was. It was obvious from the grief in his voice that Corey hadn't taken her. But, who had?

"Can you meet me?" he asked. "I'm at a practice right now, but I'll be done in an hour."

"I'm at work. And, like I said, we're having kind of a chaotic day over here."

"What about tomorrow morning?" he asked.

"I've got to trim a Pomeranian in the morning at eight."

"I'm never up at eight. Lunch? Halfway?"

"I can't leave the office that long. I have a job, Corey."

"Yeah, I have one of those, myself." He paused. "But I don't have to be at practice until four. I'll come to Brenham and meet you for lunch. We'll talk this through and maybe figure out how it happened. Will noon work for you?"

"Yeah."

"Where?"

At least I could finally get my burger fix. "Triple B's. Best burgers in town."

"I hear you guys have good beef in Texas."

I had a beef, all right, but not the kind he was talking about.

We ended the call, and I somehow got busy with the Pomeranian. I fussed and fumed for the rest of the day, my thoughts on the missing dog. Our protesters finally gave up. Weirdly, they all left at the same time. We were happy to see them gone, regardless.

Cassidy and Brianna jumped into action and placed missing posters in the lobby.

Mari reached out to all her rescue contacts in the area and asked them to be on the lookout for Sasha. I wanted to get in my car and drive around to look for her, but that opportunity didn't arrive until I got off work at six o'clock.

I crawled the streets around the clinic but turned up empty-handed. My heart nearly broke as I thought about that sweet dog out here on the streets alone.

Only, I didn't really think she was on the streets.

The more I thought about it, the more I realized someone must've taken her.

For the reward money.

Yes, news had gone out about the reward money for Sasha. Er, Ginger. Surely someone in that crowd today knew about it and took the dog, knowing she could be returned later for cash.

Realizing that to be the likely scenario, I finally gave up my search. When I pulled my car into the driveway at my little house a few minutes later, Carmela met me at the car. She waved me down, all smiles.

Until she saw the somber look on my face.

"What happened, honey?" She asked as soon as I parked the car and got out. "You look like someone died."

"I feel like it. The dog has gone missing."

"No!" She clamped a hand over her mouth. "Someone walked off with our beautiful little Sasha?"

"Either that or she escaped. She was in the play yard behind our clinic with several other dogs when our clinic was surrounded by protesters demanding we give the dog back to Corey Wallis."

"What in the world?" Carmela followed me into my house.

I tossed my purse on the table and walked to the refrigerator to grab a bottle of water. I offered one to Carmela, but she turned it down.

"I think Corey might've given his manager instructions to bring the dog back with or without our input."

Carmela gasped. "Honey, you met him. How could a man like that steal anything from anyone? He's a good guy."

"But how do you know that for real?" I asked. "We don't actually know him."

"I've lived on this planet over eighty years," she countered. "You learn a lot about people in that amount of time. I have a sense about these things."

This, coming from the woman who got taken in by an online scammer just two months ago.

I knew the real problem here. She loved football. And when one loved football, all common sense went straight out the window.

This I knew from personal experience.

I plopped down at the breakfast table and took a swig from the water bottle. "I'm half-tempted to cancel our lunch date tomorrow."

"Lunch date?" Carmela's eyes widened as she took the seat across from mine. "You're having lunch with Corey Wallis?"

"Yes. Triple B's."

"What time should I be there?"

I stared at her, unable to respond. Had she really just invited herself to my lunch date?

Okay, not a date. . .but my lunch meeting.

Meeting didn't sound right either. What would you call it when sharing a meal with a man whose dog you'd somehow lost?

"You want my opinion on whether or not he's telling the truth, right?" Carmela said. "I'll have to be there in person to know for sure."

I must've paused a little too long because she erupted in laughter. "I'm just kidding, kiddo. I wouldn't horn in on your very first date with the guy. I'll wait until you're his steady girl."

"Oh, it's not a date," I said. "And I'm definitely not going to be his steady girl. We're just meeting to discuss the dog. He seemed genuinely concerned when he heard that she was missing."

"Right." Carmela gave me a little wink and eased her way up from the chair, mumbling something about needing to take a tres leches cake out of the oven.

She had me at tres leches.

But I couldn't let that distract me. Not right now. Not when I still had to figure out what to wear to lunch tomorrow.

Not that this was a date, of course.

CHAPTER ELEVEN

Thursday, September 14

I was a nervous wreck all Thursday morning at work. I was so distracted by my upcoming lunch with Corey Wallis that I couldn't think clearly about the work in front of me.

I was also terribly worried about Sasha. I couldn't stop fretting over her. What if she was running the streets, braving the traffic? What if she ended up dehydrated? Or worse—what if she got hit by a car?

My mind wouldn't stop spinning as I pondered all the possible scenarios. Hopefully, none of those things was true. I hated the idea that she had been stolen, but that almost seemed a better choice to the running-the-streets scenario. At least she would be safe in a perpetrator's hands.

I hoped.

With my thoughts tumbling, I could hardly focus on my work. I accidentally bathed the Lab instead of the Maltese, then had to start over with the right dog.

Turned out the Lab just needed a nail clipping. He got a free bath as a result of my distraction.

When I wrapped up with both of those dogs, I found most of my coworkers in the reception area. It seemed we'd been hanging out there a lot lately. I walked in on a conversation about Corey Wallis, who had—according to Cassidy—appeared on the Wednesday evening news to share an update about Sasha. Er, Ginger.

"He had to have taken her." Cassidy paced the room, more than a little worked up. "He's got the money to pay someone to swipe her. I guarantee that's what he did. He seems like a newshound. You know? Like, he enjoys being in front of the camera."

"This is a star football player," Tyler countered. "He's in the limelight all the time. I don't think he would risk his career to take an animal. People with money don't swipe dogs. They sue the folks holding the animal, but they don't steal them."

"True." Cassidy bit her lip. "We don't need a lawsuit, that's for sure."

No, we definitely didn't. Lone Star Veterinary Clinic had been through a lot in the few years since I'd started working here. It seemed someone was always threatening something.

Such was the case with animal owners. Many of them didn't trust the medical community. Or, some would wait too late to bring an animal in for care, then blame the vet if the pet passed away.

I'd seen it all. Hopefully, I wouldn't see a lawsuit from Corey Wallis. Or any signs that he was actually the one behind this dognapping.

If, in fact, it was a dognapping. Sasha was a runner. We knew that much already. She'd run away from home in Houston. Perhaps she'd managed to slip out somehow and was roaming the streets of Brenham now.

If so, I would find her. With Mari's help, of course. She and Parker were the best at finding lost animals. They seemed to have a gift for it.

Parker interrupted our gathering. I could tell from the expression on his face that he was concerned about something.

"Guys, want to come out to the play yard with me?"

We followed on Parker's heels until we reached the backyard. He had nudged the doggy condo over several inches. Weird.

"Okay, so I moved the dog condo over and found this." He pointed to a small hole in the dirt at the base of the fence.

"It wasn't visible when the condo was in place, but there's definitely a hole here, and these look like fresh paw prints."

I knelt down and had a closer look. It did look as if someone had been digging recently.

"So, you think she dug her way out?" I asked.

"It's hard to know." Parker shrugged. "But we can't rule out that possibility."

"So, all of our concerns that she was stolen might have been in vain?" I sighed as I realized just how quickly I'd jumped into finger-pointing mode. To my way of thinking, Corey was somehow behind this.

Only, now I wasn't so sure. Had our negligence really caused this to happen? The pup had been left in the play yard alone, something that rarely happened at Lone Star. But with the chaos of the media circus and protest out front, I couldn't exactly blame Brianna for slipping back in to take care of things inside.

We all gazed her way, and I noticed the tears in her eyes.

"I'm so sorry, y'all." She offered a little sigh. "I should have brought them in. I know that. But I was so preoccupied with the protest and got distracted."

"Don't worry about it, Brianna," Tyler said. "These things happen. We're human. And we can't have our eyes on every pet every moment of the day. It's just not possible. You were doing the best you could under the circumstances."

Mari told a story about how she'd accidentally let Beau Jangles slip out of her car at a local park just a couple of months back.

"And I'd like to think I'm one of the most responsible dog owners ever." She shrugged. "But these things definitely happen to just about everyone."

Brianna didn't look convinced. I did my best to console her, then looked at my watch. 11:40. I needed to hit the road to join Corey for lunch. Should I tell the others?

Nah. They would make a big deal out of it.

"Hey, I've got an errand to run," I said. "Can I break for lunch early? I'll be back by one."

"Sure." Tyler shrugged. "See you when you get back."

I went back inside, gave myself a quick glance in the mirror, then headed out to my car. Ten minutes later I walked through the door of Triple B's, my favorite burger joint. I looked around for Corey. I didn't see him, but in the far back corner booth an older man with a baseball cap and beard flagged me down. I took tentative steps in that direction.

"Hey." Corey's voice spoke from behind what was now obviously a fake beard. "Thanks for meeting me."

"Um. . ." I stared at him, unwilling to sit down until he explained the weird getup. "What are we doing?"

"Trying to fend off the paparazzi."

I rolled my eyes as I slid into the booth. "Really?"

"I can't seem to shake them. Ever since I got to Houston, they're tailing me at every turn. Pun intended."

"Pun intended?"

"Tail. Dog. Never mind." He flashed a crooked smile. I think. It was kind of hard to tell past the fake beard.

"I can't have a sensible conversation with you looking like that." I reached for a menu. "I don't care how famous you are." I might've rolled my eyes after that last comment. I wasn't sure.

He pulled off the beard and that gorgeous face came into full view.

Stay calm, Izzy. Stay calm.

Those beautiful blue eyes weren't making it easy. They peered at me with such intensity that I felt like he could see right through me.

The young waiter appeared at the table, ready to take our order. He took one look at Corey and his jaw dropped. "You're. . .you're. . ."

"Yeah, and you're going to get the biggest tip of the day for not saying a word," Corey countered. "Do we have a deal?"

The kid nodded, wide-eyed, then took our drink orders.

Corey ordered root beer. I ordered Dr Pepper.

"Dr Pepper?" He looked my way.

"You betcha. It's my favorite."

"I like it too. It's just not one of those drinks I think to order with a meal, is all."

"You're in Texas now, cowboy," I said. "Do as the Texans do."

He changed his order to Dr Pepper and reached for the menu.

How could I explain Texas to a foreigner from Pittsburgh? Here in Brenham, we were a flag-waving, country-music-loving bunch. No denying that. A good day wouldn't be complete without a can of Dr Pepper and a scoop of Blue Bell ice cream.

And BBQ brisket. How Mari's grandmother could give up beef was beyond me. I would sooner join a convent than give up beef.

Not that I still held strong ties to my Catholic upbringing. These days Mari and Parker welcomed me with open arms at Grace Fellowship.

"Have I lost you?" Corey glanced up from his menu.

"No. Just thinking about Texas. You need to acclimate as quickly as you can."

"I guess. Life here is. . .different."

"You're welcome."

He smiled. "Okay, talk me through who was at the building yesterday when Ginger went missing. I think we need to make sure we're not overlooking anything."

I was sure he already knew but went through the list anyway.

"Your manager," I said. "Ray What's-his-name."

"Haas. Who else?"

"That same reporter from a Houston station, the one Brianna's fascinated with."

"Just one?"

"Yeah, his name is Lance Henderson. KBRT. I've seen him on the evening news. I guess some of the ladies think he's, well. . ."

"Handsome?"

I shrugged. "I guess. Definitely not my type."

"Gotcha. I'm tempted to ask what that means, but I won't."

"He had a cameraman with him," I interjected. "I recognized him from the other day. No idea about his name, though."

"Did either of them behave suspiciously?" Corey asked.

"No, but your manager did. If I didn't know any better, I'd think he was communicating with the people, telling them what to do, where to stand, and so on."

Corey looked shocked by this. "Why would you say that?"

"Because I watched him. Closely. And that woman who blocked the door with her body was definitely taking her marching orders from him. He knelt down next to her and gave her instructions. I think."

"There was a woman on the ground?"

"Yeah, don't you watch the news?"

"Only when I have to." He shook his head. "I didn't see any of the things you're talking about."

"Well, I did, and like I said on the phone, I'm half-tempted to think the two of you set this up so you could get the dog." I gave him a penetrating look.

Corey seemed legitimately wounded by my words.

"Do you really think I would have come all this way to talk this through if I took my own dog back?" He gave me a pensive look. "What would be the point of all that?"

I shrugged. He did have a point.

"If Ginger was at my house right now, I'd drop all this and just hang out with her."

"Ouch." I paused.

"Sorry." His tight expression eased. "I can see how that might have sounded. I didn't mean it like that. It's just that it's a long way to Brenham from River Oaks."

"In more than just miles," I countered.

His eyes narrowed to slits, and he appeared to be thinking through what I'd said.

"Not sure what you mean by that," he said.

"River Oaks is a whole other world from Brenham, Texas," I countered.

"If you knew me, you'd know that I'd probably fit in better in Brenham, then," he said.

The truth was, I didn't know him. Not at all. He could talk a good game, but was he who he said he was? He could be bluffing with that speech about not watching the news. Maybe he was one of those paparazzi hounds ready to do anything to make it into the limelight.

"For all I know, you guys might have set this up with the reporter for a good story."

He lifted the menu to cover his face as an older couple walked by, then lowered it once they were safely tucked away in a booth on the far side of the room.

"I'm the opposite of that, in case the beard and cap didn't clue you in. I hate being the center of attention—on the field or on camera. It's too much."

"Oh." Just one word, but it was all I could come up with.

"Yes, I've done a couple of interviews about Ginger. I want her back." His expression tightened. "I need her back. But being showcased isn't my goal. If you knew me at all you'd know that I play the best football game possible, but after the lights go out on the field, I'm ready to tuck it in and go back home." He paused, and I seemed to lose him to his thoughts.

"What?" I asked.

For a moment his eyes took on a faraway look. When he finally spoke, his words were strained. "Houston's not my home. That fancy house in River Oaks? That's not my home. My home was a tiny wood-framed two-bedroom house I grew up in, in Pittsburgh."

"Ah."

"Yeah." He paused. "And trust me when I say that nothing about that life even remotely resembles the one I'm now living. I would go back to it in a heartbeat if I could, but. . ."

My heart melted with those words. Maybe I'd completely misjudged him.

Probably.

Okay, I totally had. And the time had come to acknowledge that. I looked directly into his eyes as he delivered this next part.

"I came so that we could talk this through. I think we can both agree that we want to get Ginger back."

I softened at his words. He really had come a long way and he did seem concerned.

"Corey, I just want to say how sorry I am that Sasha—Ginger—is missing."

"Again." He sighed.

"Again," I countered. Though, I didn't bear any responsibility for the first disappearance.

And, frankly, I didn't bear any personal responsibility for the second. Though, I felt guilty every time I thought about the little doll.

CHAPTER TWELVE

I don't hold you responsible," Corey said. "Ginger's a runner. Clearly. I imagine she dug her way out of the yard and took off on a tour of Brenham. I'm praying she turns up."

"Me too."

"I drove all over the place when I got off work last night," I explained. "I finally gave up. But Mari has reached out to several local dog rescues, and we've put signs up in the lobby and other places around town."

"Thank you." His words were soft and genuine. "That means a lot to me. So, can we agree to work together on this and not against each other?"

My angst melted with those words. It felt silly now, to think he would've gone to all this trouble to drive to Brenham not just once but twice to locate his mother's little dog. . .a dog who was confused and lost because her owner died.

My heart suddenly filled with compassion for Corey. He had lost his mom. I'd lost my grandmother.

I got it.

The waiter reappeared with our Dr Peppers and a complimentary basket of tortilla chips. I took a big swig of my drink and reached for a chip.

Corey followed suit, a big smile lighting his face as he enjoyed the taste. Then the waiter took our orders. Both of us ordered burgers.

"I'm sorry everything has been crazy," Corey said after the waiter took off with our menus. "This whole thing just got completely out of hand. All I really want is for Ginger to be okay. It's hard to explain, but she's a living, breathing reminder of my mom. That might not make much sense, but—"

"It makes perfect sense. And I can see why your mom fell in love with her. She's such a sweet little dog. I'm very fond of her. I know she's only been in my life a few days, but I've gotten really attached. She's adorable. I mean, other than the part where she ate my sofa and piddled on my floor, the whole experience has been absolutely dreamy."

"Ginger ate your sofa?"

"Not the whole sofa," I countered. "Just one section. And it's not really the sofa. I exaggerated that part. It's more of a love seat. But it was my grandmother's, and it means a great deal to me now that she's gone."

"I'm sorry." His nose wrinkled, and he reached for his drink again. "I do understand the grandmother part. Sounds like we have a lot in common. We've both lost people we love."

"Yeah."

"How did you end up with your grandmother's sofa?"

I shared the story—the whole story—of how I'd come into possession of Lita's house and sofa. When he heard that the tale involved the Texans, a smile lit his face.

"Well now."

"I know." I found myself gazing at him a little too intently, so I shifted my glance to my drink.

"She was a fan?"

"Superfan," I explained. "If you came to my house you would see. There's Texans memorabilia everywhere. It's kind of. . .over the top."

He laughed. "If you came to my house you'd see almost no football decor. I'm a minimalist."

"That's crazy. But I could also show you every newspaper clipping from the morning after the big wins." I took a sip of my Dr Pepper.

"Really?"

"She drove to the store and bought the paper so she would have the actual headlines. I tried to explain how the internet works, that she could have those headlines at her fingertip any time she wanted, but that wouldn't do. She wanted a physical copy of the paper, something she could hold on to and read over and over again. That's how much those games meant to her."

"Man." The edges of his lips turned up in a smile. "I can't help but think she would've been fun to have around."

"She was." I paused to think it through, and a lump rose to my throat. I tried to envision what Lita would've said if she'd seen me sitting here, having lunch with a Texans quarterback. "She would've flipped out if she could have met you in person. That's why Carmela—my neighbor—was so over-the-top excited. She was my grandmother's best friend. Talk about two peas in a pod."

"Carmela didn't seem shy."

"Oh, she's not. She's the opposite of shy. I rather think she was enjoying those cameras and reporters. She was born for it."

"Some people love their time in the spotlight."

"I can't imagine." A shudder ran through me. What a way to live. "I'm more of a stay-out-of-the-spotlight-at-any-cost kind of girl."

He groaned. "People wouldn't know this about me, but I'm pretty introverted, myself. Public speaking is enough to make me feel sick."

"Really?"

"Yeah." He shot a glance across the restaurant at a booth on the far side of the room. "But I've been forced out of my shell the past couple years."

I had experienced something similar, though it had nothing to do with football. My shell was a protective cocoon. It had kept me safe and cozy from my ex. Until Little Lita died, anyway. Then I had no choice but to break out of it and face the world on my own.

Well, not completely alone, of course. I was never truly alone, not with God on my side.

Corey dove into a story about the move from Pittsburgh to Houston. I did my best to listen closely but found myself distracted thinking about Lita. Corey's words faded off just as the waiter appeared with our burgers.

He took a look at the oversized burger on his plate, and his eyes widened. "Whoa. That's huge."

"Welcome to Texas," I said. The edges of my lips curled up in a smile. I couldn't help myself. "We know our beef here."

"And Blue Bell," the waiter added.

"Blue Bell?" Confusion seemed to register in Corey's eyes. "Carmela mentioned that. What is it?"

I'm pretty sure the waiter and I gasped in unison. Corey really was a foreigner. Everyone knew Brenham's favorite ice cream brand.

"It's just the best ice cream on the planet," I said. "Destined to change your life."

"Oh." He shrugged. "I'm not a big ice cream person."

"Yet," the waiter said, then looked my way. "Which flavor should I bring him? Homemade vanilla? Cookies and Cream?"

"Moolenium Crunch," I said. "If it's in season."

"Ice cream...in season?" Corey reached for his burger. "Is that a thing?"

How could I explain it to him? We took our various flavors of Blue Bell very seriously. And yes, they came in season.

"Are touchdowns a thing?" I asked him.

He took a bite and then swiped at his lips with the back of his hand.

"Are gifts at Christmastime a thing?" I added. "Does it snow in Pittsburgh in the winter?"

"Yes to all of the above."

"Seasonal flavors of Blue Bell are a thing," I said. "It's a brilliant marketing strategy."

The waiter took off, all smiles. I was pretty sure this customer was making his day. Maybe his week.

We ate our burgers, and then the waiter reappeared with our ice cream. Corey didn't look particularly interested until he took that first bite. Then, suddenly, he was all in.

His eyes widened and he shoved an even bigger bite in his mouth. "This stuff is...wow."

"I know, right?"

He took a couple more bites.

"I just can't believe I haven't heard of Blue Bell before."

"You come to Texas to find the best," I said.

He looked up from the ice cream, his gaze meeting mine.

"Mm-hmm." A little smile lit his face.

I shifted my gaze to my ice cream and reached for my spoon. Time to change the subject.

"What were you saying about your grandmother?"

"Lita was a Texans superfan." I took a little nibble of my ice cream. Yum. "Lita?"

"Short for Little Abuelita. She was petite."

"Ah. A petite superfan. Cool."

I waved my spoon at him. "Only, she didn't like interlopers."

A blob of ice cream slid off the end of his spoon. He gave me a pensive look.

"Her word, not mine. She didn't like the way players got traded in and out."

"Welcome to the club." He sighed and slid the spoon back into his bowl. "Me either."

"I think you'll fit right in before long," I added. No point in making him feel even more like an outsider.

"I haven't been in town long enough to really get to know anyone," Corey said. "But I feel like every time I turn around that reporter from KBRT is there, capturing it all on film."

"He's not technically the one capturing it on film," I reminded him. "That would be the cameraman."

"Yeah, him too. Don't know his name, but I got the weird feeling he was filming me the other day after I left the clinic."

"One of the perks of being a superstar," I said. "I can't really imagine what that would feel like."

"First of all. . ." He lowered his voice as he leaned forward and placed his elbows on the table. "I'm no superstar. I'm just a guy who is blessed to play a game I love."

"A game you're really good at."

"Thank you. But my point is, as eerie as it feels to be followed around by cameras, it's even stranger that Lance Henderson is always just a few feet away when something big happens. He always manages to beat the other stations to the story."

"Maybe he's just good at what he does too," I said. "Like you're good at football."

"Well, trust me, I know my football. I—" He paused, spoon dangling. "Oh no."

"What is it?" I asked.

He gestured with his head to a table across from us.

I looked that way and gasped when I realized Lance Henderson from KBRT was having lunch with his cameraman.

Whose camera was pointed right at us.

CHAPTER THIRTEEN

No way." Everything in me rebelled the moment I saw that camera pointed at me. I started to get out of my seat, but Corey gestured for me to stay put.

"Let me," he said.

He rose and took several decisive steps in the direction of the table where Lance and the cameraman sat. A heated discussion ensued, and then he came back to the table.

"What happened?" I asked.

"They said it was a public place and they had every right to be filming. He also said that I'm news, whatever that means."

"He's right. You are news. But I'm not. And I don't want to be stuck in the middle of a story just because I happen to have a compassionate heart and I fostered a little dog." My eyes filled with tears, and Corey reached across the table to rest his hand on mine.

"I'm sorry about all of this. I'm going to go talk to the manager. He'll ask Lance to stop."

"No, if you do that, you'll draw even more attention to us."

"If I don't, we're going to end up on the five o'clock news."

"It's probably too late to worry about that," I said. "Let's just go back to our ice cream and ignore them. What's the most they can say on the news, that we're drinking Dr Pepper and eating burgers in a burger joint in Brenham?"

"Right. Good point."

So, we returned to our meal and our conversation.

Which was hard, knowing a camera was pointed right at me.

EVERY DOG HAS HIS DAY

"Ugh. I don't trust that guy." I gestured to Lance. "Such a showboat. And for all we know, he might've taken off with Ginger yesterday. He was at the clinic when it happened."

"You think so?" Corey looked up from his bowl of ice cream.

"It's a possibility," I said. "He wants a big story. The missing dog is the big story. And why is he here today? Why show up in Brenham the day after the dog goes missing? He had to have known you were coming here."

He put his hand up. "No way. I didn't let anyone know I was coming, trust me."

"Well, then, they followed you. Because how else would a news reporter have known to come to Triple B's in Brenham, Texas, on the very day—at the very time—you were here if he wasn't tailing you?"

"Okay, I'll buy that. Maybe he did follow me here. But I still don't see why you think he's got Ginger."

"I told you, to drag this out. To make a story where there is none."

"Then I'm going to go confront him." He pushed his ice cream bowl back and looked as if he might stand up.

"Wait till you've finished your ice cream," I suggested. "It's not worth ruining a perfectly good bowl of Blue Bell."

"True. This is good stuff." He pulled the bowl back and had another bite.

We somehow got caught up in conversation about the Blue Bell factory just a few miles away, and I remembered Carmela's suggestion that we invite him for a tour. Before I could stop myself, I had brought that up in conversation.

Somehow I'd lost all control over my mouth. It just kept rambling on and on about ice cream.

And football.

And Dr Pepper.

I think it had something to do with those blue eyes. Every time he looked my way, I seemed to forget myself.

And everything else as well.

He excused himself to go to the restroom a short while later, and I did my best to regroup.

"Get ahold of yourself, girl," I muttered.

Out of the corner of my eye, I realized the camera was still pointed my way. Really? Was that guy still filming me as I talked to myself about how incredibly nonsensical I was whenever Corey Wallis was around?

The front door of the restaurant swung open, and Maggie Jamison entered the restaurant. She saw me from a distance and waved.

I waved back.

Maggie was a regular at the clinic. Her dog Midnight was one of Mari's rescues. And Maggie had played a big role in supporting Mari when she first started the 501(c)3 for Second Chance Ranch.

Maggie was sporting her usual jeans and plaid button-up with her signature baseball cap flipped backward on her head. She had that rough-and-ready look about her as she ambled my way.

"Hey, stranger." Her face lit into a big smile as she drew near.

"Hey," I responded.

"It's rare to see you eating alone." Her gaze traveled to the plate of food across from me. "Oh, you're not alone. Is Mari with you?"

"Nope, not Mari."

"Brianna?"

"Nope."

"Cassidy?"

I shook my head.

Maggie laughed. "Okay, I give up. Not a coworker?"

"No, I..." I shot a glance across the crowded restaurant, hoping Corey would come back in. "I'm having lunch with someone, but he had to step out for a minute."

"Someone with a fake beard?" She leaned down into Corey's side of the booth and came up with the beard. "What is he, an actor or something?"

"No. I'll explain later, I promise. So, what brings you out today?"

A smile tipped up the edges of her lips. "I've been out Christmas shopping for Juanita all morning but decided I'd better refuel so I have the energy to hit a few more stores."

"Juanita?" I stared at Maggie, perplexed. This wasn't a name I knew.

She dove into a lengthy conversation about a ten-year-old named Juanita but lost me until she added the words, "She's from Honduras. I've been sponsoring her for years. I always shop for her in September so there's plenty of time for shipping."

Until that moment I had no idea she took care of children in Third World countries as well as dogs.

"Oh, that's wonderful." I flashed an admiring smile. "I've been thinking about doing something like that myself."

"Oh my stars, you totally should." She slid into the spot where Corey had been sitting and grabbed a tortilla chip from the basket in the center of the table. "I can't tell you the sense of satisfaction it gives me to know I'm bringing a smile to a child's face. Do you want to see pictures?"

"I, well. . ."

Corey showed up at that very moment.

Maggie was so busy scrolling on her phone that she didn't notice him at first. Her gaze still on the phone, she said, "I'll take a Number 3 with extra onions, please. And a Dr Pepper in a to-go cup."

Corey cleared his throat.

Maggie looked up from her phone and startled to attention.

"Oh, I'm so sorry. Were you. . .is this your spot?" She shimmied out of his spot and came around to my side, pressing herself in next to me. "I'm Maggie Jamison."

"Corey Wallis." He shook her extended hand.

Her gaze shot to the booth where Lance and the photographer were sitting.

"I don't know what's up with that creep in the corner," Maggie said. "I'm about to go over there and give him a piece of my mind. He keeps staring at us."

"He's a reporter," I said. "From a TV station in Houston."

Maggie squinted and then nodded. "Oh, right. I recognize him now. Lance the Legend. I'm pretty sure that's a toupee he's wearing, by the way. It's too perfect to be real."

"No idea," I said.

"And his teeth are veneers. You can tell by the way a person speaks if they're trying to hold their teeth in."

"I knew a guy with veneers once," Corey said. "He always made a clacking noise when he spoke."

"Yeah, that happens. But what are they doing here?" Maggie looked back at Lance and the photographer. "He keeps staring at me. And I think that other guy has a camera. I'm gonna go over there and put them in their place."

I knew she could do it too. Maggie was tough as nails and about as subtle as a lightning bolt.

"It's me he's after," Corey said. "Trust me, he's doing everything he can to make my life miserable."

"But why would he—" Maggie looked up from the basket of chips and gave Corey a closer look. Her eyes bugged. "Oh! Oh my stars! You're. . .you're. . .You said it yourself! You're Corey Wallis!"

"I am," Corey said.

"And I'm about as dense as a doorpost," she countered. "Forgive me. I'm so incredibly distracted today. I've been Christmas shopping for the little girl in Honduras that I sponsor."

Corey's face lit up. "Really? I sponsor a boy in Colombia. I have for the past four years. He's eleven now. His name is Lupe."

This, of course, led the two of them into a lengthy conversation about the children they sponsored. This shifted to photos being pulled up on both of their phones.

I sat there like a bump on a log, wondering about a precious little missing dog.

The one we weren't talking about.

"I'm so sorry I'm interrupting your meeting," Maggie said when the conversation hit a lull. She glanced my way. "You two were having a private lunch, and I horned in."

True. But how could I remedy that now? I glanced at my watch and realized my lunch hour was almost over. I needed to get back to work.

"We were here to talk about his missing dog," I interjected.

"The one you refused to give back?" Maggie turned my way with a motherly look on her face. "I read all about it in the paper. Why did you keep his dog, Isabel?"

I groaned. "It's not like that. He didn't have proof that Ginger was—oh, never mind."

"We have the proof now," he explained. "I gave it to that rescue lady—"

"Mari," Maggie and I spoke in unison.

"Mari. Sent her an email before I left Houston this morning. But Ginger has gone missing. . .again," Corey explained.

"No way." Maggie's mouth rounded into an O.

Out of the corner of my eye, I caught a glimpse of Lance Henderson nudging the cameraman, who looked up from his burger then glanced our way.

"Yeah, she was stolen from the backyard of the clinic yesterday afternoon when the place was swarming with reporters," I explained as I inched my way closer to the wall. "No one seems to know who took her."

"Maybe she dug her way out?" Maggie suggested. "Happens all the time at the rescue. Mari can tell you about all the little ones that slipped out under the fence. We housed the rescue dogs at my place for a while before Trina bought her property and gave the rescue a permanent home."

"That's nice of you." He gave her an admiring look.

Great. Everyone in this story was a hero. . .except for me. I got the moniker of dog thief.

"We found a hole near the fence, but it was a small one," I explained. "I suppose it's possible she could have. . ."

"You found a hole under the fence?" Corey's brow wrinkled. "Why didn't you tell me?"

"I planned to. But we don't know that it was big enough for her to squeeze through."

"Oh, those little dogs can flatten like pancakes," Maggie said. "Ask me how I know." She turned her attention to Corey and offered a reassuring smile. "But don't you worry. Those Lone Star Ladies are good. If there's a clue to be found, they'll find it."

"Lone Star Ladies?" Corey looked back and forth between us.

I felt heat rise to my cheeks. How in the world did Maggie know the name of my little text group? Mari, no doubt.

I would have to scold both of them later. If I lived through the humiliation right now, anyway.

"Kind of a long story, but that's the text group name for all the single ladies who work at the clinic." I felt like an idiot for sharing that information out loud. And even stupider once I realized the cameraman was pointing that ridiculous camera my direction once again.

"They're not all single for long, honey," Maggie said, her voice rising. "Mari's getting married, Cassidy's found her Mr. Right—that hunky game warden, Jason—and Brianna's so madly in love with Dr. Cameron that she can't see straight. That just leaves you, sweet girl."

Yep. That just left me. And now, thanks to the camera pointed my way, everyone in the Greater Houston metroplex was about to know it.

CHAPTER FOURTEEN

A nother quick glance at my watch clued me in that I needed to leave. The waiter came back, and I asked for the check. Corey looked absolutely mortified by this.

"No." He shook his head. "It's on me."

"If you're sure. I really need to get back to the clinic."

"Looks like you're not the only one leaving." Maggie gestured to the table where Lance and the cameraman were now making their move. They both rose, tossed a couple of bills down, and stepped away from the table.

Unfortunately, they headed our way.

Ugh.

Lance stopped a few feet away when Corey put his hand up.

"Come on, guys," Lance said. "I've been waiting for a breaking story for months now. I've got to get out of this dead-end job. I want to work for a national network."

"And I'm your ticket out?" Corey gave him a penetrating look.

"Maybe." Lance shrugged. "I don't know."

Corey squared his shoulders. "I'll make you a deal. What's your name again?"

"Lance the Legend, dude. Surprised you don't know it. Everyone in Houston knows Lance the Legend."

"You're in Brenham, honey," Maggie interjected. "We have the best reporter in town. Ever heard of Mollie Kensington? She's the only literary legend I know."

"Never heard of her."

The cameraman nudged him. "Yeah, you have, boss. Remember? Local gal, works for the paper?"

A hint of recognition finally sparked in Lance's eyes. "Oh, right. Well, when she's ready to go big-time, have her give me a call."

Corey cleared his throat. "I'll make you a deal, Lance the Legend. If we find the dog—and I'm sure we will—I'll let you know."

"Ahead of the other networks?"

"Yep. You'll be my first network call."

Lance didn't look convinced. "Promise?"

"Yep."

Lance turned to the cameraman. "You heard that. Right?"

The cameraman nodded. "Yep. Heard it, boss."

They headed out of the restaurant, door slamming behind them.

"Well, that was pathetic," Maggie said. "Now, I'm just going off of first-time meetin' and all, but I'd say that guy's about as worthless as gum on a boot heel."

"You think?" I asked.

"Um, yeah. Could he be any more puffed up? What's up with that Lance the Legend thing? He thinks the sun comes up just to hear him crow." She shoveled down another chip then went off on a tangent about how conceited Lance was. After she finally calmed down, Maggie switched gears on us. "And that cameraman? Why does he look so familiar?"

"Does he?" I asked.

"Yeah, I can't place him, but he's got a familiar look about him, like I've seen him before or something."

"Could be. He's been hanging around a lot," I said.

"I wish they would both go away." These words came from Corey. "I'm done with being followed."

"Honey, you're in the South now." Maggie reached over and rested her hand on his. "We're a hospitable bunch. And we look out for our own. You're one of us now, so rest easy."

A smile lit his face. "I feel like such a foreigner here," he said. "But you've made me feel at home."

"Speaking of home, I've got to get home to bake a strawberry rhubarb pie for a certain someone." She gave me a little wink and then rose. "See you later, gators."

"But you didn't get to order any real food," I said.

"I've had enough chips to fill me up. But I'll order some food to go. Might eat it later." She headed to the reception area to visit with the hostess.

Corey turned his attention to me. "It's almost like you Texans have a language all your own."

"Do we?" I shrugged. "I've lived here all my life, so I don't even notice."

"Let's just say that coming here from up north is a bit of a culture shock." A little smile followed. "In a good way."

He paid the bill, and we headed out to the parking lot. I whistled when I saw his BMW parked next to my worn-out sedan.

"It ain't nuthin', little lady," he said. "Just four wheels and an engine, like any other car."

Sure didn't look like any car I'd been in. And even less when he hit a button on his remote and the top of the car lifted.

"Oh my gosh, I love convertibles." I couldn't help the sigh that followed.

"Want to go for a drive?" he asked.

Out of the corner of my eye, I caught a glimpse of Lance and the camera guy in the KBRT truck. "Um, no. But thanks. I have to get back to work. Thanks for lunch."

"You're welcome."

I opened the door of my car, then turned back to face him. "Oh, one question."

"What's that?"

"Did you like the Blue Bell?"

A smile lit that handsome face, and for a moment all traces of angst seemed to disappear. "Loved it."

"Then you'll definitely have to come back for more."

"I'd love that. Hopefully, next time I come to Brenham it's to pick up Ginger. I won't stop praying until we find her."

Well, that certainly softened my heart toward him. He got into his car and pulled away. The KBRT van followed him. I was relieved not to be watched.

Then again, who would want to watch someone drive away in an old clunker like mine?

I drove back to the clinic with my thoughts firmly wrapped around all that had happened at lunch. I got hung up on the part where the reporter was watching us. The last thing I wanted was to end up on the evening news.

I must've had a somber look on my face when I walked into the lobby, because Cassidy stopped me.

"You okay, girl?"

"Yeah, you kind of look like you did the day your ex showed up to scare you," Mari said.

"It's nothing like that. I just had lunch with Corey, and that reporter showed up with the cameraman. They made things awkward."

"Wait, you had lunch with who?" Mari planted her hands on her hips and stared at me, wide-eyed.

"Corey Wallis." I lowered my voice, hoping to keep this private. "He met me at Triple B's so we could talk about the dog."

"Corey Wallis was the errand you had to run?" Brianna asked.

"Yeah. He wanted to help me figure out who stole her."

"I thought you blamed him?" Mari looked genuinely perplexed.

"I know. I did say that, but after talking to him, I don't think he's got her. If so, he's a great actor."

"I know a few football players, and they're not actors," Mari countered. "My senior year of high school, my drama teacher tried to put our star quarterback in the lead role of *Brigadoon*, and let's just say it didn't end well—for the football player or the rest of us in the cast. You don't even want to know what happened during one of the Scottish dance scenes." She pinched her eyes shut as if the whole experience was just too much to relive.

"I didn't realize you had a drama background, Mari."

"Chorus. Don't ask. I was never leading lady material. That was always my aunt Trina. But trust me when I say she was there for every performance at Brenham High, even the infamous one where I played the role of a horse's head."

"A horse's head?"

"*Macbeth*, the musical," she explained. "My drama teacher's own vision of the play. Don't ask. It went down in flames."

"At least you weren't the back end of the horse," Cassidy said.

"Silver linings." Mari shot her a playful look.

Tyler walked into the reception area at that particular moment, file in hand. He laid it on the reception desk. "Here's that file you were asking for earlier, Brianna."

She took it then looked back at me. "What were we talking about again?" Brianna asked. "I can't keep up."

"Football players and acting," I said. "Corey's not an actor. He's the real deal."

"My, my." Mari gave me an inquisitive look. "And we've only known him. . .what? A day? Two? Three?"

"Long enough to see he's not the one who took the dog," I explained. "That's all I meant by that."

"Inquiring minds want to know how you came to this conclusion," Tyler said. He gave me an inquisitive look.

"Oh, we had lunch just now."

"You just had lunch with the Texans' new star quarterback?" Tyler's eyes widened. "The one who's threatened to sue us?"

"I don't think he's going to sue us. That's just his manager talking."

"Well, that's a relief." Tyler shrugged. "But, you had lunch with the guy?"

"Yeah, at Triple B's. He showed up in a fake beard and baseball cap. He thought that would keep the paparazzi away. But it didn't work."

"And you said he wasn't an actor." Mari rolled her eyes. "Please."

"He's not," I said. "He's a genuinely good guy who's trying to get acclimated to Texas. Would you believe he never tasted Blue Bell before?"

Everyone gasped in unison.

"He had his first scoop in front of me. Trust me when I say his reaction was genuine."

This led to an even more intense conversation about the flavor of ice cream he'd chosen. In Brenham we took our Blue Bell very seriously.

"So, based on a stranger's random reaction to ice cream, you've concluded that he couldn't possibly be responsible for the dognapping?" Cassidy asked. "I guess that makes sense."

"There was more to it than that," I said. "I have a pretty good liar, liar radar."

They all looked at me at once. "Okay, okay, not so much when it came to Matt Foster. I'll give you that much. But my radar is much more in tune these days. I won't be taken in again by a liar. That's all I meant by that."

"Mm-hmm." Tyler didn't look convinced.

"Ta-ta, y'all. Work calls!" I went back to the grooming area and put on a clean apron before bathing my next dog, a little male dachshund.

The sweet little dog was old and somewhat frail. I'd never seen so much gray on a pup before. I was sure at some point this dog had been black and tan, but those colors had long since morphed into completely different shades.

"Come on, sweet boy." I gently scooped him into my arms. "You deserve extra TLC."

I lifted him into the bathing sink and warmed the water before adding shampoo. A couple of minutes later, I was deep in thought as I lathered him up.

The sweet dog didn't fight me at all. He seemed content to be in my arms.

I couldn't stop thinking about Sasha. Was it really just a few days ago I'd bathed her in this very spot? Unlike this dachshund, she was a handful.

My thoughts gravitated to her—how she'd chewed a hole in my sofa. How she'd curled up in the bed next to me.

How she'd trembled when the news reporters flooded the lobby of the clinic.

How much I missed her right now.

And yet, how sad Corey looked as he talked about his mother.

I rinsed off the pup and towel dried him, not wanting to scare him with the blow dryer.

Then I transferred him to the grooming station to clip his nails. Usually dogs balked at this process, but the old man was a good boy from start to finish.

Afterward, I put a fresh bandanna on him—blue gingham.

"Okay, cowboy," I said. "You're ready for the rodeo."

Only, I wasn't ready to let him go just yet. I held the sweet old boy closer for a moment, enjoying the cuddles.

"You okay over there?"

I turned as I heard Brianna's voice.

"Yeah."

She flashed a smile. "Copper's owner is here to pick him up."

"Oh, perfect timing. I just finished him."

"Want me to carry him out?"

"No," I said. "I'll come."

We made our way to the lobby, and I passed him off to his owner, an older woman named Mrs. Finch.

When she left, Cassidy called me into her office. Tyler's cat, Aggie, was sound asleep on her chair. She booted the feline off so that she could sit down.

"Aggie's moving really slow these days," I said as I watched the older cat amble out of the room.

"Yeah, I'm worried. The poor thing is locked up with arthritis, even with anti-inflammatories." She turned her attention to me. "I want to talk to you about that reporter. Lance what's-his-name."

"What about him?"

"I spent last night researching some of the stories he's done. While doing that, I stumbled across a couple of personal stories about him that were troubling."

"Like what?" I asked.

"You remember that big national story that broke years ago about the reporter who made up a story about being in the military?"

"Vaguely."

"Well, this guy is kind of like that. Everything with Lance the Legend is trumped up to be bigger than it is. He finds scandals where there are no scandals. He finds stories where there are no stories."

"Crazy."

Before we could say anything else, a couple of squeals sounded from the lobby. I rushed out to make sure everything was okay.

That's when I saw Ms. Peach—Mari's grandmother—had arrived with her cat, Hector. I could tell right away that something was wrong with the poor old thing.

Turned out the squeals were from another client whose hyper dog had tried to get a little too close to Hector. Hector didn't do dogs. And he'd apparently lashed out at the hundred-pound Bernese Mountain dog, scratching him on the nose and causing bleeding.

After making sure the dog was okay, I struck up a conversation with Peach and Mari, who were concerned about Hector's current condition. Then I somehow found myself in the exam room with our patient, something that rarely happened. I had my own grooming space at Lone Star, and exam rooms definitely weren't my domain.

Still, Ms. Peach obviously wanted me here and continued to include me in the conversation until we were all settled around the exam table with Hector the center of attention.

Poor cat. He looked thin. And his hair was falling out too.

"How long has this been going on, Grandma?" Mari said. "You didn't mention that Hector was sick when I called you yesterday."

"I didn't want to trouble you, honey. You're in the middle of wedding planning. And I know Hector's not high on your patient list."

"Now, Grandma, you know I love—tolerate—Hector." Mari reached to pet him, and he hissed at her.

Kristin joined us a couple minutes later. I offered to leave, but Ms. Peach insisted I stay. Kristin didn't seem to mind, so I stood off at a distance.

Kristin put her stethoscope in place and listened to Hector's heart and lungs. I didn't know much about veterinary work, but I could tell from the look on her face that something was amiss.

When she finally spoke, her words were laced with concern. "Mrs. Nelson—"

"Peach."

"Ms. Peach, when did these symptoms begin?"

"I believe Hector ate a slice or two of my pecan pie a couple of days back," Peach confessed, her words rushed.

"Pecan pie?" Kristin pulled the stethoscope out of her ears. "Did I hear that right?"

"Don't knock it till you try it," Peach said.

"You had me at pecan." Kristin laughed. "But that much sugar is definitely not good for cats. Especially with those strong spices."

"Yes, I know. But controlling a cat as old as Hector is like asking me to stop breathing. He gets into everything. I'm worried about my poor little boy."

Brianna chose that moment to walk in, files in hand.

"Oh, Ms. Peach! I heard that song on the radio, the one about Hector! 'The Cat Can Stay'!"

Peach groaned.

"It's just the sweetest and funniest thing ever," Brianna said. "And it's so true. When you fall in love with someone, you're taking on their quirks...and their pets."

"Trina really hit the nail on the head with that one," Mari said. "If anyone knows the intricacies of Grandma's quirks, it's Trina."

"I'm surprised my daughter still finds my life inspirational," Peach said, eyes now rolling. "Now if you all will excuse me, I'm only here to focus on Hector today, not my daughter's over-the-top musical career, wonderful as it may be. Let's stick to the matter at hand, shall we? Or have we all forgotten this is a veterinary clinic?"

We hadn't forgotten. Kristin, in particular, seemed put off by that last question.

Mari grew silent, and I could read the concern in her eyes.

I was concerned too. Something had triggered Ms. Peach. . .but what? And why?

CHAPTER FIFTEEN

Ms. Peach was definitely offended by her daughter's latest hit song. But why? It painted a lovely picture of her relationship with the good reverend. Everyone thought it was touching and sweet.

Except her, obviously. Was she really upset about it?

Nah, surely not. The song was adorable. Completely and totally adorable. Everyone in town thought so. And, from what I'd heard from Mari, it was getting nationwide attention too.

Kristin cleared her throat and continued to examine Hector, who flinched when she pressed on his upper abdomen.

"I want to run a full gamut of tests on Hector," Kristin said. "With your permission, Ms. Peach."

"Of course. Do whatever you need to do. Cost is no object. I want the best for my boy. Let's get to the bottom of this."

Mari picked up Hector, and he hissed at her, so Kristin intervened and swept the cat into her arms. Before long she was headed out the back door of the exam room, toward the lab.

Mari and I followed on her heels until we were all in the lab with Kristin and Hector. Safely out of earshot, I was finally free to voice my thoughts. "Your grandmother seems pretty upset about that song."

Mari laughed. "Don't let her fool you. She loves every bit of time in the spotlight she can get. Grandma Peach was made for stardom and so was Hector."

"But something's off today," Kristin chimed in. "She's just not herself. Is she not feeling well?"

"She's worried about Hector, of course," Mari said. "But I don't think she's slept much. She and the reverend are also concerned about their friend, Curtis Elban. I heard all about it on a phone call last night."

"Who is Curtis Elban?" I asked.

"He's a fellow church member at First Prez whose second wife passed away several months ago."

"I remember Curtis," Kristin said. "He had that little three-legged dog, Tripod."

Mari nodded. "Yes."

"Poor Tripod." Kristin released a little sigh. "He passed away a while back. We did our best to save him."

"You do your best to save all of them," Mari said. "But Curtis has really been grieving—the loss of his wife and his dog. He's been leaning on Grandma and Reverend Nelson a lot, I think. Maybe too much."

"Poor guy." Kristin sighed. "I feel for him."

"Me too," Mari countered. "But I think he's been overstaying his welcome. Grandma made a snide remark about putting in a room for him. Apparently, he's at their place. . .a lot. And you know Reverend Nelson. He's such a kindhearted soul that he wouldn't send him packing, especially under the circumstances."

"He's a sweetheart," Kristin said.

I wasn't sure if she meant the Reverend or Mr. Elban.

Kristin did a thorough examination of Hector before attempting to draw any blood. When she reached that point, Mari jumped in to help. It took the two of them to get the deed done.

"I hope Hector's okay. He's definitely off his game." Mari's words were laced with concern. "I'm so worried about how it will affect Grandma if anything ever happens to this old boy." She tried to stroke Hector on the head, but he turned to snap at her fingertip. "Okay then."

"We'll do our best," Kristin said.

To which Mari responded, "You always do."

But we all knew that some cases—even the ones that seemed simple and straightforward—could end up being anything but.

Dr. Tyler came into the room and grabbed a box of syringes from the cabinet above where we stood. "Sorry. Didn't mean to get in your way."

"No worries," Kristin said. "Just having a look at Hector. He's in rough shape, I'm afraid."

Tyler paused and gazed down at the cat. "I would help you, but the last time I tried to examine him, I ended up with scratches that took weeks to heal."

Mari sighed. "Hector's a problem child. But I don't know what will happen to Grandma Peach if he doesn't pull through. Like I said, she's already working overtime to help Curtis recover from the loss of his wife, Donna Sue. I'm just praying they find the right balance in all of this, especially with my wedding coming up. It's a lot."

Tyler looked stunned. "Do you mean Donna Sue Specklemeyer?"

Mari nodded. "Yes, did you know her?"

"I remember the name," he responded. "One doesn't tend to forget a name like Specklemeyer."

"A name she never changed, even though she had four husbands," Mari interjected. "If you want to know more about all of that, just ask Grandma Peach. But not right now, obviously."

"I was wondering why I hadn't seen her standard poodle in a while," Tyler said. "Princessa is long overdue for her shots."

"That's why," Mari responded. "Donna Sue passed away several months ago. God rest her soul."

They had lost me at Specklemeyer. This was a name I did not know. And I said so, because with a name like that I felt compelled to be in the know.

"Donna Sue Specklemeyer is the gal who stole Curtis Elban from my grandmother a couple of years ago," Mari explained.

"Mari Evans, take that back!" Peach's shrill voice sounded from behind us, and I realized she had walked straight into our conversation. Oops.

"Grandma, you're not supposed to be back here," Mari scolded. "This is an employees-only area."

"I'll do as I please." Peach planted her balled-up fists on her hips. "And for the record, I was never interested in Curtis Elban!"

"Grandma, really?" Mari shook her head then turned to face me. "She baked that man at least a dozen pies during their courtship, then he up and left her for Donna Sue."

"I refuse to further engage in this conversation." Peach scooped up Hector into her arms. "If anyone wants me, I'll be at the house, tending to my sick cat. I would think you would have more compassion on him—and the memory of sweet Donna Sue—than to start such ridiculous gossip, Marigold Evans."

Mari's grin flipped upside down. "Don't leave in a huff, Grandma," she pleaded. "I was just teasing. You know that. Besides, Kristin wasn't done with her exam yet. So you can't take Hector. You want to know what's wrong with him, don't you?"

"I told you, it's the pecan pie."

"This isn't food poisoning, Ms. Peach," Kristin said. "At least it doesn't present that way. His upper abdomen is very tight to the touch, but I believe the issue might actually be coming from his heart."

"Oh my goodness." Peach looked as if she might be ill.

"I heard a bit of fluid buildup in his upper abdominal area when I listened through my stethoscope," Kristin explained. "I can remove some of it now to relieve the pressure, but I'll have to take him to the surgery area to do it. Shouldn't take long."

"Whatever you think is best." Peach's eyes filled with tears. "Money's no object, Dr. Kristin. Do what you can to save my baby."

"I will." She lifted Hector, who never even flinched at her touch. "I'll be right back."

She disappeared into a separate exam room, and Mari went with her. I did my best to keep the conversation with Peach light, hoping she would be okay.

It took some time for Mari and Kristin to return. By the time they arrived, we'd covered every topic I could think of—from the weather to our preferences in Blue Bell flavors.

Dr. Kristin passed Hector back into Peach's outstretched arms.

"I got off quite a bit of fluid. More than I expected. He's definitely presenting with congestive heart failure, but we need to get to the root cause."

"Oh, my poor baby!" Tears filled Peach's eyes.

"We'll know more after the labs have returned. I'll be in touch with results in a day or so," Kristin said. "In the meantime, please keep him on a bland diet. Nothing with salt or sugar. And make sure he doesn't get overly excited. I'm going to give you some steroids and heart meds too."

"Heart meds?" Peach's eyes widened.

"Yes, I'm picking up on a murmur. I've never noticed it until today. But don't worry, okay?"

Ms. Peach nodded, but I could see the concern in her eyes.

Mari went to fetch the meds for Kristin, and then we all made our way to the reception desk so that Ms. Peach could pay her bill. She seemed to calm down a bit once we were out of the exam area.

"I'm sorry I overreacted about Donna Sue." Peach glanced my way as she passed a credit card over the counter to Brianna. "I'm still trying to process her death. I always thought she would live forever."

"Why is that?" I asked.

Peach sighed. "She's outlived four husbands. To be honest, I was convinced she would kill Curtis too."

"She killed the first four?" I asked.

"Well, it's just a theory." Peach offered a little shrug. "She fed them fried chicken and other fatty foods. I tried to tell her, but would she listen to me?"

"Oh my." I didn't know what else to say. After all, I'd had fried chicken a few days back at Carmela's place. And mashed potatoes with gravy. And flan. Always flan.

When Peach finished paying her bill, Mari walked her to the car. Brianna was busy helping another client, and I figured I'd better head back to my grooming area to prep for my incoming client, a bloodhound with arthritis.

I reached for the hand broom and used it to brush off the grooming station then did inventory of my brushes, shears, and clippers.

Mari showed up at my door a couple minutes later and walked straight toward me.

"Your poor grandma," I said as I cleaned my clippers. "I suppose she's at the age where many of her friends are passing away."

"Yes, but don't be fooled by her," Mari said. "I never heard her speak one kind word about Donna Sue Specklemeyer until the poor woman died."

"Oh my." I set the clippers down and reached for the broom to sweep dog hair off the floor.

"Yep." Mari nodded. "She thought Donna Sue was a little...loosey-goosey."

"I see. But at least she's finding some nice things to say about her after the fact." I kept sweeping.

"Funny how that happens," Mari countered. "We need to learn to relish the time we have together while we have it."

"Agreed." I swept the dog hair into a dustpan and dumped it in the trash can.

Mari's eyes took on a faraway look. "If only we could see the good in people while we have them with us."

My heart twisted, and I immediately thought of Little Lita. She had always seen the good in me and vice versa. I had learned that much from her, at the very least.

I knew the sadness in Mari's eyes well. She had lost her mama a couple years back. Grief was still affecting us both.

Just as quickly, my friend snapped back to attention. "Hey, speaking of Curtis Elban, he's got a dog in need of grooming."

"I thought his dog died."

"This is his wife's dog."

"I thought his wife died."

"She did." Mari paused. "Anyway, I heard all about it last time Grandma and I ran into him at Bubba's Weed & Feed."

"You seem to spend a lot of time at Bubba's," I countered.

"Duh. Anyway, Curtis was there looking for dog shampoo and seemed a bit perplexed by it all. He inherited Donna Sue's dog—some sort of large breed with curls."

"Standard poodle. Tyler just said that."

"Oh, right. Anyway, he mentioned that Donna Sue always took care of the dog's grooming with that mobile groomer you don't like."

"Danielle at Vanity Fur?" I shivered at the mention of her name. The girl had done her best to sabotage my good name last year. I had forgiven her but kept my distance.

"Right. Anyway, he was never a fan of hers and doesn't want to use her again."

"Have him give me a call. Better yet, give him my card."

"I think he lives close to you," she said. "Just a couple of blocks away."

"In that case, let me write down my address." I scribbled it onto the card. "But he'll still have to come here for the grooming."

"The man or the dog?" She laughed. "Are you a barbershop now?"

"Not even close. Though I did manage to get Corey Wallis to lose his fake beard, so there is that."

I finished up my last groom of the day and then headed to the parking lot to get in my car. I wished like crazy I had that tiny little dachshund to keep me company. Things just weren't the same now that Sasha was gone.

My heart twisted as I thought about the joy she had brought into my life in such a short time. Dogs were like that. They kidnapped pieces of our heart and kept them forever.

Kidnapped. Ugh. Had she been taken from us. . .for good? I prayed not.

Before heading home, I shot off a quick text to my mama: If you see anything in the paper about me, just ignore it. I didn't steal anyone's dog.

Trust me. I've heard all about it, she responded. Everyone in the neighborhood is talking. My phone is ringing off the wall.

Sorry, Mama. But trust me. I didn't do anything wrong.

I know you, my sweet girl. You never do.

"Never" might be a stretch, but in this case I was 100 percent innocent.

Why, then, did I feel so guilty?

CHAPTER SIXTEEN

On Thursday evening, the Lone Star Ladies met at Mario's Mexican Restaurant for dinner. Brianna was very chatty. Cassidy seemed preoccupied with her phone. Texting Jason, no doubt. And Kristin had a faraway look in her eyes. I wondered if she was thinking about Tyler.

Mari was her usual self, bubbly and fun, as we placed our orders, teasing with the waitress as she attempted to order in Spanish.

"So, you want the pollo in the bano?" the waitress asked. "You might want to rethink that."

"Oops. I meant the Pollo Adobado." Mari giggled. "And I'll be eating it at the table, not in the bathroom."

After the waitress left to turn in our orders, our conversation focused on work until Brianna finally turned the chatter to Corey Wallis. I still felt guilty every time I heard his name, as if I had somehow caused that fiasco with his dog. It wasn't true, of course, but I couldn't shake the feeling that I'd played a role in his sadness.

And my sadness. I missed Sasha—Ginger—as well.

I also couldn't stop fretting over the response of the news teams—both in the Houston area and in nearby Austin. It didn't feel good to have so many people hating on me. None of this was my fault, after all. Still, the idea that people thought badly of me was really troubling. How could the owner of the runaway dog come out of this looking like a hero while the dog foster took the blame?

Ugh.

I decided to put all this out of my mind and focus on my friends. These days, with everyone falling in love, these moments together away from the office were few and far between. Besides, we only had a couple weeks until Mari's wedding. Then everything would change.

Or not. Maybe life would go on just as it had, but with Parker and Mari living in the big house on Trina's property so they could be near their beloved pups.

That sounded and felt a little weird to me—my friend married and living with a man—but maybe I'd get used to it. Maybe someday it would happen to me too. I hoped.

Before long we had our drinks and our food, and we dove right in. I was always happy with tacos. Couldn't get enough of them, in fact, though these didn't hold a candle to Carmela's. Still, they weren't half bad. And I certainly wouldn't complain, not when I got to eat them surrounded by my besties, my Lone Star Ladies.

Brianna took a bite of her enchiladas and leaned back in her chair, her mind still on Corey Wallis. "I think he's great. He's an amazing quarterback. But I don't trust that manager of his."

"Why not?" Kristin asked as she jabbed her fork into her taco salad. "What brought that up?"

"Oh, I was just thinking." Brianna dabbed at her lips with her napkin to get rid of the enchilada sauce. "I saw him hovering around the clinic earlier in the day."

"Today?" My heart started racing at once. Was Ray Haas back to make more trouble? "What's he doing back in Brenham?"

"No." Brianna shook her head. "The day Ginger went missing."

"You're saying he got to the clinic before the picketers?" This question came from Mari, who didn't look at all pleased by this information.

Brianna nodded. "Yes, I saw him pull up in that red Tesla of his and park across the street when I first took the dogs outside to the play yard. I would recognize that car anywhere."

"Why didn't you tell us?" Mari asked. "That's important information, Brianna."

"I didn't think much of it at the time. I mean, a lot of people have Teslas, you know? And I knew—because you guys told me—that we were about to have an incoming crowd of people upset at us for not giving the dog back. Just figured the protest was starting when I saw him."

"What time was that, do you think?" Cassidy asked.

She shrugged. "I don't know." A pause followed, and then she said, "Oh, wait! I remember snapping a picture of Romeo when I was out in the yard."

"Romeo?" Cassidy asked.

"The Labrador. Belongs to the Harrisons."

"Oh, right." Cassidy took a swig of her drink.

"It should have a time stamp, right?" Kristin asked.

"Pictures always do," I said. Maybe technology would save us this time.

She pulled out her phone and scrolled until she found what she was looking for. Then Brianna flipped the phone around to confirm.

Or so I thought. Turned out it wasn't a picture of the Lab.

"Look at Sasha."

"Ginger," we all said as we took in the picture of the tiny dachshund playing in the outdoor play yard at the clinic. What a little doll she was. Very photogenic, for sure.

Brianna sighed. "She loved that little condo that Parker built so much. She ran in and out the whole time, like it had a revolving door."

Brianna pulled up another picture of Romeo and then clicked on it. "Okay, I can see now that this picture was taken at 11:14 a.m."

"That's a good fifteen minutes before anyone else arrived," Cassidy said. "I remember specifically that they arrived at eleven thirty because Mrs. Martin had just walked in the door with her bulldog—the one with the leaky bladder—and he had an eleven thirty appointment." She scrolled on her phone until she found what she was looking for. "Yep. Eleven thirty. I keep the schedule app on my phone just in case the system at work goes down."

"So, we know that he was here before the others," Kristin said. "What does that prove?"

"For one thing, that he knew the crowd was coming to protest before we did," Mari said. "Which makes me wonder if maybe he was the one who set all of that up."

"Why would Corey's manager set up a picket outside our clinic?" I asked as I wiped my fingers with my napkin. "That makes no sense to me."

"To get more publicity for his client," Mari said. "Sounds exactly like something a manager would do." She reached for her fork and jabbed it into her chicken.

"I'm more inclined to think the reporter set up the picket," Brianna said. "If he's really into drumming up stories to make them look bigger than they really are, he would want a crowd here."

I shook my head as memories flooded over me. "Y'all, I distinctly remember seeing Ray Haas talking to the woman who laid down in front of the door. So, maybe he did orchestrate the protest."

"I say we look that woman up on social media," Cassidy said.

I reached for my water glass, somewhat preoccupied. "You have her name?"

"No, but I know who does." She grabbed her phone and made a call. Minutes later, we all heard—thanks to speakerphone—what local reporter Mollie Kensington had to say.

"The woman who blocked the doorway?" Mollie asked. "Yeah, I got her name. In fact, I'm writing an article about her for tomorrow's paper."

"Really?" Mari asked as she pushed her plate aside. "She gets her own article?"

"Sure does," Mollie explained. "And here's why: She's not an activist at all. And she definitely wasn't on a hunger strike. I saw her drive through Burger King on the way out of town. Lauren Neeley works for a theater company in the Houston area."

"Are you saying that protest was some sort of acting gig for her?" Kristin asked.

"Looks like it. Someone set the whole thing up. She's not the only one I traced to that organization. Several of the other protesters are members too. And some of the others appear to be connected by a larger organization of actors in the Houston area. They're all linked."

"So, our building was picketed by an actors' group that had nothing to do with the love of dogs?" Mari asked.

"It would seem that way," Mollie responded. "I planned to call you before the article came out so you would be aware. But this is too big of a story to let go."

"Since you're on this story anyway, can I ask a favor?" Mari interjected. "I'm a little busy with wedding prep and don't have a lot of extra time to spare looking for clues."

"How can I help?" Mollie asked.

"It would be nice to know if Ray Haas has a connection to this theater group."

"Or Lance the Legend," I added. "He might be the one who set it up if Ray didn't."

"I'll see what I can find out." Mollie promised to be in touch with any information.

When the conversation ended, we all started talking on top of each other. It was in the middle of this chaos that I noticed Maggie Jamison approaching our table.

"Hey, sorry I'm late."

"Glad you could join us, Maggie." Mari's lips curled up in a smile. "Welcome to the Lone Star Ladies."

"We're going to have to change our name if I join the group." She slipped her purse off her shoulder and put it on the bench between us.

"Nah, you're as much a part of the Lone Star Team as anyone," Kristin said. "After all you've done for the rescue? Please."

"If you say so." She reached for a menu. "But this single ladies' group of yours is changing their status one at a time. Half of you are already on your way to the altar."

"Hardly." Brianna laughed.

"Check back again in a few months," Cassidy said, and then smiled.

Kristin's phone started ringing, and she glanced down then said, "Hey, I've got to take this. It's Tyler. We've got a trip to Navasota tomorrow to see my folks. He seems anxious about it."

"Anxious about seeing your folks?" Mari gave her a curious look.

"Yeah, something about fishing with my dad. I don't know." Kristin answered the call then rose and took several steps toward the front door of the restaurant before disappearing outside.

"Must be really personal if she's leaving the restaurant," Maggie observed.

"It's just loud in here," Mari countered. And it was. Crazy loud.

"Tyler's been acting a little weird lately," Cassidy observed. "Anyone else noticed it?"

"Yeah." Brianna nodded. "He was late coming back from lunch yesterday, and when he got there, he seemed really anxious."

"Weird," I said. Tyler was usually pretty easygoing. Well, when we didn't have the press or picketers outside our door.

Maggie looked a little down in the dumps, but I couldn't tell if the noise was bothering her or something else. She wasn't a usual member of our group, and I hadn't spent as much time with her to know her quirks.

I quietly asked if she was okay.

"Oh, yes." She offered me a faint smile. "I'm just worried about Juanita."

Cassidy's brow wrinkled. "Who's that?"

"The little girl I sponsor in Honduras. I just got word today that her mother passed away. Apparently, it happened over a month ago, and I'm just now hearing."

"What will happen to her?" Mari asked. "Does she have family?"

"They've moved her out of the program because she's now a ward of the state. I can't tell you what this is doing to my heart. I've sponsored her since she was three."

"How old is she now?" Brianna asked.

"Nine." Maggie paused and her eyes brimmed with tears. "And living in an orphanage now, from what I've been told. It's all just so heartbreaking."

"My goodness." I gave her a sympathetic look. "That's a lot. Why don't you go and fetch her? Bring her back. We'll turn her into a Texan in no time."

"You think?"

"Well, sure," I said. "Pray about it, anyway."

"I will." She sighed. "To be honest, I've been so preoccupied with my own stuff lately that I haven't had time to process the news about Juanita's family."

"What stuff?" Mari asked. "If it's not too personal."

"This is the Lone Star Ladies," Cassidy said. "We get personal here."

"Well, if you say so." Maggie closed the menu and set it down on the table in front of her. "You know I've been selling my homemade dog treats in shops all over the place. They're doing really well."

"I'm so proud of you." Mari beamed like a proud mama.

"Anyway, I was in the cutest little dog bakery in the Woodlands and got to talking with the owner."

"The Woodlands?" Cassidy let out a whistle. "You really are branching out, Maggie. That's a long way from here."

"Well, this is a special case. I met the owner at a Trader's Day event a few months back." Her cheeks turned pink. "He had a booth and was selling his wares. I had a booth and was selling my wares. We're both widows."

"Widower," Cassidy corrected her. "I think that's the proper term for a man who's lost his wife."

Maggie shrugged. "His wife, Julia, died four years ago after a really complicated journey with MS."

"Oh, wow. That's a hard one," I interjected. I knew that particular illness well, since my grandmother had battled it most of her life.

"The dog bakery was really his wife's idea, and he's kept it running since she passed away, but he's been thinking of selling."

"Maggie, no!" Mari let out a gasp. "Please don't tell me you're thinking of moving away to the Woodlands!"

"You're buying his business?" I asked.

"But you can't move away!" Mari said.

"Who's moving away?" Kristin walked in on the conversation, looking back and forth between all of us.

"No one," Maggie said. "That's not where I was going with this. But it's good to know your feelings are that strong on the matter. I was going to tell you that he's found a buyer and he's thinking of moving out here, to Brenham. He's looking for a place to lease."

"Oh. Whew." Mari looked incredibly relieved at this news.

I felt that sense of relief too. Maggie was a fixture at Lone Star. She'd been helping Mari for ages.

Still, I felt there was more to this story that she wasn't telling.

"So, let's get to the point." I turned to give her a pensive look. "Maggie, does this fella happen to have a thing for you?"

Her cheeks flamed pink, and she pulled off her cap.

"Well, yeah, since you asked. See. . .Chuck has asked me to marry him."

CHAPTER SEVENTEEN

M aggie! You're getting married?" Mari's hand went to her chest.
"No." Maggie shook her head, a pained expression in her eyes. "I—I
turned him down."

"Oh." Mari's smile instantly faded. "But why?"

"I've only known him a few months," she said. "That's why. But I figure
if he's moving out here, we'll have a chance to get to know each other better.
I don't want to marry a fella just because he's lonely. You know?"

I did. But didn't say so.

"Besides, I've been single a l-o-n-g time." She drew out the word.
"After Drew died, I kind of got accustomed to doing things my own way.
I don't rightly know how I'd do with a husband in the picture. He might
cramp my style."

"Understood," Mari said. "I've had that same thought. But when you
really love someone, you work all of that out." She paused. "At least, I
assume you do. I've never been married before."

"Well, that's the thing." Maggie offered a little shrug. "I have. I was
married to Drew for more than twenty years. And trust me when I say that
marriage is a two-way street. Problem is, I've been on a one-way street for
so long now that I'm not sure I've got it in me to adjust."

"Sure you can," Cassidy said. "Take it from someone who just opened
her heart to romance."

"But we won't push you," Brianna said.

"That's right," I added. "We'll pray that God shows you what to do.
And you'd better bring this guy around to meet all of us as soon as he
gets to town."

"I was kind of hoping I could bring him to your wedding as my date." Maggie's lips tipped up in a smile. "That'll be a good way to let him meet everyone at once."

"You bet." Mari nodded. "Perfect. Can't wait to meet him. But I'm warning you now, I'm probably going to slip into matchmaker mode and insist you marry him. If I approve of him, I mean." She offered Maggie a little wink. "You're like a mama to me. Not just anyone can sweep you away."

"Understood." The tenderness in Maggie's smile was a little out of character. The normally brusque gal was suddenly getting soft and mushy on us. Love could do that to a person, I supposed.

The waitress returned and took Maggie's order, and before long she had food too. By then, most of the rest of us were done eating, but we were always willing to hang around for a while and visit.

Mari's phone rang and she answered it with a quick, "Hey Parker. Can I call you back? I'm out to dinner with the girls." She paused and then looked at all of us. "He wants me to put the phone on speaker so he can tell us something."

We all agreed that was fine, so Mari did just that. A few seconds later, Parker's voice sounded.

"Okay, weird story," he said. "It's been bugging me since the other day."

"What's that?" Mari asked.

"That cameraman, the one in the mask. I'm pretty sure I know that guy. We went to school together here in Brenham."

"But he works in Houston now?" Mari asked.

"I guess." Parker answered. "I lost touch with him. He was always kind of a rough dude, getting into trouble in school."

"What's his name?" Mari asked. "I wonder if I know him."

"Joey Hansen."

She gasped. "Yeah, I know that name. He used to run with a rough crowd."

"Right. But I thought he settled down. He got married, I think."

"Yeah, he got married all right," Mari said. "And then he left Sabrina and their kids and took off for Houston."

"Oh, I know Sabrina Hansen," I said after a moment of thinking it through. "She owns a Pekingese."

"Yes, long-haired," Mari said.

I remembered it clearly. "She brought him in for a groom a couple months ago. She was really worried about paying for it, so I gave her a discount."

EVERY DOG HAS HIS DAY

"There's a reason she was worried," Parker continued. "When Joey took off, he literally left her to fend for herself and the kids. I just did some digging and found out all of this."

Parker kept talking, but Brianna decided to pull up pictures of Joey Hansen on social media. She turned her phone around to show off photos of a clean-cut young man who barely resembled the cameraman.

"I can't believe that's the same guy." Mari groaned. "No wonder he was wearing a mask. He knew better than to show his face in Brenham."

I had a feeling there was more to that story than we realized at the moment. Parker must've been feeling the same thing.

"I'm thinking we need to be extra careful at the wedding," he said. "Something about this guy just feels off. I wouldn't want him to turn up. You know? And we're getting married out in the open, so. . ."

"I say you hire security for your wedding." These words came from Cassidy, who looked more than a little worried by this conversation.

"I'm already on it," Parker said. "I made a call to Officer Dennison at Brenham PD and explained the situation. He suggested we hire off-duty officers for the big day, especially since Trina's going to be part of it. Paparazzi will likely show up because she's involved. And now that we're being swarmed with media-types because of this dachshund, we've got to be extra careful."

I sighed. Loudly.

"I didn't think about that." Mari chewed her lip. "Good grief. Maybe we should run off and elope, Parker."

"Don't you dare!" Cassidy and I cried out in unison.

"You deserve your big day, Mari," Kristin said. "If anyone does, you do. You're always taking care of everyone—and everything—else. You deserve the best."

"We'll get this figured out before then," Parker said. "Don't you worry. But be on the lookout, in case he shows up again. Now we know who he really is."

Mari ended the call. I could tell she was worried, though. I would be too. Getting married out in an open field like that was a risky move, especially with all this going on.

"I'm going to ask Grandma Peach about Joey Hansen," Mari said. "She's lived in Brenham her whole life and knows everyone. If anyone can glean more information about that family, she can."

We all agreed that was a terrific idea.

We wrapped up our meal and paid our bills, then headed out to the parking lot. As I climbed into my car, I couldn't stop thinking about how things were changing in our little group. Maggie had received a marriage proposal. Mari was getting married. Kristin and Tyler were thick as thieves. And Cassidy had Jason.

Before long, I might be the only single Lone Star Lady left.

CHAPTER EIGHTEEN

I tossed and turned for hours that night. In my mind, all sorts of scenarios played out related to Ginger. In one of them, I imagined her in a drainage pipe, hunkered down to get away from the rain. In another, I pictured an abusive dog thief withholding food and treating her harshly.

My heart twisted as I imagined her going without food, especially when I had that big bag of food in the kitchen. And sleeping on the hard ground instead of that plush bed I'd bought for her? It seemed cruel and heartless. Every scenario brought tears to my eyes and added another layer of angst to my sleepless night.

I ushered up several prayers asking God to take care of the precious little dog. I knew He cared about the beasts of the field and the birds of the air. Surely He cared for ornery little dachshunds too.

On Friday morning, we were met in the clinic's lobby by Cassidy, who was visibly upset. I could tell she had been crying.

"What's happened?" I asked, my heart doing that beat-skip-skip thing.

Her gaze shot in the direction of Dr. Tyler's office then back to us. "We need to give Dr. Tyler some space today, y'all."

"Why?" I asked.

"It's Aggie." She lowered her voice and gestured for us to join her in her tiny office. Once we were all inside, she shut the door.

"What's happened, Cassidy?" Mari planted her hands on her hips.

"Aggie passed away in the night."

We all let out a collective gasp. Aggie had been a part of us all these years. I couldn't even imagine the office without that finicky old cat.

"Tyler said he passed quietly in his sleep. He brought the body."

"Oh, this is awful." I'd never known a day at Lone Star Veterinary Clinic without Aggie in it. Things just wouldn't be the same around here. I felt the sting of tears in my eyes.

"I'll call the crematorium," Brianna offered.

"No." Cassidy shook her head. "I already did all of that just minutes after he told me. And I made a paw imprint so Dr. Tyler can keep that as a memento."

We spent a few minutes talking through the plan of action. This was just too much in light of everything else going on. And poor Tyler! No doubt he was devastated right now.

I had a chance to see for myself a little while later when we were called into an office meeting.

"I guess you guys have heard." Tyler's words were laced with emotion, something that didn't happen very often. He was our leader, our rock.

Kristin reached for his hand. "We're all so sorry, Ty."

"Thanks. Me too. I've had Aggie since, well. . .I was an Aggie." He released a lingering sigh. "He wandered into the patio of my apartment and came scratching at my window. I let him in. He kind of attached himself to me."

"That's how it is with cats," Kristin said.

"Yeah, dog lovers prep for months to adopt a dog," Mari said. "They get their house ready. Buy all the right foods. Adopt from a shelter, rescue, or breeder after filling out a ton of paperwork and waiting for approval. Cat owners are like, 'Yeah, I found this little guy on my roof.'"

"That's pretty much how it happened," he said. "But Aggie was smart enough to come to my door. I took him in. . .and it was all over after that."

"That's how it goes." I sighed, thinking of Ginger. I missed her so much.

"Life is short." Tyler's gaze traveled to Kristin. "I'm thinking we have to fully live while we can."

I wondered if his words held some sort of hidden meaning. Maybe time would tell.

Kristin wrapped him in a hug, and they grew silent.

The rest of us slipped out of the room to give them some privacy.

"That's just so sad," I said. "The office is going to seem so empty."

Just then, Mari's Cavalier King Charles, Beau Jangles, came barreling down the hallway with Parker on his tail—pun intended.

"Catch him, y'all," Parker called out. "I can't get him to calm down."

121

"So much for the office being so empty." Mari laughed as she coaxed Beau Jangles her way.

We all laughed. Still, my heart hurt.

"First Ginger disappears, now Aggie's gone. I just don't think I can take any more sobering pet stories."

"Then please don't ask me how it's going at the shelter," Cameron said. "It was rough yesterday."

"Are you doing okay juggling your work here with all of that?" Brianna asked.

He shrugged. "I'm doing the best I can, but I'm running on very little sleep." He offered a yawn as if to prove the point. "It's okay. I'm doing what I'm called to do."

"We all are." Mari gave him a tender smile. "Thank you for that, Cameron."

"Of course." He grabbed a file from the reception desk and headed into one of the exam rooms.

As soon as he was out of earshot, Brianna looked my way. "I'm so worried about Cameron."

"Why?"

"He's here as a favor to Tyler and Kristin because their workload was too much. But I think he's buckling under the pressure of juggling two jobs."

"Do you think he's going to quit?" I asked.

"I think he's torn. He told me privately that his heart is really at the shelter. But if he leaves, Tyler and Kristin will be struggling to keep up with the patient load again."

She'd no sooner said the word *patient* than the front door opened and Mari's grandma Peach entered with her little cat, Hector.

"We're here to see Dr. Kristin," she said. "I believe she's got the results of Hector's tests."

"Yes, that's right," Brianna said.

"He's really struggling, poor baby." Peach's eyes flooded with tears, and my heart twisted. "He had a hard night last night."

Oh no. Not today. Was all the news going to be bad today? Why did we give pieces of our hearts to these pets only to see them broken?

Animals seemed to have this effect on us. They grabbed on to our hearts and made themselves at home in our lives. Then, just when we suspected they would go on living forever, they slipped away from us.

Or threatened to.

I could tell Peach was nearly at her breaking point, so I rested my hand on her shoulder. "Do you want me to come in with you when you talk to Kristin?"

Her tender words almost broke my heart. "Would you? Please?"

"Yes, and I'll find Mari. I'm sure she'll come too."

We all met in Exam Room 3 a few minutes later as Kristin explained the results of the tests she'd done.

"I'm afraid the news about Hector isn't good." Kristin lifted Hector onto the exam table and listened to his heart one more time. "He's definitely in congestive heart failure, Mrs. Nelson."

"Oh dear."

"The fluid I drained off earlier is back in force, which just confirms the test results. The heart meds will help to some degree, but this sounds pretty advanced. I'm afraid I hear quite a bit of fluid built up around his heart as well. Would you allow me to do an X-ray to make sure?"

"Of course." Peach's eyes flooded with tears.

"I'm also concerned about his adrenals. I suspect he might have Addison's disease, which could have triggered the heart issues. So his condition is a bit more complex than I would have wanted."

"My poor baby." A lone tear trickled down Peach's wrinkled cheek. It was the first time I'd seen this staunch woman in such a fragile state, and it broke my heart.

I could tell it was wrecking Mari too.

"It would be best if you left Hector here for a few days so that we can take care of him," Kristin said. "We'll do our absolute best, Mrs. Nelson, I promise."

"Of course. Whatever it takes." She reluctantly released the cat into their care and then made her way out to the parking lot.

Mari went with her, and they shared a hug before Peach got into her car and drove away.

When Mari made it back to the reception area, she had tears rolling down her cheeks.

"I can't believe this is happening." Mari leaned against the desk. "I'm so upset for Grandma Peach. Hector means the world to her."

"Kristin is so good at what she does," I countered. "I'm hoping she can turn things around."

Mari sighed. "I can't believe I'm saying this, because we all used to laugh at Grandma Peach for her attachment to Hector, but we'll all be devastated if something happens to him, especially since that song just came out about him and all. The timing of all this is awful."

"I love that she loves her cat," Cassidy said, concern lacing her words. "But Mari, your big day is coming up. I hate to see that joy diminished. I know you. You're going to get so caught up in what your grandmother is feeling that you'll let it rob you of the joy you deserve on your big day."

"True." Mari sighed. "What we need is a good old-fashioned miracle. We need Hector to be healed of this awful illness so that life can move forward."

"That song of Trina's has really taken off," Parker said. "If we got the local country-western deejays to share Hector's story before playing the song, we'd have people all over the country praying."

"Parker, that's it!" Mari flung her arms around his neck and planted a kiss on his lips. She backed away and said, "You're brilliant."

"Parker to the rescue!" Brianna, Cassidy, and I said in unison.

"Yes, Parker to the rescue. . .again." Mari paused. "So, who do we call first?"

"Maybe contact Trina and see what she suggests. She might have connections that will reach more people."

"Great idea. I'm going to call Aunt Trina right now." Mari picked up the phone and made the call. "Hey, Aunt Trina. Can I put you on speakerphone?"

We caught the tail end of her "Sure, honey."

Mari went on to explain the situation, and Trina grew quiet. "Man, I knew he was sickly, but I was hoping it would just turn out to be something small."

"We all were," Mari said. She went on to share Parker's idea about reaching out to deejays.

"I think that's an amazing idea," Trina said. "And it will be best coming from me. I can make some of the calls to the bigger stations and to the ones where I know the deejays personally. How would that be?"

We all agreed that would be an amazing idea.

"Hector is a superstar," Trina said. "Thanks to that song, everyone knows him. I was doing an interview a couple of days back, and the interviewer asked more questions about that cat than she did about my wedding. Can you believe it?"

Mari laughed. "Don't tell Grandma. Her head will get so big it might explode."

"Likely." Trina laughed. "But don't you worry. I'll spread the word."

Mari ended the call and turned back to face us, all smiles. "This is going to be big," she said.

"Hopefully, Lance the Legend won't try to horn in on the action," I said.

"Ugh, I hope not either. Or Joey Hansen." Mari paused and looked our way. "Oh my goodness, I almost forgot to tell you guys. I know more about Joey Hansen now. I had a long talk with Grandma Peach late last night. She called to share her concerns about Hector, but the conversation turned to Joey."

"And she knows him?" Brianna asked.

"She knows his ex-wife's parents," Mari explained. "They go to church with her at First Prez. I'm telling you, my grandmother is a wealth of information. Who needs private eyes when you've got Grandma Peach?"

"True," Brianna said. "Very handy."

"Grandma said Joey has been in a lot of financial trouble. He and his wife split, and she won custody of the kids. He's way behind on child support, and the attorney general's office is coming after him."

"Oh my." These were the only two words I could manage.

"He told his ex-wife that he was out of work. That was his excuse for not paying support for the four kids."

"Four kids are going without food while that guy travels around with Lance the Legend, breaking news stories?" That infuriated me.

"Yeah." Mari nodded. "She said it would be just like him to turn in the dog to get the reward money."

"So, let me understand this." I paced the room. "Lance needs a story. Joey needs money. Do you think they're working together? Maybe they paired up and stole the dog right out from under our noses?"

Brianna nodded. "Sounds like we might have found our man. Or…men, as the case may be."

"So how do we find the dog?" I asked.

Mari shrugged. "Figure out where Joey lives at this current time."

"Easily done." Mari got on the computer and started searching, then said, "Bingo! Got it!"

"How did you do that?" I asked.

She smiled and quirked a brow. "I have my sources."

No doubt she did, but I had to wonder who…and where.

CHAPTER NINETEEN

Sunday, September 17

On Sunday afternoon, I got a call from Mollie Kensington.
"Hey, Isabel. This is Mollie."

"Mollie, how are you?" I kept a watchful eye on the clock. I didn't want to show up at Carmela's late. She took tardiness very seriously, especially on game day.

"You know how I told you about that theater company in Houston?"

"Oh, right. The one with the lady who was pretending to be a protester?" I scrounged through my pantry on the prowl for something to take to Carmela's, some sort of food offering.

"Right. Well, I've done a little more digging, and something's just not adding up. I'm drowning in work on this end but thought you might want to know the name of the company so you can search for more."

"Sure."

"They're called the Etapas Troupe. They have a little theater in the Montrose area in Houston called La Palencia."

"Spanish?" I countered. "*Etapas* means 'stages.'"

"I think some of their people are Hispanic. And they did some sort of performance on Cinco de Mayo, so there might be a strong link there."

"I'll ask Mama if she knows about them."

"Sure," Mollie responded. "Let me know if you find out anything."

I agreed to do that, but then ended the call. With the clock ticking, I needed to get a move on.

When I got to Carmela's house, I asked a pointed question. "Carmela, you have one of those ancestry accounts, don't you?"

She looked up from the saucepan she was stirring. "I do, honey. I've traced my family all the way back to the sixteenth century in Spain. Why do you ask?"

"Can you look up information on anyone? Like, not just people in your family but other people as well?"

"Sure. If there are public records on a person, you'll probably find them listed there. Who are we tracking down?"

"I want to look into a couple of people, actually. Folks who were there on the day Ginger went missing."

"Sure. Be my guest." She gestured for me to take a seat at her computer, which was on a desk in the far corner of the tiny living room. She managed to get me signed in to her ancestry account—though it took a couple of tries on the password—and before I knew it, a whole new world opened up to me.

Literally.

I started with *Joey Hansen, Brenham.*

Bingo. Pages of information popped up—his birth certificate, marriage certificate to Sabrina, and even information about the birth of his four children. Then, near the bottom of the second page, a divorce decree with Washington County.

Maybe I could research Sabrina later. Right now I wanted to turn my attention to someone else.

I typed in *Lance Henderson, Texas* and waited for the results to pop up. Turned out there were quite a few Lance Hendersons in Texas.

And Tennessee. And Kentucky. Weird. That couldn't be the same Lance Henderson, could it? The one on my radar lived and worked in Texas. Still, the date of birth seemed to match most of them. I would have to figure this out later.

Just about the time Carmela called me into the kitchen to eat, I pulled up information on Ray Haas.

"Oh, wow."

"Game time!" Carmela entered the living room with a bowl of salsa in one hand and a bag of tortilla chips in the other. "You ready, girlie? Corey's our starting quarterback."

I loved the way she said "our," as if we owned the Texans.

"Sure. Just one minute." I skimmed all the Ray Haas entries in Texas and paused when I got to one that had ties to both Houston and another town, not far from Brenham. Navasota.

"Okay to print a few pages?" I asked.

"Sure, honey, but be quick about it. It's almost kickoff time."

I printed the information and then turned off the computer and headed to my spot on the sofa. I couldn't stop thinking about what I'd printed. Would Carmela mind if I snuck a peek at it? Nah, I'd better not.

Twenty minutes later we were already eating chips and salsa and shouting at the TV, our norm for each game.

"My blood pressure's going through the roof," she said. "Corey is really good, but he's keeping me on the edge of my seat."

I felt her pain. Intensely. Or maybe that was just heartburn from the salsa. It was exceptionally hot tonight. How many jalapeños did she add to it, anyway? Seemed like Carmela just kept upping the heat.

I watched closely, as always, but kept a watchful eye on Corey Wallis. Now that we'd met in person, I felt obligated to pay close attention to his career.

The Texans were having a bit of an off night until Corey pitched the ball while running an option-based offense. This move eventually led to a touchdown for the Texans.

"Whew!" Carmela rose and paced the room. "This game is so nerve-racking."

The clock counted down the minutes to halftime, and she headed to get our dinner together. Just as I offered to help, I heard the sound of a vehicle pulling up.

I peered out the window but didn't recognize the truck, which had just pulled into my driveway next door. "Carmela, I need to go outside. Someone's at my house."

"Really? Were you expecting someone?"

"No. I don't have any idea who it could be." I headed out the front door and crossed over to my driveway. I was surprised to see an elderly man easing his way out of the truck.

I took a few steps in his direction, trying to figure out who he was. The man was short—probably five-foot-five with a rounded belly and a nearly bald head. He smiled as he looked my way. "Are you Isabel Fuentes?"

"I am."

He extended his hand. "My name is Curtis Elban. I'm a friend of Reverend and Mrs. Nelson."

"Grandma Peach!"

"Yes, Peach Nelson."

"What can I do for you, Mr. Elban?"

"Please, call me Curtis." His gaze shifted to Carmela, who had made her way out to her front porch. "I actually live right around the corner." He pointed to the stop sign three houses away.

"Oh?"

"I stopped by because Peach told me that you were the one who grooms dogs up at the clinic where Mari works."

"Yes, that's right."

"Well, I have a dog—a rather spoiled one, to be precise—and she hasn't been groomed since my wife passed several months back."

"Oh dear."

"Yes. I was hoping you could help me out."

"Sure. Just bring her by the clinic on Monday. I'll be glad to—"

"I have her with me now." He shuffled to the car and came back with a standard poodle so overgrown that I actually gasped aloud.

So did Carmela, who apparently had a thing for standard poodles. Who knew? She came bounding our way, all smiles.

Carmela lit into a lengthy dissertation—in Spanish—about how beautiful the dog was just as she was, with all her long curls.

Curtis didn't seem to understand a word, but he smiled at her enthusiasm.

"My goodness," he said after Carmela leaned down to give the pooch a scratch on the head. "I haven't heard anyone talk to Princessa like that since Donna Sue passed, God rest her soul."

"Princessa is a beautiful dog, Mr. . . ."

"Elban." He extended his hand in Carmela's direction. "Curtis Elban."

"Your wife's dog is lovely."

"Poor pup is really missing all the attention the Mrs. used to give her. I hate to say the pooch is spoiled, but Donna Sue had a way of catering to her every whim. And trust me when I say she has a lot of whims."

Like now, for instance. The dog took to whining. Mr. Elban reached inside his pocket and came out with a treat.

"She just needs an exciting night of football," Carmela said. "Do you like football, Curtis?"

"I do. My wife wasn't a fan, so I didn't catch many games since we married a couple of years back."

"Do you like tacos?"

"Tacos?" His eyes widened.

"Yes." A smile lit Carmela's face. "Come inside and bring Princessa with you, Curtis. Izzy and I are watching the Texans game, and they've got a new quarterback. He's Izzy's special friend."

"Oh, I. . .well, he's not really my friend," I said. "He's more of a—"

"She stole his dog."

Curtis glanced my way and held a little tighter to Princessa's leash. "Oh? I think I heard about that on the news."

"I didn't steal his dog. The dog was a runaway, and I fostered her. There was a misunderstanding and he just thought I. . .oh, never mind."

"Come inside, Curtis," Carmela said again. "I've got homemade salsa, chips, tacos, and some wonderful horchata."

"I have no idea what that is, but anything homemade sounds good to me right about now," he said. "I've spent way too many hours at the local cafeteria eating overpriced fake battered fish."

"It's cinnamon milk," I explained. "Delicious."

"Come in, come in." She grabbed him by the arm and practically led him inside.

It didn't take long for the two of them to dive into a conversation about how good the queso was. Before he knew what hit him, Elban was also enjoying a plate full of tacos and sipping from a cup of homemade horchata. Princessa was curled up on the floor at his feet.

"I haven't eaten like this since. . ." Curtis paused. "Well, you know."

"How long has your wife been gone, Curtis?" Carmela stopped dishing up the salsa long enough to ask the question.

A somber look passed over him. "Nearly six months. She died three weeks after my little dog, Tripod, passed. It's been a rough season."

"I'd say." Carmela paused, and I could read the sympathy in her eyes. "I've been without my Rudy for three years," she said after a moment's silence. "And right after that, I lost my best friend, Izzy's grandma."

"I'm sorry to hear that," Curtis said.

"It's been an adjustment, but I'm still here and doing my best to keep going." Carmela's eyes filled with tears. "That's what they both would have wanted, for me to be happy."

"Amen," Curtis said, and then took another bite of his taco.

"This sweet girl here. . ." She looked my way and smiled. "Well, she's been the icing on my proverbial cake these last couple years. Since she moved in next door, the sunshine has returned."

"For a dog thief, she seems like a pretty nice person." Curtis offered me a playful wink and then went back to eating.

The game started back up, and before long we were all hollering at the TV. Well, I was hollering because Corey was tripped by another player and took off flying through the air, landing on his right leg, which twisted underneath him as he hit the ground.

CHAPTER TWENTY

Monday, September 18

Monday morning everyone seemed preoccupied, even our clients. Parker and Tyler were anxious over what they'd witnessed during last night's game. In fact, several of us were. Was Corey going to be okay? I sure hoped so.

"They're saying it's his hamstring," Tyler explained as he looked up from his phone. "According to this article, they think he'll be rehabbed and go right back to the game. But they're saying it might be a couple weeks or more."

"I feel terrible for him." Mari sighed. "He lost his mom, he lost his dog, he's really been through it."

I felt sick every time I thought about our decision not to return Ginger to him that first day. If we had done that, she wouldn't have disappeared twenty-four hours later. She would be in his house in Houston, probably curled up in his lap right now, bringing the comfort that only a dog could bring.

Before diving into my work, I texted a quick Hope you're okay.

To which he responded, Will be. With time.

I responded with the praying hands emoji.

Around noon Trina stopped by to talk to Mari. I happened to be in the break room with Mari when they were meeting. I offered to leave, but they both insisted it was fine to stay put.

JANICE THOMPSON

"Hey, I wanted to let you know to be on the lookout for that reporter who was here the other day."

"Which one?" Mari said. "There were a bunch of them."

"Lance the Legend. He's kind of tall, has sandy-colored hair. Nice looking."

"Yeah, definitely remember Lance the Legend." Mari laughed. "The one with the fake hair. Why am I supposed to be on the lookout for him?"

"I don't know." Trina eased her way down in a chair at the table next to us. "He somehow got my new address and showed up outside our gate this morning. Wyatt gave him the boot."

"How in the world did he get your information?" Mari asked.

Wrinkles formed on Trina's brow. "I have no idea. None whatsoever."

"Trina, I didn't give it to him, if that's what you're thinking. I would never do that."

"None of us would," I chimed in.

"No!" Trina put her hand up. "I'm not saying that. I know that he's slippery. I've dealt with him before. And I know it's easy for people to find addresses online these days."

"Yeah, I do it all the time," Mari said. "A paid service."

So, that answered that question. Mari had turned into a supersleuth.

"You've dealt with Lance the Legend before?" I directed this question to Trina.

"Yep." She nodded. "Kind of hoped to avoid him once I moved to Texas, but I guess that's impossible. He really gets around."

Cassidy and Brianna chose this moment to join us for their lunch breaks.

"Are we interrupting?" Brianna asked.

"We can always eat in my office," Cassidy said.

"No, please stay," I countered.

"We're talking about Lance the Legend," Mari explained.

"Ugh, I can't stand that guy." Cassidy opened the refrigerator and grabbed a meal from inside. "I stopped watching the news because of him." She popped the meal into the nearby microwave and pressed some buttons.

"Are you serious?" Brianna asked. "But he's so handsome."

"On the outside, maybe." These words came from Trina. "But when you get to know him as well as I have—"

"You know him, Trina?" Brianna slipped into the one empty chair at the table. "How?"

133

"He used to work for a network in Nashville." Trina's gaze shifted to Mari. "Did you know that?"

Mari looked Trina's way, mesmerized by this. "No, I thought he was a Texan through and through. He makes a big deal of his Texas roots."

Trina shook her head. "Nope, he's definitely not a Texan. The first year I lived in Nashville, a local station sent a reporter out to interview me, and guess who showed up."

"That's crazy," Mari said.

That certainly explained my search results on the ancestry site. Man, you really could find anything you wanted online.

"What's crazy is he was eventually investigated by the station because of some sort of accusations made against him." Trina sighed.

I gasped. "What sort of accusations?"

"You don't mean sexual harassment, do you, Trina?" Cassidy took her meal out of the microwave and squeezed in another chair at our little table.

"No one really knows for sure because it was swept under the rug. I wouldn't know myself except that my publicist at the record label happened to know him personally at the time, which is how I got the interview. It's kind of rare for the new kid in town to get TV coverage her first month in Nashville."

"He didn't hit on you or anything like that, did he?" Mari asked.

Trina shook her head. "No, other than being a showboat, he seemed like a pretty typical reporter, which is why I was so shocked when I heard he was being let go from the station."

"And you don't know why?" I asked.

"Just that there were some sort of accusations against him."

"Well, we're going to find out what they were." Mari pulled out her phone and started doing some research online.

I reached for my phone too. I started by entering his name, but that only brought up recent stories from the Houston area.

Then I remembered his moniker, Lance the Legend. I typed in that and got a completely different list of stories featuring the reporter.

Including one in Nashville that was six years old. "Ooh!" I read the headline then skimmed the story. "I think I found it, y'all."

"What?" Trina asked.

"So, it looks like he was investigated for lying about his background. He told the station that he was a veteran, that he served in Iraq. But he was never in the service."

"What kind of person would do that?" Cassidy asked as she removed the lid from her lasagna. Steam came rushing out.

Trina's eyebrows elevated. "The kind who loves a good story. And he's still looking for a good story."

"I found a completely different article about him." Mari read aloud from her phone: "Lance Henderson, known to his fans as Lance the Legend, reported on a fire at a Marathon Village office complex, but investigators discovered the facility was actually linked to the zealous reporter. Turns out Henderson has part ownership in the building and was actually witnessed on site just before the fire began."

"He burned down his own building?" Cassidy asked.

"I like him less every passing minute." Brianna sighed. "Good looks can only take you so far when you're secretly burning down buildings."

"Especially with a toupee like that," Trina said.

Brianna sighed. "I can't believe that beautiful hair is fake."

"Oh yeah." Trina nodded and gave her a knowing look. "It's as fake as he is."

"It looks like they never had enough evidence to pin the fire on him." Mari glanced up from her phone. "But the fact that he reported on the event and didn't mention the building belonged to him raised suspicions at the station. So, he wasn't just let go because of the lie about his military service. Looks like this story might've contributed as well."

"The man really, really loves to weave a big tale," Trina said.

Which raised a thousand suspicions in my head, even now.

Had Lance taken the dog so that he could report on the stolen dog? Was this some sort of ploy to make himself out to be a hero by reporting on Houston's new star quarterback?

"Who brought up Lance, anyway?" Brianna asked.

"Me," Trina explained. "I stopped by to let Mari know that Lance showed up at our gate this morning. And if he knows my new address, no doubt he knows my old one too. So, be on the lookout for him, Mari."

"I'm going to end up hiring security for my wedding. I can feel it." Mari sighed.

"No, I'll hire the security," Trina said. "You just relax and enjoy your big day."

"I hope I can." Mari released a lingering sigh.

I felt bad for her. That Lance guy had better not try to show up on her big day. Joey Hansen either.

As I worked, I couldn't stop thinking about Lance the Legend. Yes, he had worked in Nashville. But what if his story actually began elsewhere? Something about that story wouldn't let me go.

After grooming a particularly feisty basenji, I reached for my phone. It took some digging—starting on social media—but I was able to trace his story back not just to Nashville but to a small town in Kentucky where he apparently still had family with the same last name.

I had to give that ancestry site credit. They had tracked this guy all the way back to his birth. A little more research revealed that he'd grown up in abject poverty. An early interview he'd done with a local paper in Kentucky revealed much of his story.

So, this was a "small town boy makes it big" story.

With *big story* being the key words.

Lance the Legend was always looking for the big story, wasn't he? And maybe, just maybe, he'd found one in a little, tiny dog named Ginger.

I smiled as I realized I'd finally come to terms with her real name. Now to find her and get her back to her owner.

When we got ready to close up shop, I managed to find the whole staff together in the reception area. Perfect. I took the opportunity to share what I'd learned.

"Y'all, I did more research on Lance."

"Who's Lance, again?" Kristin looked up from the computer.

"The reporter from KBRT."

"My aunt Trina came by earlier to warn us about him," Mari explained.

"Warn us?" These words came from Tyler, who also looked up from the computer. "Why does this story require a warning?"

"Trina told us earlier today that she knows him from Nashville," Mari shared. "Apparently, he showed up at her house."

"In Nashville?" Kristin asked.

"No, here. Her new house, the one she and Wyatt live in." Mari squeezed some hand sanitizer into her palms and rubbed them together. "He only got as far as the gate."

"I did a little more digging and found out his story goes back to a small town in Kentucky," I said. "He was the editor for a local newspaper there. From there he worked at a news station in Danville. Then he got the job in Nashville but was let go because he fabricated his time in the military."

"Ugh. That's awful." Kristin looked as irritated as I felt knowing that information.

"Who lies about their time in the military?" Tyler's eyes narrowed.

"Apparently, Lance Henderson," I countered. "He also has a history of getting attention for covering sensational stories. . .like the building that burned down in Nashville that incidentally belonged to him."

"He burned down his own building?" Tyler shook his head.

"It wasn't proven," I said. "But that's a hunch I'm working on. So, I'm thinking the way to find out if he's up to no good is to entice him."

"Deliberately trap him, you mean?" Mari didn't look convinced.

"I'm guessing it wouldn't be that hard to trap a hungry reporter," Parker said. "We just need a big story."

"Are you saying we should get him here under false pretenses?" Mari still didn't appear to be won over by this idea.

"Not necessarily," I countered. "I'm just thinking that. . ." I wasn't sure what I was saying. This one would take a bit of finessing. "We know someone with a story."

"We do?" Mari asked.

"Yeah. Corey Wallis."

Tyler gave me a pensive look. "You want to somehow involve Corey Wallis just so we can find out if Lance Henderson is up to no good?"

When he put it like that, it didn't make a lot of sense.

But then again, when had I ever allowed a lack of common sense to stop me? I decided to place a call to Corey as soon as I got home.

He picked up on the third ring and listened quietly as I laid out a plan.

"Lance wants a story," I said.

"Right."

"You've got an injury."

"I do. Are you suggesting I invite him in to interview me about my hamstring injury?"

"Maybe? At your house? Kind of a homey environment. Let's make him feel comfortable."

"My home isn't exactly homey. It's pretty empty, actually."

"I'm sure it's fine."

"No, you haven't seen it. I don't think my house is ready for a made-for-TV moment." He went off on a tangent about all the things he had yet to do to his house.

"You should let my dad come help you," I suggested. "He's a whiz with that kind of thing. He's a skilled carpenter."

"He is?"

"Yeah. But I don't think you need to worry about all that before having a reporter come by. Just call him up and invite him to interview you on your turf."

"Why am I doing this again?" Corey asked.

"So we can get a closer look at him. See what kinds of questions he asks. See if he talks to you about Ginger."

"You called her Ginger."

"I did."

"So, when do you propose I do all of this?"

"How long did the doctors say you'd be out of the game?" I asked.

"Probably a couple of weeks."

"Do you have to go to practice?"

"Not for a few days," he explained. "I'm supposed to be resting my leg a couple of days, and then we start rehabbing it."

"Perfect. Then call Lance up and have him come right away."

"If I'm doing this, you're coming too."

"Why me?" My heart quickened at the very idea.

"Because it's inevitable he's going to ask about Ginger, and you're the one who was fostering her. If he sees we're on the same team, it might just change the whole dynamic."

"I see." Were we on the same team?

For the first time, I had to conclude. . .we were.

"So, can you come this way?" he asked. "Maybe tomorrow?"

"I think I can readjust my schedule." It would take a bit of work, but I would manage. I still couldn't believe I was agreeing to drive into Houston to spend time with Corey Wallis, though. Carmela was going to flip when she heard.

"I'll see if that works for Lance, and I'll be in touch." He gave me his address, and we ended the call. Had I really just promised to go to Corey Wallis' house on a random Tuesday?

Why, yes. Yes, I had.

CHAPTER TWENTY-ONE

Tuesday, September 19

Corey texted the following morning to say that Lance and the photographer would both be at his place at noon. I told him I would arrive by 11:50. He responded with his full address.

I couldn't quite believe Corey had invited me to his house.

Neither could my parents.

I called Mama on my way to River Oaks to meet up with Corey. She was tickled pink that I was headed to Corey's house but was also a little put off that I had no plans to stop by her place on my way into town.

"You're coming to Houston without seeing us?" she argued.

"I know, but this is important, Mama."

So important that I'd jumped in the car straight after church and pointed myself toward Houston without eating any lunch. I hadn't even had breakfast, for that matter.

"Too important to see your parents?" she countered.

"We're in the middle of figuring out who stole his dog. Oh, and I'm going to be on television."

"You're going to be on television?"

"I think so. The reporter is really coming to interview Corey about his injury, but if the subject of the dog comes up, I'll probably end up in the interview as well. I've dressed appropriately, just in case."

"Oh good. That last time I saw you on TV, you looked like a hot mess."

"Thanks, Mama."

EVERY DOG HAS HIS DAY

"So, the interview is about the dog you were taking care of? The one you refused to give back to him?"

I sighed.

"It's so exciting that you're going to be on television," Mama said. "What are you wearing? Tell me everything."

This led to a lengthy discussion and several suggestions. I explained—once again—that it was too late for any last-minute changes.

"Surely you can find time to stop by and say hello after you're done with all of that," she said. "Your father is working on the yard today, but I'm canning salsa and tomatillo sauce."

I told her I would try but made no promises.

"Promise you'll take pictures of his fancy River Oaks house, honey," my mother said.

"Take me with you," my dad hollered out from behind her. "I'll just pretend I'm not there."

This was my first clue Mama had me on speakerphone.

"Pretty sure that whole pretending to be invisible thing won't work for you, Dad," I said. "But if you want to meet Corey, I'm sure it can be arranged."

"Corey, eh?" I heard the grin in his voice. "You're on a first-name basis with him?"

"Sure, we're working together to try to find his dog."

"The one you stole," Pop countered. "I saw that story on the news."

"I didn't steal his. . ." Never mind. What was the point?

"It was a headline sports story on Telemundo," Pop said. "I'm proud of my girl for making the evening news, even if it was as a dog thief."

"I'm not a dog thief, Dad. Someone else stole that dog."

"Whatever you say, honey."

We ended the call, and I finished the drive to River Oaks, following the directions on my phone. I finally arrived at the monstrous white house—the ultramodern one framed out in front with massive oak trees.

Man.

My dad would've flipped. Mama would've grabbed her camera and started snapping pictures.

Oooh, pictures. I had promised that much, anyway. Better get it over with before the others arrived. I reached for my phone and snagged a quick one of the front of his house. . .

Just as Corey stepped out onto the front porch and waved at me.

I shoved the phone into my purse.

Out of the corner of my eye, I caught a glimpse of a small blue sports car slowing at the end of the driveway. I turned and caught a glimpse of the man behind the wheel.

Lance Henderson. Either I was late or he was early.

Another car pulled up behind mine. I was surprised to see Corey's manager, Ray Haas, get out of his red Tesla.

I got out of my clunker and slammed the door. The handle rattled, as always, and I did my best not to let my embarrassment show as I took several steps in Corey's direction.

"These are some digs," I said.

He shrugged. "Honestly? I was a lot more at home hanging out in my grandmother's little place in Pittsburgh. But this will do in a pinch."

"Then pinch me now."

Had I really said those words out loud?

Lance and Ray joined us, and Joey Hansen pulled up in a medium-sized white SUV. He came up the front walk a couple minutes later, laden down with cameras.

"We headed inside?" he asked.

Corey nodded, then led the way.

I couldn't stop thinking about what I'd learned about Joey. He looked like an ordinary camera guy from where I stood, but knowing he had left behind a wife and kids to fend for themselves really got me upset.

I tried to put it out of my mind. Staying focused was key today.

We followed Corey inside, and I was completely overwhelmed at the sheer size of the entryway. I'd been in whole houses smaller than his massive foyer. Or maybe it just looked bigger because it was two stories high.

My gaze traveled to the sweeping stairway that curved up from the left to the right in a beautiful arch. I'd seen stairs like that in fancy hotels, but in a house? An ordinary house?

On the other hand, this house was far from ordinary. He led the way from room to room in the modern architectural wonder, and I tried to imagine what it might feel like to live in a place like this.

Honestly? It felt a bit sterile. I wasn't sure I could get used to it. And judging from the sparse furniture and decor, Corey was having a hard time too. I could sooner picture him in his mama's tiny wood-framed house in Pittsburgh than a stark place like this. A guy with as much personality as Corey needed a home that reflected that.

Ray's phone rang, and he took the call then moved to the far side of the living room to talk to whoever was on the other end of the line.

Lance let out a whistle as he took in his surroundings. "I heard you were in the Cunningham place."

"Cunningham place?" Corey looked confused.

"Yeah, the Maxwell Cunningham family lived on this property for years. But they tore the old house down and built this one a couple years back, just before old Mr. Cunningham kicked the bucket."

Kicked the bucket? Who talked like that about the deceased? My opinion of Lance Henderson dropped even lower than before, simply because of his disrespect for poor Mr. Cunningham. Whoever he was.

"Was there a Mrs. Cunningham?" Corey asked.

"I think she's living in a senior center now." Lance offered a slight shrug. "Something like that. But this is a neighborhood I know really well. I live just a few blocks from here, off of Kirby."

"Oh, wow."

"Yeah." Lance handed him a business card. "Feel free to stop by anytime, especially if you have information about the missing dog."

Ray joined us, shoving his phone into his pocket. "Sorry about that. Just talking to Coach about your PT, Corey. They've got you set up for ten every morning this coming week. I'll send you the address."

He nodded.

"That was a tough injury," Joey said. "I watched it in real time."

"Could've been worse." Corey shrugged. "But it's time for me to get off this leg, so come on in to the living room and sit down, everyone."

I looked straight at the camera guy and extended my hand. "Isabel Fuentes. I don't believe I ever got your name."

"Oh." He coughed. "I'm—"

A weird silence filled the air between us before he said, "Ian. Ian Gentry."

Ian Gentry. Interesting.

"Ian's been working at KBRT for the past six months," Lance said. "He's my sidekick for all the big stories."

A sidekick who stumbled over the use of his own name. And who looked better without a beard.

I said nothing but managed to maneuver my phone from my purse. I silently snapped a picture of Joey—Ian—whatever—from a weird angle. I would send it to Parker later to verify that this was actually the same guy he grew up with.

It took a few moments for Lance and Ian to get their stuff set up, but a few minutes later we were up and running. Well, Corey was. They'd seated him in a chair opposite the sofa, where he had his leg propped up on a footrest. Thank goodness they hadn't asked for my participation, at least not yet.

During the interview, I managed to send the picture of Ian to Parker. I was glad I'd remembered to mute my phone before the interview started, because Parker wrote back with three words:

"That's the guy."

So, Ian was really Joey Hansen, a.k.a. deadbeat dad from Brenham. Yet, here he sat in Corey's living room, filming his every word.

Corey did well with the interview. Lance did too, for that matter. His questions were practical and kind, honing in on the injury.

"Are you hurting?" Lance asked.

Corey paused a moment before responding. "Yeah, the leg aches. It's better when I rest it. But the doc said that ice would help, and it has. The PT I have scheduled should help too. We're just waiting for the swelling to go down before attempting that."

It didn't take long before the conversation shifted to Ginger. At this point they placed Corey and I side by side on the sofa. He rested his foot on the coffee table.

I did my best to answer Lance's questions, which seemed fair and balanced. There was nothing accusatory about them, at least this time. I found myself relaxing and all the more when I caught a glimpse of Corey smiling at my chatter about how sweet Ginger was.

After we finished, Lance extended his hand in Corey's direction. "I'm grateful for the one-on-one, Corey. I'm not sure why you called me, but I'm glad you did. I hope you feel better soon."

"Thanks."

And just like that, Lance, Ian, and Ray took off.

Corey closed the door behind them then turned back in my direction. "Well, I'm glad that's over."

"Me too." I shrugged. "He actually seemed pretty okay."

"Yeah, I was kind of surprised. After what you said before, I was expecting him to be really aggressive. Pushy. He was anything but."

Still, I wouldn't let my guard down just yet. "We haven't seen the interview go live yet. Who knows what he'll do with it."

"True." Corey shivered. "I can't tell you how many times reporters have twisted my words over the years. It's very frustrating."

This led to a conversation about his years in Pittsburgh. Corey and I visited for several minutes, and I finally started to relax. Sometime around four, my stomach started rumbling.

He must've been hungry too. Corey led the way into the kitchen and opened the fridge, which looked to be pretty empty. "Do you want some water?"

"Sure." I pointed to the barren fridge. "You don't cook much?"

"Cook? What is this word *cook* you speak of?"

"How do you survive?"

He laughed. "I have most of my meals delivered. There are so many services these days for drop-off." He seemed to lose himself to his thoughts for a moment. "I haven't had a real home-cooked meal since my mom died."

"I'm so sorry."

We walked back into the living room, and Corey pointed to the coffee table. "Looks like Lance the Legend left his sunglasses."

"Those look expensive."

Corey picked them up and whistled. "I'll say. They're Bose."

"Whoa. Maybe you should call him. He gave you his card, right?"

"Right." Corey placed the call, but no one answered. He looked my way with a shrug. "Want to go for a ride?"

"What. . .right now?"

"Sure." A smile lit Corey's face. "A drive will do us good. Unless you have plans this afternoon."

"No."

"We'll go by Lance's place and drop these off. Then maybe I can take you for a little spin around the neighborhood."

In his BMW convertible, it turned out.

With the top down.

Five minutes after getting in the car, we pulled onto Kirby Drive. We arrived at Lance's place a couple minutes later. It was a nice-looking older house but nothing close to the monstrosity Corey lived in.

"Want to come with?" he asked me.

I wasn't sure why he wanted me to, but with those beautiful eyes gazing into mine, I would be a fool to say no to the man.

When I nodded, he sprang from the car, came to my side, and opened the door like a true southern gentleman.

I couldn't help but chuckle. "If I didn't know any better, I'd say you were born and raised in Texas."

"Nope. Definitely not. But thank you for considering that as a possibility. I hear southern fellas are true gentlemen."

"Some of them." I shivered as I thought of my ex. "Not all." My gaze shifted to the driveway. "Hey, Lance's car's not here."

Corey shrugged. "Maybe it's in the garage?"

"Could be."

We walked up the path to the front door and rang the bell. Right away, we heard yapping from inside the house.

No one answered.

"Corey, listen." I leaned in to put my ear by the door. "Ring it again."

He did, and the dog inside went crazy.

"Ginger used to do that," he said.

"I know. Carmela rang the bell at my house when Ginger was there, and she completely lost it."

When no one answered, we turned around and headed back to the car. Before pulling away, Corey gave the house another look.

"I think it's a little weird that he lives in my neighborhood."

"Why is that?" I asked.

"Because I made the rounds to several of the neighbors early on. As soon as she went missing. I'm starting to wonder if he knew she was missing before other reporters got wind of the story."

"Could be."

"What if that barking we heard just now was Ginger?"

"You think it is?" I asked.

"Sure sounded like her. I mean, what if she's at his house right now, at this very minute?"

"You're saying he took her to keep the story going?"

"He was there at the clinic on the day she went missing the second time, right?"

"Well, yeah, but. . ." I paused to think through my response. "He was pretty busy that day, interviewing that woman doing the sit-in. Or lay-in. Or, whatever you call it. She was blocking the clinic door. She turned out to be a fraud."

"She did?" Corey looked perplexed by this.

"Yeah. Long story."

"Still up for a drive?" Corey started his car, and I adjusted my seat belt.

"Sure."

He pulled out onto the road and pointed us toward a major street, Shepherd. Then he turned left onto West Gray. We passed several restaurants and some shops.

"Are you hungry?" he asked when we approached a well-known steakhouse.

Was I ever. But an idea hit me, one that wouldn't leave me alone. "Yes. But don't stop at a restaurant. I've got a better idea."

"Oh?"

I grinned. "My parents live just a few miles from here, in a neighborhood called Lindale, just north of 610."

"I have no idea what any of that means, but okay. I'm game."

"I think they would flip if we stopped by. And trust me when I say there's always food at Mama's house. Though, it's not restaurant quality."

"Oh." He offered a little shrug. "That's okay. I don't mind."

"No, you're misunderstanding me. It's not restaurant quality. Mama's home-cooked meals are ten thousand times better."

"Well, all right, then." Corey laughed. "You had me at home-cooked meals."

CHAPTER TWENTY-TWO

Had I just invited Houston's star quarterback to my family's humble home to meet my family?

Yep. Sure had. And he looked thrilled by the idea.

Should I warn him about my mom and dad? They tended to run a little on the loud side. Corey seemed anything but. Nah. He could just discover the Fuentes family on his own, without any preconceived ideas.

Mama met us at the door looking a little frazzled. The smell of her homemade salsa emanated from the house. I watched as Corey stopped and sniffed the air then turned my way, eyes wide.

Mama's eyes were pretty wide too. She recognized Corey immediately and started stammering. "I—I—I—"

Her three little Chihuahuas all met us at the door as well. Phoebe, the mean one, started yapping the moment she saw Corey. She went straight for his ankles, so I scooped her up in my arms to prevent any catastrophes. She knew better than to snap at me. We had an understanding, Phoebe and I.

Tika and Muffy were a little slower on the draw. Muffy was 110 years old—in dog years—and didn't have the energy to bark at incoming guests anymore. Tika was just overweight and a little on the boring side.

Mama, however, was anything but.

Well, anything but boring.

"What in the world?" My mother stared at Corey for a moment then turned my way, jaw dropping. "Isabel! Warn a person when you're bringing a guest over! The house is. . ." She wiped her hands on her apron.

"Perfect," I said. Mama's house was always perfect. Except for a handful of dishes in the sink from the homemade tortillas she was making, of course.

And the salsa, which she happened to be in the middle of canning. And the boiled chicken in the pressure cooker nearby. And the tomatillo sauce, simmering on the stove.

The kitchen was in more of a state than usual. She invited us in but fussed around cleaning up her mess as she carried on about how excited she was to meet Corey.

"Where's Pop?" I asked.

She gestured to the backyard. I opened the sliding glass door and heard the hum of the mower in the distance. Then I caught a glimpse of him, rounding the side of the house.

Pop was mowing the back lawn with the same mower he'd used my entire life. And, as always, he was dressed in basketball shorts, no shirt, and a grimy sweatband wrapped around his head to keep off the sweat, one he probably borrowed from the Bee Gees in the 1970s.

Okay, maybe it didn't date back quite that far, but the sweatband was a permanent fixture in my dad's life. He refused to give it up.

Nothing much had changed over the years.

Pop stopped when he saw us and turned off the mower. When he realized I'd brought Corey over, he yanked the sweatband off his forehead and sprinted our way, eyes wide.

"You're Corey Wallis."

"Yes, sir." Corey extended his hand.

Dad grabbed it, unfortunately with the hand that still held his sweatband.

Corey didn't seem to mind. He probably saw his fair share of sweat on the field. Still, it was nice of him not to react.

"Saw you in that last game," Pop said as we all headed back into the kitchen. "How's the leg?"

"Just a pulled hamstring. Doc says I'll be back in the game in a week or so. I start physical therapy soon."

"Good to hear. I just went through physical therapy myself, for a frozen shoulder."

"How did you injure it?" Corey asked.

"Don't ask." My five-foot-five father slapped six-foot-four Corey on the back. "Let's have a glass of horchata. You like horchata, son?"

"I don't know. But I'm willing to try it to see."

I was really hoping Pop would put a shirt on, but apparently he didn't see the need. Corey didn't seem to notice or care, but Mama fussed as my father took a seat in his sweaty basketball shorts and leaned his elbows on the kitchen table.

"Guillermo!" She called out his name with that same stern tone I'd heard so many times, myself. "You're dripping on the Formica!"

That was another thing. We were probably the only family in town that still had a Formica table. In my house, nothing got thrown away. Ever. That table had come from my mother's grandmother and would keep its place of honor in my parents' home until it was one day passed to me.

At which point I would likely donate it to Goodwill.

Pop headed to their bedroom to clean up and change then arrived back in the kitchen looking more presentable.

Mama gave us glasses of her infamous horchata, which Corey guzzled down. Before long he and my father were deep in a conversation about the kind of grass in our backyard. Turns out we had St. Augustine. He was accustomed to ryegrass in Pittsburgh. Who knew.

The conversation shifted to the Texans, and Mama kept working on the salsa.

"You hungry?" she said after she moved the tomatillo sauce aside to cool. "I'm going to make tacos for dinner."

"Starving," I said for both of us. Corey would understand after he'd eaten one of Mama's tacos.

And that's when the magic happened. The food magic, anyway. Mama did what she was known for—whipped up a meal no restaurant could rival—and we all settled in at the Formica table and ate until we almost made ourselves sick.

I kept a watchful eye on Corey, who seemed lost in a state of foodie bliss. Every now and again he would look my way and smile.

And I would immediately shift my gaze back to my plate, feeling the heat in my face.

Somehow it came out during dessert that my father's recent shoulder injury had come from trying to start the old lawn mower.

"Pop's not one to give up on something easily," I said. "He'll tug and tug on a busted mower's cord a hundred times before he finally calls it quits."

"Hey, mowers are a lot of money," he said. This led to a lengthy discussion about a new brand of mower he hoped to buy before Christmas. I knew my father had been saving up for this mower for some time, and I planned to contribute as part of my Christmas gift to him.

Before long we switched gears and were talking about the interview we had done with Lance.

"Lance the Legend." My mother laughed. "That guy is something else."

"How so?" Corey asked.

"Well, for one thing, he's only a legend in his own eyes. His ego's so bloated you could fly to the moon on it."

"I heard he was almost let go from that job last year," Dad said.

"Really?" This was news. "He had trouble at the Houston station too?"

"What do you mean *too*?" Pop asked.

I filled them all in on Lance's history in Nashville.

"How do you know all this, honey?" Mama asked as she rose to clear the table.

"Trina Potter told me." I stood up and tried to help Mama, but she waved me back down to my seat.

"Trina Potter the country-western singer?" Pop looked my way, wide-eyed.

I nodded.

"Have you heard her new song?" he asked. "The one about the cat?"

"I have. Kind of a long story, but I actually know that cat. He's really sick right now."

"Yes, I heard all about that on the radio station," Mama said. "We've been praying for Hector."

"I've never been a fan of cats," my father said. "So, this is my first time to usher up a prayer for a cat."

"I lit a candle for him in church," Mama said.

Turned out, Corey wasn't a cat fan either. Now he and Pop actually had something tangible in common.

I shifted gears, ready to get back to the conversation about Lance. I still had a lot of unanswered questions. "So, why did they almost let Lance go last year?"

"I think he was trying to dig up some dirt on one of our city councilmen." Pop took a sip of his horchata and leaned back in the chair. "Only, it turned out not to be true, as I recall. But he wouldn't let it go. So, the mayor got involved and threatened to sue Lance if he kept up the false reporting."

"Oh." I glanced Corey's way. "So, he does have a shady history in Houston too."

The conversation carried on for a good hour, shifting from topic to topic. My father then showed off our very quaint house to Lance. Quite a contrast to his River Oaks mansion. But he had only kind remarks, especially when they got to my room, which still looked exactly as it had every day of my life. Mama wouldn't change it for anything.

"I think she secretly hopes I'll move back home," I said, after Corey and I were back in his car, headed to his place.

"You're an only child?"

"Yep. They always said they kept at it until they achieved perfection." I offered a crooked grin.

"You made it easy on them, eh?" He flashed a warm smile my way.

"Guess so." I laughed. "But trust me when I say I was far from perfect."

"Oh, I don't know." He tapped the brakes as we approached a stop sign. "You seem pretty perfect to me."

"Well, tell that to my mama. She always seems to find flaws."

"She makes a mean tortilla, though. And that tomatillo sauce was amazing."

"The woman can cook."

"Did she pass that skill down to you?"

"*Yo quiero* Taco Bell!" I offered.

He laughed. "You want Taco Bell?"

"That's about as close as I come to preparing Mexican food. But don't tell my mama, okay? She'd like to think I got the cooking gene. Truth is, I'm happy to mooch off of Carmela and my folks."

He hit the gas, and we took off down the street, finding ourselves in the middle of Houston's late-afternoon traffic. "Well, next time you come into town, invite me over again because that was some good mooching."

"You've got it. And I think she liked you. In fact, I'm pretty sure she liked you more than me."

"Now you're just being silly."

"Maybe." Still, I liked being silly with him. He made it easy. "But there is one thing I want to discuss with you that's not silly. I was waiting until the timing was right."

"What's that?"

"That cameraman. I didn't want to tell you, but he's using an alias."

"Using an alias?"

"Yeah." I nodded. "He actually grew up in Brenham. His name is Joey Hansen, not Ian Gentry."

"Are you sure?" Corey glanced at the GPS on his phone, which was guiding him back home to River Oaks.

"Yep. Parker—one of our vet techs—knows him. Joey looks different now. Different hair color. Beard."

"And he goes by Ian now. That's kind of weird."

"Yeah, well I think I know why," I explained. "From what I learned, he's claiming that he's too poor to pay child support for his four children."

Corey's expression tightened. "That guy who was at my house is a deadbeat dad?"

"Yeah. That's the story from Grandma Peach."

"What's a Grandma Peach?"

I laughed. "Mari's grandmother. The lady who owns Hector."

"Hector, the infamous cat."

"Yes. Peach is kind of the matriarch of Brenham. She found out—through the grapevine at First Prez, mind you—that Joey and his wife divorced and he moved away, leaving the four kids behind."

"What's a First Prez?"

"First Presbyterian, where Reverend Nelson leads the faithful," I explained.

"I would ask about Reverend Nelson, but—"

"Married to Ms. Peach. Anyway, according to his ex, he hasn't paid child support in ages."

"Reverend Nelson has an ex?"

"Joey Hansen." I paused to refocus. "Joey hasn't paid child support in all that time and has been claiming he doesn't have a job."

"But he works for a major network."

"Under a different name. And, if you noticed, he was wearing a cap and mask when we saw him in Brenham."

"Lots of people are still wearing masks in public," he said.

"I suspect there's more to it than that. He came to Brenham knowing he might be recognized, so he went incognito." I pulled up a picture of him from his social media site, one without a beard, and passed it Corey's way just as we arrived at a stoplight.

"Wow. That looks nothing like him." He gave the photo a closer look.

"Right. He's dyed his hair and is wearing a beard now. And he's put on weight."

"So, you think he's hiding?"

"That's what I want to get to the bottom of. I have his address, thanks to Grandma Peach."

"She's your grandmother?"

"No." I shook my head. "She's Mari's grandmother."

"Mari, the one who rescued Ginger."

"Yep. Anyway, I'm dying to know what kind of house Joey lives in. I looked up the address, and I don't think it's very far from here."

"Are you suggesting we drive by and see how—and where—he's living?" Corey asked.

"Maybe?"

"I'm in."

Turned out it wasn't far at all. Joey's house was in Montrose, a neighborhood about five miles from Corey's house. It wasn't exactly River Oaks, but neither was it shabby.

We pulled up to a perfectly respectable wood-framed house, not unlike the one I'd grown up in, and Corey slowed the car almost to a stop. "You want to snap a picture?"

"How did you know?"

"Just figured. That's what I'd do. You can show it to—"

"Grandma Peach."

"Who isn't your grandmother."

"Right." I snapped a picture and then gave the house a closer look by enlarging the photo on my phone.

I glanced back at the real house, then in Corey's direction. "Let's get out of here," I said. "I feel kind of weird. What if he's home already and sees us here?"

"Right." He hit the gas and we took off.

We turned onto a smaller side street and found ourselves in a rougher-looking area. Corey put on his signal to turn at the next light, and I happened to glance up as a small, run-down building in front of us came into view.

"Oh, look!" I pointed. "It's La Palencia."

"La Palencia?"

"A theater. Those protesters who came to our clinic that day were actually actors from that troupe."

"Are you serious?"

"I am."

He hit the brakes. "Should we check them out?"

"No." I put my hand up. "I think we've had enough adventure today, don't you?"

"I guess so."

We somehow transitioned the conversation back to my parents, and minutes later we were driving past a Taco Bell. I shouted, "Yo quiero Taco Bell!" and he laughed. A lot.

Before I knew it, we were back at Corey's house in River Oaks. He pulled into the driveway and parked then came around to open my door. I could tell his leg was bothering him, and I felt bad that I'd kept him out for so long when he needed to be resting. Good thing Ray wasn't here to see this, or I'd get a scolding.

"This was a fascinating day," I said as I eased my way out of the convertible. "I had fun."

"Me too." He flashed the most beautiful smile. "Thanks for introducing me to the city of Houston. I discovered some new neighborhoods. Oh, and thanks for pointing out the Taco Bell. Now that I know where it is I'll—"

"Think of me when you drive by it?"

He laughed. "Well, maybe. But it feels good to finally feel like I'm settling in. Now, if only. . ." His words drifted off.

Was he thinking about Ginger, perhaps?

"Now if I can just get past this injury and get back in the groove when it comes to my game." He shrugged. "I feel like I've been off ever since I moved here."

"Now that Houston is your home, you'll settle in." I flashed a smile. "But I should probably go. I've got an early appointment in the morning."

"I hate that you have to drive all the way back to Brenham alone."

"I do it all the time. I'm in Houston at least every other weekend to see my parents. And don't even get me started on the cousins."

"Do you think your parents would like tickets to an upcoming game?"

"Is this a trick question?"

"No."

"My dad would flip. Though—between us—he and Mom are really more into the Astros. Baseball's kind of their thing."

"Maybe I can convert them?"

"Away from the Astros?" I laughed until my sides hurt. "That's a good one. But thanks for playing."

"Happy to be of service. And, by the way, I want you to come too."

Okay, I had to admit, that was pretty cool. I'd never been invited to a pro football game by an actual player on the team. Of course, we had to get him healed up first.

"That would be amazing. Thank you. But Corey, please take care of that injury. You've been on that leg too much today."

"I will, I promise. I've got physical therapy in the morning and every day after that. I'm in good hands."

We had a lovely moment as our goodbyes were spoken when I got to gaze into those penetrating eyes of his. He seemed to be gazing my way too. A light smile was all I offered him as I turned and headed for my car.

Well, that and a quick "Thanks for a fun day."

It had been fun. We weren't any closer to finding Ginger, but at least I was winning Corey's trust. . .and vice versa.

I climbed into my car and was about to slip it into gear when he tapped on my window. I rolled it down, and he leaned his head inside.

"I just wanted to say, I think you're pretty amazing, Isabel."

"I. . ." I wasn't sure what to say in response to that but managed a quiet "Thank you."

I thought he was pretty amazing too, but it seemed weird to echo back what he'd just said to me. Instead, I flashed him a shy smile.

"This was a great day."

"Definitely," I responded. "But I'm so sad we haven't found Ginger yet."

"Me too, but we'll find her. I have a good feeling. And in the meantime, we pray."

"I have been, trust me. And I won't stop. I'm a firm believer in the power of prayer."

"Me too." He rested his hand on my shoulder, and I felt little tingles go all the way down to my toes.

"I'd like to do this again sometime."

"You'd like to do a TV interview, snoop on potential suspects, meet my parents, and drink horchata while my dad sweats all over the Formica?"

"Yes." He laughed. "To all of that. Except maybe the interview part. I could've done without that."

"Yeah, me too." Crazy, that being on TV was my least favorite part of the day. But, with Corey gazing directly into my eyes, I had to admit. . . it sure was getting easier to see the good parts.

CHAPTER TWENTY-THREE

Wednesday, September 20

I didn't get much sleep on Tuesday night. I kept thinking about all that had transpired with Corey that day. Every time I thought about him, my heart did that weird skip-a-beat thing. He seemed to have that effect on me.

I wanted to consider the possibility that God had brought us together for more than just friendship, but with the looming problem of his missing dog in the picture, I just felt like a key piece to the puzzle was still unsolved. I couldn't allow myself to go there until I found Ginger.

When I finally dozed off, it was after two in the morning. I sure didn't feel like waking up when the alarm went off at six, but I yawned and stretched and then did my best to wake myself up with a long shower.

On the way to the clinic, I decided to give Mama a call. She was still pretty giddy after my visit with Corey yesterday.

Turned out she'd already told the whole neighborhood.

And my cousins.

And my great-aunt Esperanza in Albuquerque.

When that part of the conversation played itself out, I turned my attention to the reason for the call.

"Mama, have you heard of a small theater in Montrose called La Palencia?"

"La Palencia?" She paused. "It's not ringing any bells."

"I'm just trying to learn more about the theater troupe. They're called the Etapas Troupe."

"Oh, that sounds weirdly familiar. I don't know why, though."

"Some of the actors from that troupe showed up at our clinic pretending to be protesters."

"Paid protesters?" she asked.

"I guess. We didn't realize it until after they were long gone. But a local reporter in Brenham found out they weren't real protesters. They're from La Palencia in Montrose, part of this theater troupe called Etapas."

"Still can't figure out why that sounds so familiar," she said. "But if I think of it, I'll let you know, I promise."

"Thanks, Mama. I have to let you go. I'm almost to the clinic now."

"Have a fun day, sweetie. Let me know if you find Corey's dog."

"I will, I promise."

I arrived at work a couple of minutes before eight, just as my first client arrived—a hyper Jack Russell terrier. Minutes later I had the pup in the grooming station, doing what I did best.

While I worked, I replayed certain incidents from the day prior.

Seeing Corey's home.

His expression when my pop sweated his way into the house.

The kindness in his voice as he spoke to my mama.

The kindness in his voice as he spoke to me.

Had I really suspected this guy of stealing back his own dog? Crazy.

As I worked on the Jack Russell, my thoughts shifted back to that first morning when I'd bathed and tended to Ginger's grooming. I'd fallen for her right away.

Kind of like I was falling for her owner right now.

If only we could add her back to the story, then maybe things could progress naturally. Right now there was a lingering pit in my stomach every time I thought about that sweet missing pup.

When I finished grooming the terrier, I went to the reception area to see if Brianna had heard from my next client.

"Nothing yet," she said. "But they're not the only ones I haven't heard from."

"Oh?"

"Kristin and Tyler are both running late this morning."

"Weird."

"I tried to call him," Parker said, "but he's not answering."

"I think they were in Navasota yesterday after we closed," Cassidy explained. "I'm pretty sure they were having dinner with her family. You don't suppose they stayed, do you?"

"Surely not," Parker said. "That would be totally out of character for Tyler to miss work, even for a family event."

A couple minutes later, the front door opened and both vets walked through together.

"Sorry we're late," Tyler said as he took several steps in our direction. "My truck broke down, and Kristin had to come and rescue me."

"Yep," Kristin said. "That took a little while."

"It's just the battery," Tyler said. "I'll pick up a new one during my lunch break." He shot a glance her way, grinned like a Cheshire Cat, and then looked back at us.

That explained their tardiness, but it didn't explain why they both looked like they were hiding something. Kristin couldn't seem to stop smiling. What were these two up to?

"What are you not saying?" Parker asked. "Something's up."

"Something happen back in Navasota?" Cassidy asked.

"We did have very special business in Navasota last night," Tyler explained. "That's true."

"Everyone in your family okay?" Mari asked.

"More than okay." Kristin's whimsical smile broadened, but she seemed to tuck it away just as quickly. "Mama's giddy."

"Really?" Mari asked. "Why would she be. . .oh!" Mari let out a squeal and pointed to Kristin's left hand. "You're wearing an engagement ring!"

Kristin laughed and stuck her hand out for us to observe the beautiful diamond ring. "I thought you'd never notice!"

"Tyler proposed?" I asked. "Tell us everything."

We all started talking on top of each other, and all the more when some of our clients walked through the door for their morning appointments. They dove right in to the chaotic congratulations. We were all as giddy as Kristin's mama.

"Let me take care of my client first. I know they've been waiting awhile." Kristin gestured for Mrs. Kenner—the owner of a quirky little mixed breed dog called Holly—to join her in an exam room, and the woman headed that way.

We all got to work and then, around nine thirty, gathered in the break room to quickly talk through how—and where—Tyler had proposed. Everyone in the office was on pins and needles, anticipating the story.

"I had no idea," Kristin explained. "I just thought we were going to have dinner with my family, as usual. But it turns out Tyler wanted to go to Navasota to ask my dad's permission."

"That's so sweet," Brianna said.

"Yeah, Mama kept me distracted in the kitchen talking about her chicken-fried steak, and Tyler disappeared into the living room with my dad. I didn't think anything of it at the time."

"How did that go, Tyler?" Parker asked.

He grinned. "Great. I told him how much I love his daughter, and he said, 'I'm not blind, son. I know that,' and we kind of went from there."

"So, he said yes, obviously," Kristin said. "Only, I was in the kitchen, completely oblivious."

"I was a nervous wreck the whole time we were eating dinner," Tyler explained. "But I wanted to propose in a certain place outside, so I had to wait until we finished."

"Yes, I've never seen him eat my mama's strawberry pie so fast." Kristin giggled. "Afterward, he took me for a walk out to the fort by the pond, the one I played in as a kid. Got down on one knee and asked me if I'd marry him. And all of this perfectly timed at sunset."

"Oh my," I managed. The whole thing just sounded so over-the-top romantic.

"I think it's so sweet that he asked your dad first," Mari said.

"Me too." Kristin's lips turned up in a smile. "Afterward, my parents were over the moon. Would you believe me if I told you that my mama whipped up a cake while I was out there getting proposed to? The woman is a wonder in the kitchen. Almost as good as you, Brianna," she added.

Brianna's cheeks flushed pink. "I would be honored to bake for your bridal shower. You are having one, aren't you?"

"I think it's wise if we let Mari and Parker have all the attention for now," Kristin said. "We can talk about all of that after their big day. But yes, I would be honored if you would bake for my bridal shower. As long as my mother isn't put off by the idea."

Which, of course, led the Lone Star Ladies into an intense discussion about where the shower would be held and what decorating theme we would choose.

Kristin moved on to take care of another patient, but my thoughts were firmly locked on her good news.

Good grief. If everyone around me kept getting engaged, I was destined to be the only single lady in the group.

Ugh.

Still, I wanted to be happy for my friend. She deserved it. So did Tyler. They were such a perfect couple and deserved the very best.

My thoughts shifted at once to Corey. No, I'd better not let a football player consume my thoughts or plant any seeds of hope in my heart. Besides, we still had to find Ginger. Nothing would be right until that happened.

After lunch I went back to work on the next dog—a state agility champion named Remington. His owner, Reese Atkinson, was all abuzz at the news about Tyler and Kristin.

"I just think it's the best news ever," she said. "I mean, it's so romantic. Like a rom-com you'd watch on the big screen. Two vets meet and fall in love in veterinary school, start a business together, and then end up married?" She sighed.

On and on she went, talking about how perfect it was that the two of them were now going to become husband and wife.

It was perfect. Only, all this talk about weddings was suddenly starting to feel a little depressing.

The wedding talk went on over lunch as we gathered in the break room to share fajitas, compliments of Tyler. I wasn't sure when he'd ordered them, but he had enough for an army.

The fajitas were delicious, don't get me wrong, but the meal I'd shared with Corey yesterday at Mama's table was better.

Much better.

"You okay over there, Isabel?" Mari nudged me with her elbow.

"Hm?" I startled to attention. "Yes. Sorry. Preoccupied today."

"Thinking about Corey?" she asked.

"Yeah, how did it go at his place yesterday?" Kristin asked.

"Oh." I paused and tried to think of where to start.

"Why are your cheeks turning pink?" Mari asked. "Or do we want to know?"

"They are?" I rested my fingertips on my cheek and realized it did feel warm. "Is it hot in here?"

"Nope." Cassidy laughed. "Good try, though."

"Yeah, tell us everything." Brianna took a seat at the table and gestured for me to sit beside her.

So, I told them about my day.

"When I got to his house, Lance, Joey, and the manager were just getting there."

"How did that go?" Cassidy asked.

"I got the picture of Joey," Parker said. "He looks nothing like I remember from high school."

This, of course, led to me showing all of them the picture that I'd taken of Joey just yesterday and comparing it to his social media photo, the clean-cut one.

"So weird," Brianna said.

"Yeah, but even weirder, he's going by a different name now. He said his name is Ian. And I don't think Lance has any idea who 'Ian' really is."

"So, we've proven that Joey is hiding his identity, but that doesn't mean he took off with the little dachshund." Tyler pulled up a chair to the table. "Right?"

"Right." I set my fajita down and leaned back in the chair. "But something weird happened with Lance that I didn't tell you guys about. The interview went well, but he left his sunglasses, so we stopped by his place afterward to drop them off. When we got there, he wasn't home, but we heard a dog barking on the other side of the door when we rang the bell."

"So, he has a dog." Tyler shrugged. "So what?"

"Nothing, except that he told us that first day that he isn't an animal person."

"Oh, that's right." Brianna nodded. "I remember that."

"So, Joey is Ian, Lance has a dog. . .anything else?" Cassidy asked.

"Yeah, remember how Mollie told us about that theater troupe?"

"Our so-called protesters?" Tyler rolled his eyes.

"Yep. Mollie called me the other day to tell me that the troupe operated out of a theater called La Palencia in Montrose."

"Where's Montrose?" Kristin asked.

"A neighborhood in Houston, not far from Corey's place. It's actually pretty close to where Ian is staying."

"A coincidence. . .or something more?" Mari asked.

"Good question." I paused to think it through. "Anyway, we happened to drive by it, and it kind of gave me the willies. It's in a rough part of the neighborhood. But here's the crazy part—I called my mom on the way to work this morning to ask her if she'd ever heard of it, and she said it sounded familiar. She's going to look into it."

Everyone started talking at once, and then the chatter finally leveled out.

"Yeah, what's Corey's house like, Isabel?" Cassidy asked. "Everything you imagined a River Oaks house to look like?"

"I guess?" I shrugged. "It's big. Kind of empty. I get the feeling he's existing there but not really living, if that makes sense. He's definitely not looking settled in the place. It's kind of. . .sterile."

"Needs a woman's touch, eh?" Mari quirked a brow, and everyone laughed.

I felt heat rise to my cheeks once again. Instead of answering, I said, "I think he felt more at home in my parents' little house, actually."

"Wait." Mari put her hand up. "You took him home to meet your parents?"

"Well, yeah. He was hungry, and Mama was cooking."

"Oh boy." Parker laughed as he reached for more chips. "Guy lives alone, probably eats out every meal, then along comes a gal who offers him a local family with home-cooked meals."

"He doesn't stand a chance." Tyler reached for his drink. "That poor guy's a goner, and he doesn't even know it."

CHAPTER TWENTY-FOUR

That's how Kristin won me over," Tyler said. "She introduced me to her family over a huge home-cooked meal. Have you guys ever tasted her mother's strawberry pie?"

"You're marrying me for my mother's strawberry pie?" Kristin feigned offense at this.

"No, but it didn't hurt." He pulled her into his arms and gave her a kiss on the cheek. "Especially since she's passed down your grandmother's recipe book to you."

This led to a lengthy discussion about pie, which somehow led back to Brianna asking for my mother's salsa recipe, which then led to a discussion about Mari and Parker's upcoming wedding.

"How are things going with the plans?" Kristin asked. "Anything we can do?"

"We'll know more after the workday this coming Saturday." Mari said. "So far, no problems to speak of, unless you count the part where there's a 20 percent chance of rain that day."

"On the day of the wedding or this Saturday?" Parker asked.

"This Saturday." Mari laughed. "I don't think I'll start worrying about the weather on our wedding day until a couple of days before."

"The weather on our wedding day will be perfect," Parker said. "I have it on good authority." He pointed upward.

He wasn't the only one praying about that. The Lone Star Ladies had been pounding heaven's door, asking God to rain down sunny skies on the thirtieth of September.

"Hey, speaking of problems. . ." Tyler reached for another flour tortilla, then filled it with beef and onions as he spoke. "Remember when I got back from lunch late the other day?"

"I do," Cassidy said. "You seemed upset by something."

"I was." He shoved some pico de gallo and sour cream in on top of the meat, then tossed on some grated cheese. "I had taken Kristin's engagement ring to be sized and was supposed to pick it up at twelve fifteen that day. Only, when I got there, they hadn't sized it yet. The jeweler was running behind. So, he said I'd have to come back the next day. Which was impossible. I had surgery all day that day, so I had to send Parker."

"Parker!" Mari slugged him. "You knew Tyler was proposing to Kristin and you said nothing?"

"Well, yeah." He gave her a "duh" look. "When I give my word, I mean it. I told Tyler I wouldn't breathe a word."

"Thanks for that." Tyler offered a nod. "Couldn't have done it without you."

I couldn't help but smile as the two guys dove into a lengthy conversation about how good it felt to pull one over on the ladies. They really were something, weren't they?

For that matter, all my coworkers were the best. God had blessed me abundantly by planting me in such a great clinic with remarkable people who cared so deeply about each other.

My coworkers made me want to be a better person. With their help, I could be.

Carmela would say, "You already are, girl!" But I knew my penchant for distrust and insecurity. After the fallout with Matt, I had been guarded. Maybe too guarded. Letting pieces of my heart go was tough these days.

But these friends of mine definitely made it a little easier.

When our lunchtime drew to a close, I managed to get a couple of minutes with Kristin alone.

"Hey, I wanted to tell you something I learned."

"What's that?" she asked.

"I did some digging on Carmela's ancestry site and found something interesting about Ray Haas. He has ties to Navasota."

"Really?" Kristin's eyes widened. "Corey's manager has ties to my hometown?"

"Yes, he has family there."

"I know. I was wondering if you would call them to see if they're acquainted."

"Why? Do you suspect him of something?"

"Maybe? I'm not sure. But first can you call your mom?"

"Sure," Kristin said. "I'll try to remember to give her a call. What am I asking her, again?"

"If she knows a family named Haas and if they happen to have a dachshund that looks like Ginger."

Kristin's eyes widened. "Oh dear." Her eyes lit with recognition. "Wait. I was raised in Navasota and definitely know a family named Haas. I went to high school with Lindsey, the oldest daughter."

"Are they still there?"

"I think so. I don't remember the dog part. Meaning, I don't know if they're dog people. But my mom knows Mrs. Haas, for sure. They used to be in the PTA together, I think. Or maybe it was when I was in Scouts? I honestly don't remember."

I was intrigued that she actually knew the Haas family. Maybe we would be able to find out if they had taken Ginger.

"Do me a favor and ask about Ray, will you?" I said.

"Of course. What are you thinking?"

"I don't know. It just strikes me as odd that he's linked to Navasota."

"No kidding." Kristin shook her head as she walked out of the room to meet her next patient.

I slipped on my grooming apron, deep in thought about the Haas family. Then, as I bathed my next client, a cattle dog, my thoughts shifted back to the day Corey and I had spent together. I ushered up a silent prayer that God would quickly heal his leg so that he could get back to the game. Hopefully, that would happen soon.

I went about my workday, pausing only to respond to a text from Corey.

ANY WORD ABOUT GINGER? he asked.

NOTHING. I followed that up with a sad face emoji.

I FIGURED. He followed up with a crying face emoji.

WHEN DOES OUR INTERVIEW AIR? I asked. I WANT TO BE PREPARED.

TONIGHT AT FIVE, he responded. I HEARD FROM LANCE THAT HE HAD TO TRIM IT BACK TO MAKE THE NETWORK HAPPY. NO TELLING WHAT THEY'VE CUT.

HOPEFULLY NOT THE GOOD PARTS, I countered.

I sure hoped they left in the parts where Corey talked about his mom.

At five minutes till five, I wrapped up with my last dog and walked to the lobby.

"Hey, Brianna, would you mind turning the TV to channel 2? Maybe text me if my interview is about to come on? I've got some cleaning to do in the grooming area."

"Sure." She flipped the channel and promised to keep a watchful eye on the TV so that she could text me when the sports came on.

I got the text at 5:17 and left my broom and mop to rush to the lobby. I found most of my coworkers gathered together to watch the interview.

I had to admit, the piece on Corey seemed well balanced. Most of the conversation was about his injury, after all. The few words that were spoken about Ginger were mine, and the camera angle was funny so I looked about a hundred pounds heavier on film than I was in real life. Okay, maybe not a hundred, but at least ten or fifteen.

Mama would be quick to point that out, I imagined.

I turned to my coworkers as soon as the bit ended, and they were all delighted with my performance.

"You go, girl!" Mari gave me a high five. "Thanks for mentioning the rescue."

"You're welcome. I was glad they put up a picture of Ginger so that people can be on the lookout for her."

"I'm just glad they didn't say anything awful about the clinic." Tyler seemed to be breathing a sigh of relief as he spoke those words.

I was glad about that too. But I was mostly glad that I had the opportunity to do something with Corey that had actually worked out well for a change. People could now see that we were on the same team, working together, not against each other.

My phone buzzed immediately after the interview ended, and I saw Corey's name on the screen. I stepped back into my grooming room to take the call.

"Hey," I said.

"What did you think?"

"It was okay. I looked very. . ."

"You looked great! And I was so proud of you for saying what you did about Mari's rescue. I think Houston will see that we're on the same team now."

"That's what I was just thinking. I hated the idea that people might think we were, well. . ."

"Diametrically opposed?" He laughed.

"Not sure I would've phrased it like that, but yes. I'm glad we're working together. And I'm praying, Corey. Really praying that Ginger is found and returned to you."

"Me too." He paused. "I wanted to let you know that the physical therapy is going well. The therapist thinks I'll be back on the field in a week or so."

"That's great. I know Carmela will be thrilled. She's been so anxious."

"Carmela. . .your neighbor? The one who likes to cook?"

"She's almost as good as Mama."

"Everyone you know is a good cook." He released a sigh. "I need to be in your inner circle."

Had Houston's star quarterback just said he wanted to be in my inner circle? Well, honey. . .fling wide the gate! Let him in!

In that moment, the craziest idea occurred to me. I asked him if I could call him right back, and he agreed.

Then I shot off a text to Carmela with the question ARE YOU IN THE MOOD TO COOK TONIGHT?

She responded with a quick ALWAYS.

CAN I BRING A FRIEND? I asked.

She responded with WHOEVER YOU LIKE.

Oh boy. She had no idea.

I called Corey back, a nervous wreck as I asked if he had plans tonight.

"Other than resting and ordering takeout, no," he said. "How come?"

"Feel up to a drive? Carmela's making homemade tortilla soup, and I think there's tres leches cake for dessert. And don't even get me started on her coffees."

"What time should I be there?"

Turned out, seven was the perfect time. And when I walked into Carmela's place with Corey Wallis next to me, Carmela almost fainted dead away.

She sashayed around her kitchen, all smiles, as she continued to cook, cook, cook. And Corey, God bless him, hung on her every word.

When he wasn't flashing shy smiles my way.

Was I picking up on flirtatious vibes? Why, yes. Yes, I was. And I didn't mind it one little bit. In fact, I returned the favor with a few shy smiles of my own.

Carmela knew just how to keep a guy interested. She handed him a ladle and asked him to dish up the tortilla soup. Then she opened the oven to pull out a pan of freshly baked enchiladas and asked him to pass the oven mitts.

I had a lot to learn from Carmela.

She filled our bowls with soup and handed us plates to scoop steaming enchiladas from the pan. I would have offered to do the honors, but she was still using Corey's willingness as a cue.

Should I remind her that he was supposed to be off his foot?

Maybe.

"Carmela, he's got an injury," I said.

"I nearly forgot." She laughed and then said, "Oops! I suppose if you're down for the count a few extra days it'll be my fault."

"Nah, I'll be fine."

Though he did look relieved to finally take a seat at the table once the glasses of tea were poured.

Just as Carmela took her seat, a rap sounded at the front door. I offered to get it, which was good because Carmela was busy fussing over our guest. I made my way through the living room and into the foyer where I opened the door to discover Curtis Elban standing on the other side.

"Mmm. Smells good in here." He sniffed the air. "Am I late?"

Considering I didn't even know he was coming? "No." I offered him a welcoming smile then ushered him inside. "We're just sitting down. We're having enchiladas and tortilla soup."

"Oh, I know. Carmela called earlier and told me the menu. I rushed right over." He shrugged. "Well, as much as you can rush at my age." A little wink followed.

I led him into the kitchen to the table where Carmela and Corey sat arguing about a particular move in a recent football game she'd watched. Go figure. Corey was responding with a smile, but Carmela was all in, ready to take him down.

Curtis took one look at Corey and almost lost his marbles. He took several steps in Corey's direction and extended his hand with a chipper, "Well, look who the cat dragged in!"

I was glad there were no real cats in this story. The current guest list was quite enough for me, thank you very much. Still, as I took my seat at the table, as my eyes met Corey's, I could tell he was already having the time of his life.

It didn't take long for the four of us to dive into a dinner straight from heaven. And the dessert! I'd never seen anyone enjoy tres leches cake the way Corey did. Unless it was Curtis Elban, who couldn't seem to take his eyes off of Carmela once he downed a full helping.

We spent the whole time at the table, eating, laughing, and swapping stories. With no game tonight, we were free to just enjoy each other's company. And boy, did I know how to pick my company.

Several times during the evening, Corey glanced my way and smiled. I could tell he was really enjoying himself.

I was too. Not a bad way to spend a Wednesday evening, I had to conclude. Just yours truly, a pro football player, and an elderly couple who looked somewhat twitterpated with each other. Or maybe Curtis was just infatuated with Carmela's cooking.

At one point Mr. Elban looked Corey's way and said, "Young man, I can't believe we actually met in person. I feel so blessed."

"No, I'm the one who's blessed," Corey countered. "It's great to meet you, sir. I'm always glad to bond with other football lovers."

"You betcha."

The two men got to talking more, and that's when it hit me.

They had both been through horrible losses. No wonder they seemed to bond so quickly.

Grief was a fickle friend. It left its mark. But it also bonded you with others who were walking through it as well.

This I knew from my own experience, having lost Little Lita. Carmela and I had bonded over our shared grief. It had drawn us together because we understood what the other was thinking and feeling.

I had the sense that Corey had benefitted from his time with Mr. Elban this evening. And, no doubt, so had I.

As we ended the night, I walked Corey out to his car. When we got there, he reached for my hand and gave it a squeeze. "I owe you a lot, Isabel."

"No. I was so glad you could come."

"I had a blast." He held tight to my hand and gazed directly into my eyes. "But then again, I always seem to have a blast when I'm with you."

"I feel the same."

"You've made this move to Houston so much easier. I came knowing no one except my manager and a couple of the players. And the coaches, of course. But even then, I barely knew them. I've been so. . ."

"Lonely?"

"Yeah." He sighed. "And feeling out of place. It felt good to have the city rally behind me when Ginger went missing, but the honest truth is, my house feels empty without her. There's been a lot of emptiness leading up to this move."

"I'm sorry."

He slipped his arm around my waist and pulled me to him. "I was...but now I'm not. Nights like this make me—"

"Wish you still lived in Pittsburgh, away from the chaos?"

"No." He laughed. "Make me realize how good life can be, no matter where I live. I've come all the way to Houston, and God has still surrounded me with people who get me."

Oh, I got him all right. Especially as he held me close. I locked my arms around his waist and rested my head against him.

In that moment, the sun, moon, and stars collided.

Well, not technically, but in my heart they all came together in flashes of brilliant light.

Nope, wait. Those flashes? They were coming from the photographer who stood at the end of my driveway, snapping pictures of the two of us.

CHAPTER TWENTY-FIVE

Thursday, September 21

A couple of crazy things happened in the time that followed the airing of my interview with Corey.

First, several different reporters, TV stations, and radio stations reached out to me for more comments about Ginger's whereabouts. Okay, so it started with the photographer at the end of my driveway, the one who wasn't Joey Hansen. Turned out, he was just a local kid hoping to catch a few minutes of my time. Boy, did he.

That photo of Corey and I was widely circulated, not just in our local Brenham paper but in Houston papers as well. Of course, Lance had to take on the story as if he'd somehow created it. So, a story about our supposed blossoming romance aired on Tuesday's news at five.

Turned out there was only one thing the city of Houston loved more than a sports star. . .a sports star with a new gal on his arm.

And apparently I was that gal.

Only, we hadn't really established that. Not in any real sense. Okay, so we had feelings for each other. That was certain. But with the missing dog, Corey's injury, and Carmela's tres leches cake, we hadn't really had time to voice any emotions.

So the people were doing it for us.

Some folks argued—this, I read online—that I was only trying to get on Corey's good side because I'd lost his dog.

Others were seeing the truth, that the two of us were thrust together due to a sad experience that started with the dognapping and kind of went from there.

Not that we knew for sure that Ginger was stolen from the clinic's play area. She could just as easily have wriggled her way out. And don't think I didn't think about her every single day, dozens of times.

Which, of course, I told every reporter who reached out to me in the days that followed our photo appearing in the paper.

Perhaps the best thing that came out of that photograph was the sudden interest in Mari's rescue. Second Chance Ranch had seen an influx in donations that week as a result of our story.

Something else happened that week. Trina's song about Hector went viral. Like, over-the-top viral. I couldn't walk into a restaurant, grocery store, or other public establishment without hearing it playing on the radio overhead.

And every time I got into my car to drive to work, the store, or someplace else, it seemed "The Cat Can Stay" was playing. I had latched on to it. I even caught myself singing the words in the shower one morning. People all over the place were doing the same.

Well, maybe not the shower part. Not everyone sang in the shower like I did.

Deejays were making much of the song, especially with Hector's current illness. They had asked for prayer, and my oh my. . .were people ever calling in to radio stations to say that they were keeping Hector on their prayer lists.

One lady started a prayer chain online; www.prayersforhector.com had become a gathering place for people to place individualized prayers—both for the cat and his owners. On other social media accounts, the hashtag #prayersforhector was growing more common by the day. The women at First Prez were diligent, some of them taking shifts at various times of the day and night to pray for the ornery feline.

The world had gone absolutely crazy. . .in a good way.

There was talk of some sort of a Hector award at the upcoming Country Music festival. Trina was on our local country station talking about that one, though I couldn't make heads or tails of it.

Pun intended.

Grandma Peach promised to keep him away from the pecan pie, which was—it turned out—loaded with salt. And Hector seemed to be responding in a good way. He still wasn't out of the woods yet, but Kristin was doing her best. The nation responded with encouraging remarks on Hector's website.

I was thrilled to hear that Kristin had managed to help Hector through the worst of his illness. He was no longer in a place where she feared they might lose him.

With the use of diuretics and other meds, Dr. Kristin managed to pull off the majority of the fluids that had built up around his heart. Hector still had a long journey ahead of him—lots of meds and rest—but we were feeling more hopeful now. We all breathed a collective sigh of relief when Kristin told us privately that she felt he would pull through and go on terrorizing the community for months—if not years—to come.

I happened in on a conversation between Mari and Grandma Peach on Thursday morning in the reception area. I wasn't sure when Peach and her husband had arrived, but they were making quite a scene. The older woman seemed deliriously happy about something, but I could barely make out her words, they were so rushed and loaded with emotion.

"Slow down, Grandma," Mari said. "I'm having trouble making sense of what you're saying."

Peach released a slow breath and then said, "I've. Had. A. Call. From. The. Governor."

"A call from the governor?" Mari blinked a couple of times and appeared to be thinking this through. "Of the state?"

"Well, yes, of course." Ms. Peach laughed. "The governor of the state of Texas called me on the telephone just this morning."

"It wasn't actually the governor," Reverend Nelson explained. "It was his assistant."

"True." Peach nodded. "The phone rang just as I was heading into Hector's catio to check on him early this morning. I almost didn't take the call when I saw the word *Austin* on the screen. Thought it was one of those political calls, and you know I can't tolerate those, no matter which way they swing."

"Amen," Mari said.

"Anyway, I'm mighty glad I picked up. It was the governor's assistant asking for me, personally." Peach beamed as she shared this news. By now, several of our clients were listening in and hanging on her every word. They knew who Hector was, of course. Everyone in town did.

And, apparently, everyone in the state.

"Grandma, tell a person!" Mari's eyes bugged. "If the governor calls, that's a big deal."

"It's really Trina's fault," Peach explained. "That song of hers has gone...what do they call it? Feral?"

"Viral?" Parker said.

"Yes, viral. And apparently it's a favorite with the governor. So, when he heard that Hector was under the weather, he asked his assistant to call up to say he's praying for him. He and the...Mrs. Governor."

"First Lady," Reverend Nelson said.

"Right." Peach giggled. "The assistant said they are big fans of Trina's. And they heard on the radio about Hector being sick and all."

"I'm so glad we've got a praying governor." Mari smiled. "That does my heart good."

"Mine too. From what I understand, they've left a special prayer on Hector's site." Grandma Peach now addressed the room. "Did you all know that Hector here has his own site?"

A couple of our clients chimed in that they had left prayers on the website as well. Before long Peach was seated next to a woman with a sick rat terrier, praying over the little dog.

Afterward she rose, tears in her eyes, and said, "I figure this is my new calling in life—prayers for animals. If folks can take time out of their busy day to pray for my cat, I can certainly take time out of mine to pray for their animals, in return."

"Takes the term *prayer chain* to a whole new level." Reverend Nelson grinned.

Peach pulled out a measuring tape from her purse and measured the rat terrier, then promised to make him a Halloween costume in any design the owner wanted. Because that wasn't weird.

From there, she made the rounds to our other customers, praying and measuring until everyone in the room was giddy over having spent time with the indomitable Peach Nelson.

She was something else. So was her husband, who trotted along behind her, clearly onboard with her current prayer and clothing ministry to dogs.

That's how I wanted to be when I grew up—compassionate and loving to all I met.

Now all I needed was someone to make the journey with me.

Oh, who was I kidding? I'd found him. He was standing right in front of me Wednesday night in my driveway. With his arms around my waist, pulling me close. Telling me that I'd made him feel at home in Texas.

It did my heart good to know that I'd somehow played a role in making Corey feel wanted here.

Even if I had lost his dog.

The more I thought about Corey, the more hopeful I became. What was God up to here? Would this story blossom and grow? If so, I surely hoped it had a happily-ever-after ending, one that included a tiny red dachshund with a white spot on her front left paw. That would send me over the moon.

"Please, God," I whispered. "You know where she is. Bring her back to us."

"You okay, Isabel?" Mari seemed concerned as she glanced my way.

"Oh, yes." I startled to attention and remembered where I was. "Better get back to the grooming area. Just remembered I have to bathe a shih tzu."

"Now those are words I don't hear every day." Reverend Nelson flashed me a broad smile.

I spent the rest of the day hard at work. When I got ready to leave that evening, I met up with the others at the reception area to say goodbye. From the looks of things, Dr. Cameron was exhausted. I could tell from the haggard look on his face that he wanted to get home.

"You doing okay, Cameron?" Cassidy voiced the very words I was thinking.

He glanced her way. "Yeah." A long yawn followed. "Sorry. Long night at the shelter last night. We brought in thirty dogs from a hoarding case in Greenville."

"Oh no." That made me so sad.

"We had to do intake on all of them. I was there until two in the morning."

"Why didn't you say anything this morning when you got here?" Tyler asked. "I could've covered for you."

Cameron shrugged.

"You poor thing." These words came from Brianna, who looked more than a little worried about him. "And you had surgery here this morning on top of all that."

"It's okay." He smiled. "They're worth it. The animals and the people."

"You're not thinking of running away to some high-paying office job, are you?" Cassidy asked.

Cameron laughed. "No. I'm not easily enticed by money. If I were, I definitely wouldn't be working at the county shelter."

I had to give it to him. The guy was juggling two jobs—twenty-five hours a week at the shelter and another twenty here. And I suspected—based on what he'd just said—that he actually clocked a lot more than twenty-five hours at the shelter each week.

I knew I would.

Most everyone headed out to their vehicles, but I found myself visiting with Brianna and Cameron in the parking lot for a few minutes before getting in my car.

"I've been meaning to run something by you, Isabel," Cameron said. "This is asking a lot, but we're having a volunteer training soon, and I need someone to walk them through how to bathe a dog, clip nails, and so on. I was wondering if you—"

"I would love to. Just let me know when."

"The training is this coming Sunday afternoon at five. If that doesn't jibe with your schedule, we might be able to juggle it a little."

"Pretty sure I'm free." The only thing I planned to do after church was take a nap.

"Maybe get Corey to come with you." Cameron offered me a hopeful glance.

"Wait. . .what? You want me to bring a football player to the animal shelter to help me bathe dogs and clip their nails?"

"Yeah, it would be a great promo for the shelter. Big-time quarterback helps local shelter. That sort of thing."

I wasn't so sure about that. Corey didn't seem like the bathe-a-dog-and-clip-its-nails type. But I would ask him. He might laugh me out of the dog park, but I would ask.

Turned out, he had a game at one.

"I'm sidelined, but I have to be there anyway," he explained. "I could come as soon as it's over."

"Do you think you could be there by five?" I asked.

"I'll do my best. I want to try, anyway."

I thanked him profusely and then ended the call.

I had no doubt in my mind Lance the Legend would be there too. No doubt with that photographer. Well, let him. And let the manager come too. Let them all come.

CHAPTER TWENTY-SIX

Saturday, September 23

We were all gathering at Mari's new house—which we'd all taken to calling the Great House—the following Saturday afternoon after working a half day at the clinic.

I had the strangest feeling I was being followed. I made a quick turn off onto the small country road that led to the ranch, hoping the older model SUV behind me would keep going straight.

Instead, it almost hugged my bumper, making the turn just as quickly. I pulled into the driveway at the property and stopped to check in with a security guard—an off-duty officer from Brenham PD that I recognized.

"Isabel Fuentes," I said.

He glanced down at a clipboard in his hand and nodded. "You're on the list. They're all in the big house."

"Okay." I glanced in the rearview mirror and caught a glimpse of the white SUV. The guy driving it looked weirdly familiar. It took a moment to realize it was Joey Hansen, a.k.a. Ian Gentry.

But by the time I'd pulled up closer to the house, he was long gone, headed down the road out of view. I breathed a huge sigh of relief. Being here on Trina's property made me feel safe at least for now. The last thing I needed was a photographer following on my tail, taking pictures of our workday.

Still, I should probably warn the others.

I got out of the car and walked up the steps to the front door. Before I could even ring the bell, Mari met me, all smiles.

"Welcome to our workday!" She gestured to the grand living room with its beautiful furnishings. Stacked all around the room were boxes, ready to be unloaded. "The guys brought my furniture over from the guest house as soon as they got here, so we're down to the small stuff."

"Awesome."

Something in my expression must've alarmed her.

"What's happened?" she asked. "Is something wrong?"

"Remember that photographer?"

"Joey Hansen?"

"Yeah, I'm about 99 percent sure he followed me here."

Her eyes widened. "You saw him here at my place?"

"I did. He pulled onto the street and would've followed me through the gate if the security guard hadn't been there."

"Then I'm glad Trina decided to go ahead and hire security for this weekend as well as next." Mari took me by the arm. "Tell me what kind of car he was in, and I'll go talk to Dennison about him."

"It was a white SUV, an older model."

"Okay. No worries. You wait here."

"No, I want to come with you."

We made the walk to the gate, and Mari gave Dennison a wave. She had me explain the situation, and the officer nodded.

"Yeah, I saw that white SUV too," he said. "It was a Chevy Equinox. I wrote down the plate numbers, just in case."

"Thank you." Mari offered him a warm smile. "You want some cinnamon rolls? Maggie made them."

"Is this a trick question?" he asked.

No one in their right mind would turn down Maggie Jamison's cinnamon rolls.

We headed back to the big house together, and she took the cinnamon rolls out to the officer.

When she got back, Mari squared her shoulders. "There. All done. Trust me when I say that no one is getting onto this property unless he or she is on the list."

Only, it didn't quite work out that way. Turns out, Grandma Peach's name wasn't on the list. Neither was her husband's. Dennison held them at the gate until Mari and Trina assured him they were safe.

"Did you invite Mama?" Trina asked, as we all made our way out to the front porch to watch Peach and the reverend pull up.

"Nope." Mari shook her head. "I might've mentioned we were having a workday but hadn't thought about involving her in the manual labor. She's not exactly the furniture-moving type. Neither is Reverend Nelson, especially after that incident last year where he injured his hip falling out of the tree house."

"Oh, I'd forgotten about that." Trina shook her head. "Don't ask me how I forgot about it, but I did."

"Well, you have been busy," I said. "Writing all those hit songs and all."

"Working on another." She gave a wink and then headed down the steps to help her mama, whistling an unfamiliar tune.

Turned out, Grandma Peach hadn't come to help move furniture or set up bales of hay. She had come specifically to deliver bride and groom costumes for the dogs.

This was my first clue there were dogs involved in the wedding. I should have guessed. Trina and Wyatt gathered armloads of the costumes—why so many?—and headed into the house.

"I baked some pies," Peach called out as she popped open the trunk of the car. "And I brought some sandwiches. And chips. Figured y'all might need the sustenance. And lots of bottled water. It's hot out here."

Okay then. Looked like she'd already put in the work ahead of time. God bless Grandma Peach.

And God bless Reverend Nelson, who helped her unload it all from the trunk of their car. He worked alongside her, all smiles. The man was truly smitten with his wife.

I felt guilty watching them haul in all that stuff so I offered to help. So far all we'd done was nibble on cinnamon rolls and chips and homemade queso, provided by Carmela.

"How's Hector doing today, Grandma?" Mari asked.

Peach's expression softened at once. "I believe he's rallying, honey. I'm so pleased. Kristin's got him on those new meds, and I'm very hopeful. We've certainly got a lot of people praying, thanks to that song and all the radio coverage. I'm so blessed that folks care so much."

"Well, sure they do."

The conversation shifted to Corey. Turned out the ladies had a ton of questions about my more recent outing with him. I was more than happy to fill them in.

"I haven't seen you this happy in a long time, Isabel." Mari planted her hands on her hips. "Are you smitten?"

"I don't know." I hadn't stopped to think it through. Still, I couldn't stop smiling, so maybe smitten was the right word. It felt right, anyway.

"I want you to invite him to my wedding." Mari gave me a motherly look, as if daring me to argue.

"Are you crazy? I don't know him well enough for that."

"Of course you do. I think it would be a lot of fun to have him there."

"So now we're having a wedding in an open field with a well-known country superstar and a star quarterback of an NFL team?" Parker asked. "That doesn't worry me at all."

"Thanks to your concerns, we've got security and lots of it. Trina is springing for that. And Officer Dennison has collected a whole group of off-duty officers to work the gig as an extra job. Trust me when I say we'll be surrounded by security." Mari slipped her arms around Parker's neck and gave him a little kiss on the nose. "Besides, I want him to come. Could turn out to be a magical night, one we'll never forget."

"Hopefully for all the right reasons," Parker said, and then headed out to Peach's car to grab the quilts the Presbyterians had been working on for the bales of hay.

"Corey's probably busy that night," I said, hoping to change her mind.

Mari's eyes narrowed to slits. "It's not a game night," Mari said. "Pro games aren't held on Saturdays."

I knew that, but I was hoping she didn't.

"Call him right now, Isabel. Ask him to come." Clearly, she wasn't taking no for an answer.

So I picked up the phone and called him. He answered on the second ring.

"Hey, I was just thinking about you," he said. "Any news on Ginger?"

"No, I wish. You busy?" I asked.

"Just finished a rehab session. You?"

"I'm out at Mari's ranch, getting things ready for her big day."

"When is that?" he asked.

"One week from today. It's kind of why I'm calling. Do you have plans next Saturday evening? Feel free to say you're busy."

"I'm not busy. We don't have a game that day. Why?"

"Well, like I said, Mari is getting married. She's marrying Parker, one of our vet techs."

"Right."

"I'm actually going to be a bridesmaid."

"Fun times." He laughed. "You're not calling to ask me to make the wedding cake, are you? Because that one lesson I had from Carmela isn't enough to—"

"No, no." I laughed. "Mari and Parker wanted me to invite you to their wedding."

"Me?" He chuckled. "Why?"

"Like you said the other day, we're all on the same team."

"And this team happens to have a wedding coming up?"

"It does." I sighed. "Again, feel free to say you're busy."

"But I'm not busy. We've established that. What should I wear?"

"It's in a field. You'll be sitting on a bale of hay."

"Is that a thing?" A nervous laugh followed.

"You're in Texas now, cowboy."

"Right." He paused. "So, jeans?"

"And a button-up shirt. And preferably a cowboy hat if you own one."

"One would think. . .but no."

"Then you must buy one ASAP. And boots, if you don't have them."

"I have a torn hamstring. Not sure this is the right time to wear boots."

"Right. That might be problematic."

"Should I bring my lasso and branding iron?" he said. "In case there are party games after?"

"Um, no." I couldn't seem to help the giggle that escaped. "But good try."

We couldn't talk much longer. The noise in the background on his end was too much. Still, hearing his voice and knowing that he was perfectly willing to come to the wedding with me next Saturday was great.

"Don't forget tomorrow," I said before I hung up.

"You think I could forget I'm driving all the way to Brenham to bathe dogs at an animal shelter?"

"It's going to be good press."

"Right." He sighed. "Guess that means you-know-who will be there."

"Lance the Legend," I said with as much enthusiasm as I could muster. "We'll work around him. And that cameraman too. Will your manager be there?"

"My manager?" He grew quiet and the noise from the background got louder. "I wouldn't imagine so. Why?"

"Just curious. I happen to know someone who's connected to his family in Navasota. Did I tell you that?"

"What's a Navasota?"

I laughed. "It's a town not far from Brenham."

"Do I need cowboy boots to go there too?"

"Honey, this is Texas. You need cowboy boots to go everywhere."

"I see."

Only, why I'd included the word *honey* I could not say. Habit, no doubt.

We ended the call, and I went back to my friends, who were hard at work unloading boxes and eating pie.

"Well?" Mari asked.

"He asked if he should bring a lasso and branding iron."

"I hope you told him yes," she countered.

"Nah. But he's coming. Thanks for including him."

"Of course." Mari looked back and forth between us. "Now, is everyone ready to get to work. . .or what?"

CHAPTER TWENTY-SEVEN

W hat can I do to help?" I asked as I looked around the chaotic scene in front of me.

"I have a bunch of dishes that need to be unpacked in the kitchen," Mari said. "But I'm guessing everyone is starving. Why don't we eat some of those sandwiches Grandma brought, and then we'll make a plan to unpack and put things away. I hope to be done with all of that by three so we can head out to the field to map out the area where the ceremony will take place. Then I want to show you what we're thinking about doing in the barn for the reception."

I was glad she mentioned food. I was starving, after all.

We shoveled down a few sandwiches, then Ms. Peach dished up giant helpings of her pecan pie. In the middle of all that, her phone rang.

"Would you get that, sweetheart?" She gestured in my direction toward her phone on the counter.

"Sure." I picked it up and handed it to her.

After a quick hello, she said, "Hold on a minute, honey. I can't hear you. Let me put you on speakerphone. My hearing's not what it used to be." She fumbled around with the phone and finally managed to get it on speaker, then set it down on the counter and went back to dishing up jumbo servings of pie.

"Mrs. Nelson?" The deep voice on the other end of the line was familiar, though I couldn't place it.

"Yes?" She plopped a piece of pie onto a plate and passed it my way.

"This is Governor Abbott calling you from Austin."

"Well, for pity's sake!" Peach picked up the phone but fumbled. It slipped off the edge of the counter and hit the floor below. She grabbed it and said, "To what do I owe the honor, Governor?"

"Cecilia and I heard about your little cat, Hector."

"Oh, yes." Her eyes widened as she began to pace the kitchen.

"My wife, God bless her, has fallen in love with that song your daughter wrote, the one about how the cat can stay."

"Thank you, Governor Abbott," Trina called out.

"Is that you, Trina?" he asked.

"It is," she countered.

"Let me put this call on speaker so Cecilia can hear you."

His wife came on the line and carried on and on about how much she loved "The Cat Can Stay."

Trina thanked her profusely then gestured for her mother to carry on with the call on her own. Reverend Nelson chose that moment to walk in on the conversation.

"I hear a lot of folks are enjoying Trina's song." Peach slid down into a chair at the table, looking a bit pale.

"It's made Hector quite the overnight sensation, I would imagine." These words came from the governor. "And now that he's sick, it's really brought his situation to the attention of the public."

"Yes, it has." She sighed.

"We've been praying," Cecilia called out.

"Yes, so I was told. Your assistant called me a while back."

Reverend Nelson looked Mari's way and whispered, "Who's she talking to?"

Mari mouthed the words, "The governor!" and the reverend eased himself into a chair at the kitchen table.

"Well, this time I felt I should do the honors, myself," the governor said. "I'm not much of a cat person, but Cecilia here just loves them. So, she's heartbroken to hear that Hector's not well. She's hoping you can come for a visit and bring Hector once he's up and running again."

Peach rose and began to pace the room, suddenly looking a lot younger than her years. "Governor, are my ears hearing this right? Are you inviting me to come to the governor's mansion with my little Hector?"

"As soon as he's well enough," he said. "Of course, my schedule is a little congested, but we can probably wiggle in some time for y'all to come and spend a few hours with us. Do you like chicken salad?"

"I do."

"Good. Our cook makes a great one. Southern style. It's got pecans in it. Do you like pecans?"

"Governor, I know you won't believe this, but I'm standing here dishing up slices of pecan pie."

"Well now."

"Do you like pie, Governor?" Peach asked.

"Do I!" He laughed. "Born and raised in the South, so you can probably guess the answer to that."

"What's your favorite?"

This led to a lengthy conversation between the two of them. He vacillated between coconut cream and pecan but settled on pecan.

"That's just perfect," Peach said. "Now I just have to get Hector well so we can come for that visit. But I promise when I do I'll bring that pecan pie."

"Perfect. We'll enjoy a big slice after eating some chicken salad."

"Should I bring my husband, Harold?"

"Of course."

"Thank you, Governor Abbott," the reverend called out.

"Assuming you're Mr. Nelson?" The governor laughed. "Otherwise we're really gonna be in a pickle."

"I'm Mr. Nelson."

"Well, you're more than welcome to join your wife. Just bring Hector when you come, or I'll never hear the end of it from my wife."

Reverend Nelson wrinkled his nose.

"Harold's not much of a cat man, himself, Governor, so you'll feel right at home," Peach said. "But I do believe you'll see, sir, that cats grow on you."

"Like a fungus," the good reverend whispered under his breath.

I did my best not to laugh out loud.

They had a few more words, and then the governor ended the call. Peach set her phone back down on the kitchen counter.

"Well, that was rather unexpected," she said.

"Grandma Peach!" Mari let out a squeal. "You're famous!"

"No, Hector's famous, not me." She sighed. "I have a famous daughter and now a famous cat."

"And a famous you," I said. "The governor of the state of Texas just invited you to lunch."

"We just have to make sure Hector is well enough to travel." She looked more than a little worried about this part.

"Yes, and you'd better leave him crated while you're in the governor's mansion," Mari suggested. "You know how he is."

"Heavens, yes," she said. "The cat can open doors. It's a special gift he has."

"He opens doors?" I wasn't sure I'd heard that correctly. What sort of cat opened doors?

"He made a phone call once as well," Mari said.

"Saved Mama's life." Trina gave me a knowing look. "He's got skills."

"He. . .what?" I asked.

"Mama was incapacitated at the time," Trina explained. "And Hector placed a call to Wyatt, who came to her rescue."

Okay, I had never known Trina to lie, but this story was too much.

Only, it turned out that story was completely true. Somehow the cat had accidentally placed a video call to Wyatt on Ms. Peach's laptop that day and saved her life. . .by accident.

Or by divine act, as the case may be.

Peach went on and on about what she would wear to the governor's mansion. Trina decided a shopping trip to Houston was in order, preferably to the Galleria or other large shopping mall.

Mari thought the outlet mall in nearby San Marcos was a better choice, and Peach chimed in that we had perfectly good stores here in Brenham.

I sat back and listened to them squabble—multiple generations of women from one family. This was missing from my life. With Lita gone and my parents in Houston, I rarely had days like this.

"No point in making any plans just yet," Peach said. "I have to wait until Hector is well enough to travel." Her gaze shot to Kristin. "When do you think that will be, Kristin? I do hate to keep the governor waiting."

"I'd give it another week or two, and then we can talk."

"All righty then." Peach beamed. "Looks like we'll be hitting the road in that new RV sooner than I thought."

"You have an RV?" Mari looked shocked by this. "When did this happen?"

"Technically it's a fifth wheel," Reverend Nelson said. "We've been looking at them for ages now."

"But. . .a fifth wheel?" Mari looked back and forth between them. "Who's driving it?"

The reverend raised his hand. "That would be me. I've been practicing."

"We had planned to hit the road as soon as Hector is well," Peach said. "It's been on the agenda for ages now, but that call from the governor sealed the deal. Austin will be our first stop." On and on she went, talking about the governor.

"But Mama, you're supposed to be focused on Mari's wedding, not the governor," Trina said.

"Oh, that's it! We'll invite the governor to your wedding, honey. Hector can come too."

"Now the governor's coming to my wedding?" Mari looked absolutely petrified by this notion.

"He's probably too busy." Reverend Nelson shrugged. "I would think."

"Mama." Trina put her hands on her hips. "Now I absolutely insist that you *not* invite the governor to Mari's wedding. It's already going to be chaotic enough with security having to be called in. If you invite the governor and First Lady, the security detail will outshine the wedding party."

"I suppose you're right." Grandma Peach sighed. "I'm just excited, is all."

"I don't blame you," Trina said. "And you'll have the most wonderful trip to the capital when the time is right. But everything from now until next Saturday night is all about the happy couple." She gave her mother a pensive stare. "Promise."

"Yes, honey. Of course."

We somehow managed to get back to work. I offered to help out in the kitchen. Mari pointed out several boxes on the far side of the room that needed to be emptied.

I opened up the expansive cabinets and was shocked to find top-of-the-line pots and pans lined up in perfect order. Heavens, Trina had good taste.

"You're not taking this stuff with you?" I asked her.

Trina grabbed a box and shook her head. "Nope. We've got everything in the truck that we were hoping to get today. I'm headed out now with this last box, and that will be it."

She paused to set the box down in the living room so that she could give Mari a hug. The two of them exchanged some sweet words—Mari so overcome she almost started crying.

"No, ma'am." Trina wiggled her index finger in Mari's direction. "Don't you do that. No tears today."

"Only happy tears, I promise." Mari offered a weak smile.

I might've had a few tears, myself. Family caring for family? There was nothing better than that.

Trina grabbed the final box and headed out to her new place, stating that she would be back later to help with wedding prep.

"I just can't believe she left all this." Mari gestured to the great room, which was beautifully adorned with that heavy Texas furniture we all loved so much.

Brianna released a sigh. "It's all magazine worthy. And it's yours, Mari."

"Good thing it's all stuff I like," she said. "There's nothing worse than inheriting furniture and decor that you can't stand."

Why this statement made me think of Little Lita, I could not say. Okay, so she'd left me a lot of stuff, much of which I would have never picked out for myself. Still, I wasn't going without anything.

I turned my attention to the boxes in front of me. Who needed two or three sets of pots, pans, baking dishes, and so forth?

Turned out there was plenty of cabinet space for everything. Trina had taken more than I realized. So, I did my best to put "like" things together—pots and pans in lower cabinets, plates and bowls in uppers, and baking dishes and mixing bowls in the only place left over, the cabinets nearest the stove.

As we worked, we laughed and talked and shared all kinds of stories. I told all about how I'd ended up in Little Lita's house with all her original decor.

"I've been thinking about making it my own," I said. "But it's so hard."

Cassidy offered me a smile. "Well, when you're ready, let us know. We'll do this again at your place. I think it would be fun to shop for your own dishes and stuff."

"Yeah, probably." I had to admit, Lita's kitchen items were mostly from the 1980s. Still, I didn't have room to keep both hers and anything new I might buy, so I had to keep that in mind.

Still, the idea of setting up house suddenly sounded very appealing.

We carried on with our work, and before long we'd made a big dent in getting Mari's things set up. She paused to look over the great room with its beautiful furnishings. "It's finally coming together."

It was. . .and it looked great.

Afterward, we headed out to the field, where we came up with a plan for where the bales of hay would go. There was a big debate about whether or not the guests should be facing the setting sun during the ceremony, but we finally settled on a plan to have the sun off to the side, not directly in front of us.

The guys got busy hauling bales of hay—not an easy task, I learned—and we ladies headed off to the barn to talk about the layout of the reception.

But this time Trina was back and had slipped into wedding planning gear. She and Wyatt seemed completely thrilled to help—with anything and everything. Not in an over-the-top pushy way. No, Grandma Peach was filling that roll. But I could tell Trina had a calling on her life to organize things, and I was glad Mari agreed.

When we wrapped up our day, I was exhausted but thrilled—for my friends and for me. I'd once again shared a day with people I loved, and I couldn't be happier.

Until I headed home and realized that white SUV was right behind me.

CHAPTER TWENTY-EIGHT

Sunday, September 24

I managed to shake the white SUV and arrived home safely a few minutes later. Still, I couldn't shake the fear that Joey was watching me. On Sunday morning, I awoke exhausted but managed to make my way to church anyway. The service was great, especially the worship music.

I wanted to stay focused but couldn't stop thinking about Joey Hansen. Why was he following me? Should I be worried? I shot a glance around the sanctuary to make sure he wasn't here. When I didn't see him, I breathed a sigh of relief. . .then wondered if he would show up at the shelter this afternoon.

After church, Mari and Parker invited me to lunch, as they often did. But this time I had to turn them down. I had plans—big plans—and they involved a certain quarterback.

I rushed home to watch the game with Carmela. She had prepared an amazing meal, as always. Unfortunately, the game was a real downer. Without Corey in the mix, the Texans didn't seem to have their usual spark. They lost. . .by a lot.

Oh well. I wouldn't bring it up when I saw Corey at the shelter.

I headed home to touch up my makeup and grab everything I would need for the upcoming training session. Then, just after four thirty, I headed out.

When I arrived, I saw a van from an Austin TV station. No sooner had I pulled into the parking lot than another one arrived, this one from Houston. Before long a San Antonio news van was there as well.

Had Cameron called these folks in? I didn't particularly mind, but I had to wonder how Corey would feel about it.

Turned out, he didn't really mind since it was for a good cause.

I was surprised to see that Brianna was at the shelter when we arrived. She and Cameron were working together tag-teaming to bring the animals from their kennels to the grooming area, where they were placed in crates to await their groom.

Interesting, that she was sticking so close to Cameron these days. I was beginning to suspect it wasn't just my overactive imagination at play. She was interested in him.

And, from the looks he kept sending her way, Cameron was interested in her too.

I found myself distracted when Lance Henderson showed up wearing his expensive sunglasses.

"Hey, you got your glasses," I said.

"Yeah, Corey dropped them by a few days ago."

"We stopped by your house last Tuesday after the interview to bring them to you, but you weren't home."

"Right." He took hold of the edge of his glasses and bounced them up and down on his nose. "Corey told me."

"We heard a dog barking inside your house."

"Yeah? What of it?" He stopped messing with his glasses and gave me an inquisitive look.

"You told us that first day at the clinic that you're not a dog person."

"I'm not."

"So, why do you have a dog at your house if you're not a dog person?"

He groaned. "Ask my date. Her name is Amber. Would you believe she showed up with her dog? When we left for the restaurant, I insisted she leave him at my house. I think she would've been happy to take him with us. Can you believe people actually do that?"

"I don't think many restaurants allow it."

"She called that little monster a service dog, but he wasn't wearing any sort of badge or anything. Anyway, when we got back from our lunch— which was dreadful, thanks for asking—the dog had eaten my favorite shoes. I paid over six hundred dollars for those shoes. Real Italian leather."

"Oh my."

"Yeah, tell me about it. I can never have them replaced. They don't make them anymore."

"What happened to your date?"

"Amber?" He sighed. "She snapped at me for snapping at the dog. I have a terrible record with women, and it's getting easier to see why. My ability to pick someone I'm compatible with is getting tougher the older I get."

"I have a question, Mr. Henderson."

"Please, call me Lance."

"Lance. Your cameraman has been following me."

"What?" Worry lines creased his forehead.

"Yep. He followed me out to Trina's property yesterday and was there to follow me home last night. Why is he following me?"

"You think I set that up?" Lance's eyes widened.

"I do." I planted my hands on my hips and gave him the sternest look I could manage.

"I have no idea why Ian would do a thing like that, unless he's hoping to get some shots of you and Corey together."

"We weren't together. I was with my friends."

I didn't have much longer to focus on Lance because Ray Haas showed up. Terrific. Just what I needed to make me feel calm, cool, and collected.

"Corey's not with you?" I asked, looking around.

"Nah, I can't stay long. Just wanted to be here in case there were any questions from the press."

"This is just a dog grooming training," I said.

"Press will be here, and I'm Corey's manager." Ray gave me a stern look, meant to shut me down, no doubt. "He's coming straight from a game to do this for you guys. I just want to make sure it goes smoothly."

Thank goodness Corey arrived on the heels of this conversation, which meant I had a good excuse to step away. I greeted him with a smile, but it didn't take long for Ray to take over, nudging me out of the way.

He gave Corey a handful of instructions and then turned his attention to the incoming reporters and cameramen. Cameron then led us to the grooming area at the back of the shelter.

I always had to brace myself as I walked past the kennels. The smell was overpowering. I could tell a handful of the press members were put off by it too. And even a few of the volunteers, who filed in behind the press.

We reached the grooming area, and I assessed my work space. Not bad, really. But I also saw a dozen or so crates in the room, each with a dog inside. Looked like this was going to be a busy day.

Everyone started talking at once, and I wondered how—or if—we'd get this ball rolling. My stomach went to my throat when I saw Joey Hansen walk in. He met my gaze, and I did my best to speak words of warning to him with my expression.

Cameron finally called the room to order.

"We're here today, first and foremost, to draw attention to the Washington County shelter," Corey spoke to the cameras. "But of course we've got to mention my little dachshund, Ginger, who has been missing for the past week and a half. She disappeared here in Washington County, and we've had no sign of her. We're asking the public to be on the look-out for her. She disappeared from the Lone Star Veterinary Clinic midday on the thirteenth."

I cringed when he named the clinic. Hopefully, this wouldn't bring us bad press. I sure hoped not.

The reporters started hollering out questions—a couple for me. They wanted to know what I was doing on the day Ginger disappeared, mostly.

"I was at work, grooming dogs, as always."

"Wasn't there some sort of protest or something?" another reporter called out.

"Yes." I nodded.

"And the dog disappeared during that protest?"

"We think so, yes," I said.

"You don't know? Don't you watch your animals up there?" a reporter inquired.

"Of course we do, and Ginger was in an enclosed play area when she went missing. We're still not sure if she slipped out or someone took her."

I shot Corey a frantic look. I didn't like the direction this was headed. And this definitely wasn't why I'd given up my day, to be lectured or accused.

He jumped in. "I've been to Lone Star, and it's a great clinic. Brenham is lucky to have the caring people it has. We don't know how Ginger got out, but we know that someone out there has to know something about her, so we're asking the public to keep an eye out."

"You two are friends now?" another reporter asked, pointing first at Corey and then at me. "Because there was a time when the press was playing you as foes."

"We're not foes." He offered me a shy smile, and I felt my cheeks grow warm.

Cameras clicked.

"No," I said. "We're working together to get the word out—about Ginger and about this shelter, which is why we've invited all of you here today." I switched into work mode. "We've gathered here so that I can train a host of volunteers how to do a proper bathe and nail clip so that they can continue to assist the good people here at the shelter. We want to give you the tools to be of benefit to them."

I felt rather proud of myself for turning the conversation around. I was tired of answering questions when I had nothing to do with Ginger's disappearance. Reporters, I had learned, could twist just about anything you said and make it into something else. I didn't need that in my life. Right now, I needed to stick with what I knew best—dog grooming.

We gathered the volunteers near the front of the room so that they would have a great view of the goings-on. They were given an opportunity to introduce themselves and tell why they wanted to volunteer at the shelter.

A couple of them had me in tears, especially the lady who had adopted a geriatric spaniel mix from the shelter a couple of years back and walked her through her final stages of cancer.

"No one wanted that sweet dog," she said. "But I did. And ever since then I've been looking for the ones that don't stand a chance, the ones that get overlooked."

Her story brought tears to my eyes.

Which, apparently, made for good TV, as Ian zoomed in on me with his video camera. Ugh.

Now came the moment I'd been waiting for. Cameron brought up the first dog to be bathed—one of the homeliest-looking mixed breeds I'd ever seen. The pooch's name was Calypso. My heart went out to the sweet fella right away. I motioned for Corey to join me at the sink.

"So, what am I doing again?" he asked.

I demonstrated the proper technique for getting a dog in and out of the sink. Then Corey had his turn, picking up the dog and easing him down into the large stainless-steel sink.

I helped him clip the dog's leash to the hook above then directed my instructions to the crowd.

"First we check the temperature of the water. Then we make sure he's completely wet."

Corey helped with this process, all smiles. Okay, so he went a little over-the-top with the whole "getting the dog wet" part, actually splashing me in the process.

In the distance, cameras clicked madly. The crowd sure loved this guy.

I could see their fascination with him. He was most assuredly growing on me too. And, if the smile on his face was any indication, he felt the same about me.

I hoped.

I quirked a brow, and he laughed at me then said, "Oops. Sorry."

"Sure you are." I paused and tried to get my bearings. I didn't want to get too far off course here, not with cameras snapping photos of every little thing.

"Okay, time to lather him up," I instructed. "Grab that dog shampoo over there."

He reached for the shampoo, but the bottle slipped out of his hand and fell into the sink below, which caused the dog to jump. The poor pup got alarmed and growled at the back of his throat.

I did what I could to speak soothing words to calm him down, but it took a moment.

"Sorry!" Corey looked nervous.

"Don't worry. Sometimes that happens," I explained. "This is part of the learning curve, getting to know the dog. I doubt this sweet fella has any aggressive tendencies, but he's feeling stressed right now."

I was too, but I wouldn't say that.

I handed Corey the bottle of shampoo. He opened it and applied some to the dog's back. He put on way too much. I helped him work it into a lather and then added more water to the mix to thin things down a bit.

Just about that time, Calypso decided to shake off the moisture from his coat. He went into that crazy shaking thing that wet dogs sometimes do, and Corey ended up covered from head to toe in bubbles. I couldn't help but laugh when I saw the soap in his hair, in his eyebrows, and all over his shirt.

Which, of course, caused the cameras to start clicking again.

Not that I minded. This was actually starting to get fun.

CHAPTER TWENTY-NINE

We managed to calm things down—with the dogs and our audience—and got Calypso rinsed off. I chuckled every time Corey shot a look my way out of the corner of his eye. I could tell he was having fun with this.

I was too. Only, I needed to stay focused on Calypso. I applied a conditioner and then rinsed that off, doing my best to appear professional.

You can do this, Isabel. Seriously. Deep breath.

Afterward, I transferred Calypso to the grooming station and used the blow dryer on low heat. Then I passed it off to Corey, who finished the job. When we were done, I asked Corey to tie a cute Washington County bandanna on Calypso, who was happy to be done with the process.

We lifted him down, and Corey promptly proclaimed him to be the handsomest dog in the state.

With Cameron and Brianna's help, Calypso posed for a few pictures and seemed to enjoy the attention.

It was time for our volunteers to learn the process. I did the best I could under the circumstances. Corey ended up on the far side of the room playing with Calypso and talking with Lance the Legend, who couldn't seem to remember to keep his distance as we had instructed all the paparazzi to do.

Even Cameron seemed a bit distracted by the reporters. I could tell he was glad to have them there. No doubt because their coverage could bring in necessary supplies, donations, and volunteers.

It took a while to get through all the volunteers, but I managed. By the end of the session, my back was killing me and my shoulders hurt from lifting so many dogs up and down.

When we finished up our work, Cameron addressed the cameras personally. I couldn't help but notice that Brianna hovered nearby. She'd been doing a lot of that lately, hadn't she?

"Folks, you can help the Washington County shelter out in several ways. You can volunteer like these great folks are doing here today." Cameron pointed to the volunteers. "Or you can donate to their website."

"It's a great cause," Corey added as he walked their way, holding tightly to Calypso's leash. The dog dutifully followed behind him and even allowed Corey to lean down and scratch him behind the ears.

"Yes, you can also drop off food, blankets, toys, or treats to our facility Monday through Saturday," Cameron chimed in. "We're always looking for help with those things. And of course we love our volunteers. We even choose one volunteer every month to feature on our website."

"What he said." Corey grinned.

I had a feeling the shelter would have a lot more female volunteers if they thought Corey was going to be here when they showed up.

We wrapped up the filming, and most of the reporters left, though I noticed Lance and Joey hung around. I couldn't help but notice that Joey was wearing his mask and cap again today. And the beard seemed even fuller than the last time I'd seen him. And he seemed to be hovering near the back of the room, something that was making Lance unhappy.

When we ended, Joey started packing up his stuff. I watched as a woman in her forties approached him, eyes wide.

"Joey Hansen?" The lady's excited voice rang out. "Is that you?"

Joey turned around as the name was called but stopped short when the woman seemed to recognize him.

"Cheryl Peterson." She grinned. "We went to Brenham High together. Graduated in the same class. Remember? Your wife, Sabrina, was my best friend. I haven't seen her in months. How's she doing?"

He shook his head then returned his attention to his bag. "You've got the wrong person."

"That's impossible." She shook her head. "I never forget a face. You played tight end for the Brenham Cubs. I was a cheerleader. Remember? You invited me to homecoming my sophomore year."

"Nope. Name's Ian." He shook his head and then headed out away from wandering eyes.

"If that's not Joey Hansen, my name's not Cheryl Peterson." She shook her head and stared after him.

I stepped in her direction, ready to get to the bottom of this. "You said Joey Hansen, right?"

"Yeah, I suppose it's possible I have the wrong guy, but if that's not Joey, then he has a doppelgänger."

"You're not the first person to tell me that's Joey Hansen," I explained. "What do you know about Joey?"

Cheryl shrugged. "Kind of a rough kid in school. Got in trouble a lot. But he was great on the field. Always loved football. And he was good. We thought he would get a scholarship to A&M. But he..." She paused, and then her gaze shot to the direction he'd gone. "He ended up getting Sabrina Cortez pregnant. They got married right after the baby was born."

"I did hear that he was married."

"I don't think it's a great marriage," Cheryl said. "I ran into Sabrina a couple years ago, and she looked really down in the dumps. I hardly recognized her." Cheryl shrugged. "Then again, we've all changed since high school, haven't we?"

"I know I have." These words came from Corey, who stepped into the spot beside me.

Cheryl's eyes widened. "Corey. . .I. . .I. . ." She fumbled for words. "Would you sign my grocery store receipt?" She extended a tiny slip of paper along with a pen. "I know it's silly, but it's all I have with me."

"Sure." He took it, along with the pen she offered, and added his signature. Then he handed it back. "Don't feel bad. I've been asked to sign all kinds of things. One young mom even asked me to sign a disposable diaper."

"Hopefully an unused one," I said.

"Yeah." He laughed. "She reached into her bag and came out with a diaper, then shrugged and handed it to me."

"That's weird," I said. And he nodded.

"Oh, and once someone asked me to sign a check in their checkbook. That didn't happen. I didn't want to go to jail."

I couldn't tell if he was kidding or not. Okay, a second glance revealed that he was kidding.

I had to admit, the guy had a terrific sense of humor. And he was really cute when he smiled. . .which he did. A lot.

I was smiling a lot too, actually. Other than the part where the reporter tried to make me feel good about Ginger going missing, this had been a lovely day, and I was tickled to spend it with Corey, even if it meant I had to spend some time in the limelight, something I usually dreaded.

After the crowd thinned, we hung around to help Cameron clean up. He thanked us profusely for our help. I noticed that he was every bit as kind and gracious to me as he was to Corey. That made me feel good. I didn't have superstar status, but to the dog lovers in town, I was a hero.

"Could you tell how nervous I was?" I asked.

Cameron shook his head. "If you were nervous, you covered well."

"You think?"

He and Corey both nodded.

"You just look like a natural to me," Corey said. "I figured you did this kind of thing all the time."

"I do this kind of thing. . .never." A nervous laugh followed. "Trust me when I say I'd ten thousand times rather be behind the camera than in front of it."

"One more thing we have in common, then," Corey said. He turned his attention to Cameron. "I really appreciate what you guys are doing here." Corey gave Cameron an admiring look. "I've only been in an animal shelter a couple of times in the past, so this isn't a world I know much about."

"It's a world, all right." Cameron sighed. "One filled to the brim with incoming dogs and cats. Our intake department is overwhelmed right now. You should see how many dogs and cats we have."

"Could I?" Corey asked. "Can we look around at the dogs before we leave?"

I suspected he wanted to make absolutely sure there were no tiny red dachshunds in any of the kennels. Cameron was happy to oblige.

We made the rounds from room to room. As always, seeing the dogs—large and small—cowering in their kennels, wishing, hoping, praying someone would take them home—was more than my heart could take.

"I would take every one if I could." I paused in front of the kennel where Calypso now slept on a mat in the corner.

"Me too," Corey said. He stared through the chain-link fencing at the dog. "He's a sweet dog. Do you think he'll find a home?"

"He's one of the lucky ones," Cameron said. "He got his picture taken by lots of photographers today. And there was some video footage of his bath, which was a lot of fun. Trust me when I say he'll find a home quickly."

I had a feeling Cameron was right. Probably by tomorrow calls would be coming in about Calypso.

"It's the others I'm worried about," Cameron said. "Some of these dogs have been here for months with no interest at all. A couple were adopted and then brought back because they were too much trouble. We see that a lot. We have to resign ourselves to the fact that some of these poor pups won't ever have families."

I could've erupted in tears right then. "At the clinic we feature one dog at a time on our board in the lobby," I explained. "We call it our wanted poster. Only, it's kind of opposite. The dogs are in want of an owner."

Corey gave me an admiring look. "Do me a favor and send me a snapshot each time you put up a new one, okay? I'll put it on my social media." He shrugged. "You never know. People might see it and respond."

As popular as this guy was? I had a feeling a lot of people would respond.

"I think we'll get a lot of new volunteers after today's session," Cameron said. "I can't thank you both enough for coming. It means a lot to me."

Brianna appeared from the hallway and signaled for Cameron to join her outside. I knew they still had a lot of work to do before they could go home, and it was already getting late.

I also knew that Cameron was scheduled to operate on a Chihuahua tomorrow morning at eight. How the guy kept up with it all, I couldn't say. I was wiped out.

Then again, it had been quite the week, hadn't it? Yep, and all the better with this sweet quarterback by my side.

CHAPTER THIRTY

Monday, September 25

Mama called bright and early Monday morning, bubbling with excitement.

"Sweetheart, your father and I saw you on the evening news with Corey."

"Oh?" I sat up in the bed, still half-asleep.

"Yes, honey. We were so proud. And I have to admit, the two of you look just darling together working at that animal shelter. Everyone says so. We just loved that one scene where the dog covered Corey in bubbles."

"Scene?" Did she think that was all scripted? "Mama, who's everyone?"

"What, honey?"

"You said *everyone* says so. Who's everyone?"

She paused. "Oh, you know. Your great-aunt Rosa and your cousin Luis."

"Luis says I look cute with Corey?"

"Well, he didn't say cute, exactly. But he was excited that someone in the family was dating a pro ball player. He told me to ask if you can get tickets to the next Texans game."

"I wouldn't say we're dating, Mama. I hope you're not saying that. And no, I'm not going to ask Corey for tickets for Cousin Luis. I would never do that." Though, Corey had offered tickets for my parents. And me. Maybe, if I woke up fully, I could tell her that.

"Luis has done a lot for you, Isabel," Mama said. "Remember that time he said he would come and take care of Matt for you?"

"Mama, I hardly think that threatening to put a hit on my ex-boyfriend was an act of kindness on Luis' part." Should I remind her that he was still on probation?

"I'm just saying, now that you're dating Corey—"

"I wouldn't say we're dating, per se."

"Well, if you and Corey aren't dating, what would you call it, then? You've been together at his house, at our house, at Carmela's—"

"Wait, how did you know about Carmela's?"

"We saw that adorable picture of you taken in her driveway. Her name was listed in the article."

Oh boy.

"Well, I still wouldn't exactly say we're dating," I said. "Though, I guess I should tell you that Corey is—by coincidence—coming with me to Mari's wedding this coming Saturday."

"See there?" Mama giggled. "You're really giving him a proper introduction to Texas, aren't you? He's been to ball games, a dog shelter, and now a wedding. All that's missing is the outdoor BBQ."

"He'll be getting a twofer at the wedding. They're serving BBQ."

"Of course they are." Mama laughed. "Well, you go right on building your relationship with him, honey. You father and I really like him. He's a sweet guy and seems like the real deal."

He did. Indeed. Whether he was on the field or clipping a dog's nails.

"Just don't promise Luis or any of the other cousins anything, Mama."

"Okay." She sighed. "But do you think maybe Corey will eventually invite you to a game?"

"He already has. But not the cousins. I draw the line at the cousins."

"Just remember how much your parents love football," she interjected.

"Mama, you and Pop are baseball fans. You're addicted to the Astros. You always thought my fascination with football was silly."

"I did not!" She countered. "I just didn't want to hurt your father's feelings. He tried out for the football team in high school and didn't make it, so football is kind of a sore subject around here."

Who knew? Pop was a football failure? How had I never heard about this? No wonder he was into baseball.

"Hey, speaking of Luis, I realized why that theater troupe from La Palencia sounded familiar."

"Why is that, Mama?" I sat up in the bed and looked at the clock. 7:14 a.m.

"Luis."

"He's an actor?"

"He fancies himself one. He was in some kind of performance over there on Cinco de Mayo. I heard all about it from your aunt Lucinda. She doesn't like him hanging out with those people. She thinks they're..."

"What?"

"Alborotadors."

"Troublemakers? Really?"

"She seems to think they're more than a theater troupe. I told her I would pass along that information in case it meant anything to you."

"Thanks for letting me know."

"You're welcome. Lucinda says Luis has a friend named Peter at the theater company. Want me to track down his information for you? I think he's some bigwig in the group."

"Sure, that would be great, Mama. I'm curious to know if Peter had anything to do with those protesters who showed up at our clinic a while back."

"I sure hope not. That would be awful."

We ended the call, and I managed to shower and dress and head out by 7:50, nothing short of a miracle. I pulled into Lone Star Vet right at eight, just in time to meet my first client of the day.

My morning was so busy, I didn't have time to think much about what Mama had said. But when I finally took a break at noon for lunch, my coworkers were all abuzz over some article in this morning's paper that I hadn't even seen yet.

Mari passed it my way. "You're going to be a superstar if this keeps up."

"Um, no thanks." I skimmed the article about my visit to the shelter with Corey and shrugged. It was nice, but I didn't want to overreact to it. I sure didn't want my coworkers to think any of this was going to my head.

I glanced up, noticing that Cameron and Brianna were noticeably missing.

"Have you guys noticed anything kind of...odd going on between Cameron and Brianna?"

"Odd?" Cassidy laughed. "Isabel, we'd have to be blind not to see. She's been in love with him since the day she first laid eyes on him."

"Right, but has he shown signs of liking her too? Because yesterday at the shelter..." My words faded off as Brianna and Cameron came back into the room.

Cameron saw me and grinned. "Hey, Isabel." He reached for the newspaper and held it up to show off my photo. "Guess you saw this?"

"Yep."

"The last time I saw you, you were bathing a dog."

"With a quarterback by your side." Brianna's eyebrows elevated mischievously.

Cameron nodded. "Speaking of which, I wanted to tell you that bringing Corey along was the best thing you could have done. You wouldn't believe how many people have donated to the shelter over the past forty-eight hours. It's kind of crazy. And people are signing up to volunteer too. Oh, and I just heard that a lady came in today with a bunch of blankets and towels and things to donate. So, thanks for bringing him along for the ride to inspire the crowd."

"It was your idea," I reminded him.

"Yeah, but he wouldn't have come if I'd asked."

"You're welcome." I offered a little shrug as I thought it through. "It was good to have him there. We're both doing everything we can to draw attention to Ginger. We're hoping someone will recognize her photos."

"I hope so," Cameron said. "But the whole thing has given me the idea of using more sports figures—or folks like Trina, in the music industry—to share the work of what we're doing at the shelter."

Cameron was talking more and more about the shelter these days. Clearly, his heart was there. I didn't blame him. They were doing a good work. A very good work.

"Anyway, I just want to say thank you again, Isabel." Cameron flashed a warm smile. "You didn't just shed light on what we're doing at the shelter; you helped spread the word about Lone Star Veterinary Clinic as well."

I shrugged. "Hey, happy to be of service."

He passed the newspaper off to Mari, who gave the photo a closer look.

"This is a really cute picture of you and Corey." Mari glanced up at me and smiled. "Kind of natural-like."

"If you call being covered in soap bubbles natural," I countered.

"Just saying, you two look really adorable standing side by side."

I cleared my throat. "Shouldn't you be focused on your wedding? How's all of that coming, anyway?"

"Good try, girl." Mari laughed. "The wedding plans are coming along great, as you well know, since we spent Saturday together getting ready for the big day. Now, let's go back to talking about you and Corey."

"Isabel and Corey?" Tyler asked as he entered the room. "Have I walked in on the middle of a conversation again?"

"They're in the paper." Cameron shoved the newspaper in Tyler's direction.

He skimmed it, then looked my way with a smile. "Thanks for the nod. I think it's nice that you mentioned the clinic."

"Of course," I said. And I hoped the conversation would end there. It didn't. Of course.

"Good picture of you and Corey."

"Thanks." Only, I'd had enough attention for one day, thank you. I finished my lunch and disappeared back into my grooming room to take care of an incoming Afghan hound. Afghans weren't on my favorite-to-groom list. They were long legged and wiry.

Arlette was extremely hyper this morning but so was the owner, Mrs. Bricker. She reached into her bag and came out with a newspaper, which she pressed in my direction. "You're a star, Isabel! And you've been hanging out with a pretty handsome one too." She gave the paper a closer look and sighed.

"Oh, you read the article?"

"Read it?" She laughed. "It's all we could talk about at breakfast this morning. My son wants to know if you can get him tickets to the next Texans game."

"Oh, I really don't think I can—"

"What's Corey like? He seems so totally normal and sweet. I saw that photo of the two of you in the driveway kissing a while back."

"We weren't kissing. We were—" What were we doing, anyway? Right now I couldn't seem to remember.

"Sure you weren't." Mrs. Bricker giggled. "Anyway, think about those Texans tickets, will you? My son would be so excited. Oh, and he wants an extra one for his little cousin. They both play football."

Before I could say, "I'm not asking any such thing," she was gone, leaving Arlette behind.

I reached down to lift the oversized dog into the bathing sink and muttered, "What about you, girl? What would you like for me to do for you? Oh, seats at the fifty-yard line? Sure, why not."

"Yes," a voice sounded from behind me. "Sounds like a great wedding present."

I swung around to discover Parker had entered the room.

"Hey." He grinned. "Did I scare you?"

"No." But Arlette was now trembling.

"I thought you would want to know that someone from an Austin news station called looking for you. Brianna told them you were busy."

"Thank you." The last thing I felt like doing today was talking to the press again. This wasn't my life. I wasn't the sort of person to stay in the limelight for long. I was much happier hiding in my grooming room or in a darkened living room with a football game on the television.

"Oh, one more thing." Parker gave me a pensive look. "I heard on the news this morning that Corey's doctors have released him go back to the game."

"Really?"

"Yep." He grinned. "Think you can get me tickets to the next game?"

Before I could say a word in response, he shot out to the door, whistling all the way.

At least Parker was kidding around. He would be on his honeymoon next Monday. But the others weren't, especially Mama.

Which is why I found it ironic that Corey texted less than an hour later to offer me five tickets to next Monday's game—one for myself, one for Carmela, one for Curtis Elban, and two for my parents.

Was he reading my thoughts or something? If the guy mentioned my cousin Luis, I was really going to flip out.

"It's a Monday night game," he said. "I'm not sure if you can get here in time."

"I can probably rearrange my schedule," I countered. "Are you sure, Corey?"

"Of course I'm sure." He paused. "In case you haven't figured this out yet, Isabel Fuentes, I'm looking for any excuse I can find to spend more time with you."

My heart swelled with joy at these words. "Even dog bathing and nail clipping?" I asked.

"Even that. I'm a little sorry that I'll be on the field and not sitting next to you, but hopefully you'll enjoy the game. Your parents too."

"I'm sure they'll be thrilled. I'll pick them up on my way to the stadium."

He gave me the rest of the details related to our seat arrangements then promised to email me the information so I would have it handy.

By the time I ended the call, I could barely believe my good fortune. I made a quick call to Carmela to make sure she was available next Monday night. . .and she was. I'd never heard her sound so excited.

I had just started to ask if she would call Curtis to ask if he could come along when I heard Curtis' voice in the background. Turned out the two of them were at our local cafeteria, eating lunch. That explained the noise in the background.

I somehow regrouped and got back to work, grooming two more dogs. Around four o'clock Brianna popped her head in the door. "Isabel, you have a call on line two."

I stopped cleaning and brushed my damp hands against my apron before taking the call.

"Isabel Fuentes," I said after picking up the receiver.

"Hey, you don't know me," the female voice on the other end of the line said, "but I'm hoping you can help me."

"I'll try. What kind of dog do you have?"

"Oh, no dog," she countered. "I don't have any animals."

Oh dear. Hopefully not someone else looking for tickets.

"Someone in my family sent me a picture that was taken at the local animal shelter yesterday," the woman said. "It was in the morning paper. Do you know the photo I'm taking about?"

"I do. We were just looking at it."

"Well, I want to ask you about one of the guys in the photo. I'm hoping you know him."

"Who's that?"

"He's medium height. Full beard. Holding a camera."

Oh, wow. I hadn't noticed Joey was in the photo. Crazy.

"Cameraman," I said. "Works for KBRT. Goes by Ian Gentry." I didn't want to say more. This phone call could be some kind of setup.

"Ian Gentry?" The woman sounded confused.

"Well, I've been told that's an alias," I explained. "I think his real name is—"

"Joey Hansen." We spoke the words in unison.

"Yes," I said.

"I've been trying to track him down for months now," she explained. "Joey is my ex-husband."

Oh boy. Mrs. Ex-Hansen.

I dropped into a chair and moved the phone to my other ear. "I wasn't 100 percent sure, but I guess you've just confirmed it."

"He took off months ago and left me with four kids."

Should I tell her that I knew as much?

"Why is he on the run?" I asked.

"A couple of reasons. He's several months behind on child support. We had a temporary agreement with the courts when we separated."

"Oh, I see. What else?"

"Well, that's easy," she said. "He has a warrant out for his arrest."

CHAPTER THIRTY-ONE

Tuesday, September 26

Knowing Joey had a warrant out for his arrest made me very uneasy. I fretted over it for the rest of the day and even after I got home that night.

By Tuesday morning, I'd convinced myself that his ex-wife had already contacted Brenham PD to let them know where he was working and his new home address. Maybe he would be arrested soon. But I was still on edge, thinking about it. Especially since he'd been following me in that white SUV of his.

On Tuesday morning, I called Corey and filled him in. I wanted him to be careful around Lance and Joey, just in case.

"No wonder the guy's always trying to fly under the radar in that mask," he said. "He knows if they catch him, he's going to jail."

"Which is exactly where he needs to be, according to his ex-wife," I said.

"Any idea what the warrant's for?"

"No." I'd imagined all kinds of things but had no idea.

"Could just be traffic violations or something like that. If you have unpaid tickets, they'll eventually put out a warrant for your arrest. Happened to a guy I know."

"Yeah, happened to my ex."

"You have an ex?"

An awkward silence hung in the air between us.

"Yeah, sorry. Thought I told you about that. Kind of a bad guy. But he's turned his life around and is involved in some sort of street ministry in Houston. Parker ran into him at the last outreach, I think."

"Wow." An elongated pause followed. "Just goes to show you that people can do a 180 if they do it God's way."

"Right." But it didn't mean I needed to go back to that situation. Ever.

"I tell you what. . ." Corey paused, and I could almost hear the wheels turning. "I'm going to make a few calls and see if I can find out what Ian—Joey—is wanted for."

"How do you do that?" I asked.

"I can call the courthouse and ask. I think some counties make that information public."

"And if not?" I asked.

"Then I call a bail bondsman in your area. He would know. And I'm guessing he would be perfectly willing to share."

"Awesome. Let me know what you find out, okay?"

"Sure."

I didn't have much time to think about it. My schedule was crazy full. By the time I had a break for lunch, it was almost twelve thirty.

I made my way toward the break room but happened upon Mari and her grandmother in the lobby with Hector.

"Hey." I stopped and gave them a smile. "How's our local hero?"

"Why, I'd say you're the local hero this week," Peach said. "I've seen your picture in the paper and even saw you and that hunky quarterback on the evening news a while back."

I felt heat rise to my cheeks. "I. . .I meant Hector."

"Oh my stars and garters!" She shifted Hector from one arm to the other. He hissed in my general direction, and I took a little step backward. I'd heard about encounters with this particular cat, and some of them had ended with bloodshed.

"I'm telling you, Hector is all the rage," she said.

With all the hissing going on, *rage* seemed an appropriate word.

Before she could say anything else, Kristin called her into the exam room. I headed to the break room to eat some leftovers. I had exactly twenty minutes before my next appointment, and my back was killing me from standing all day. My feet weren't feeling much better.

As I ate, I thought about Hector. It seemed like the whole town of Brenham was going crazy over Mrs. Nelson's invitation to the governor's mansion. Local radio stations couldn't get enough of the story. And from what Mari had told me, all the ladies from First Prez had put up signs around town.

Also, #prayersforhector was still trending on social media, thanks to those signs.

Mollie Kensington stopped by the clinic just about the time I was going to head back to my grooming area to clean up. She asked if she could interview Kristin and Tyler about Hector's progress. Turned out they both had a few minutes free, and we all ended up in the exam room to hear what Kristin and Tyler had to say. Mollie seemed to want the whole group's participation, and I was, well, nosy. It was nice to be included.

"I hope you don't mind that I called Mollie and asked her to come." Peach offered an impish smile. "She's been dying for a follow-up on Hector."

"Yes, how's it looking for the little guy?" Mollie asked.

"We've diagnosed him with two different diseases," Kristin explained. "Congestive heart failure and Addison's disease."

"My goodness." Mollie scribbled something down on her little notepad.

"We've gotten him past the worst of the congestive heart failure," Kristin explained. "Now we're tackling the Addison's disease. It's an illness affecting the adrenal glands."

Mollie took copious notes, scribbling fast and furiously. She was also recording the session.

"Is this common in cats?" she asked.

"No, it's very rare, in fact," Tyler interjected.

"Leave it to Hector to get something rare." Mari laughed. Then, just as quickly, the laughter faded. "I'm sorry. I do feel really bad for him."

"The symptoms first presented as congestive heart failure—fluid buildup around the heart—along with weight loss, lethargy. . .vomiting," Kristin said. "His upper abdomen was tender, so I suspected a kidney infection or gastritis, but that turned out not to be the case. Those things would have been easier to treat."

"What's the long-term prognosis for a cat with. . ." She paused. "Did you say Addison's?"

"Yes." Kristin glanced Tyler's way then looked back at Mollie.

"This is thought to be an autoimmune condition," Tyler explained. "And treatment depends on the severity. When Mrs. Nelson brought the cat to us, he was in acute congestive heart failure. We removed a lot of excess fluid."

"I was so scared," Mrs. Nelson said. "I hardly slept for days."

"I'm sure." Mollie gave her a compassionate look. "I know how much you love this little cat."

"Why, yes, I—"

"We all do." Mollie stuck out her hand to pet Hector, who hissed and snapped at her.

She pulled her hand back at once.

"After we got the lab results, we kept him in the clinic for a while," Kristin explained. "We wanted to keep a watchful eye on him. Emergency steroids were in order as well."

"My goodness. He's really been through it." Mollie looked up from her notes.

"And will continue to go through it," Tyler said. "This is a lifelong disease."

"I see."

"We're looking at doing hormone replacement therapy," Kristin explained. "If we can keep him on good meds, that will hopefully level out his potassium, electrolytes, and sodium levels."

"So, Ms. Peach is going to have to stay on top of this." Mollie offered Mrs. Nelson a compassionate smile.

"Yes."

"Was there some sort of connection between the congestive heart failure and Addison's?" Mollie asked.

"Very good question!" Mrs. Nelson gave her an admiring look. "I asked that very same question, myself."

"Yes, the heart failure could have come as a result of the adrenal failure," Kristin said. "We see that sometimes in our patients with Addison's."

Mollie turned her attention to Peach. "I hear you're about to start traveling in an RV. Will the cat go with you?"

Everyone looked at Peach for the answer to this question.

"That depends on his condition, of course. If he's not doing well, I suspect Harold and I will have to wait awhile to begin our travels. But we can't keep the governor waiting forever, you know."

"Family first." Mollie flashed a smile.

"Especially if that family is a cat named Hector." Mari gave her a knowing look. "Let's just say he holds a place of honor in the Nelson home."

"I would imagine." Mollie glanced at her notes then back up again. "How old is he?"

"Twelve," Kristin responded. "He's been our patient since we took over the clinic from Dr. Bishop."

"Oh." Mollie's face lit up. "I remember Dr. Bishop. I used to bring my cat to see him when I was a kid. He was here forever."

"Yes. Great vet," Tyler said. "And a wonderful human being."

"I know that Hector is in good hands here. You guys have saved so many." Mollie turned her attention to Mari and asked a couple of questions about the rescue and about the upcoming wedding.

Before we knew it, Mari was inviting Mollie to the wedding and even told her to bring a date.

"Oh, I wouldn't want to horn in," she said. "And I don't know who I'd ask."

"Lots of single gals will be there." Mari pointed to me.

Well, terrific. As if I needed any more attention drawn to the fact that I was one of the few single Lone Star Ladies left.

And just when I thought it couldn't get any more awkward, Mari went and said just that. She explained about our single ladies' group and invited Mollie to join.

Because that's all we needed—a reporter in our little group to share the news of our ups and downs with the world.

Only, Mollie seemed genuinely interested in this. Relieved, even.

"I've lived in Brenham for a few years now, ever since I graduated from A&M," she said. "And I love working for the paper, but it's mostly guys over there." Her nose wrinkled. "Not any I would date. A bunch of them are sour older guys who ignore their families, chasing after stories."

"Oh?" I gave her an inquisitive look. "Is that what it's like in the news business?"

"Not everywhere," she said.

"But Lance the Legend seems like that," I said. "He's always chasing a story."

She shrugged. "I don't think he's that bad, to be honest. He's kind of. . .I don't know. . .cute?"

He was handsome. I would give her that. And he knew it. He played off that suave, debonair thing.

"At least he's not cheating on a wife," Mollie said. Her cheeks flamed pink. "I did a little digging and found out he's single."

"Well, I still don't trust him," Mari said. "And he won't be invited."

"And I sure don't trust that photographer he travels with," I interjected. "He's got a warrant out for his arrest, you know."

From the look on Mollie's face, she didn't know. Then again, how could she?

"Isabel?" Mari planted her hands on her hips. "Joey Hansen has a warrant out for his arrest?"

"Did I forget to mention this?"

"Yeah."

"His wife called me yesterday morning," I explained. "She saw me in the paper and—"

And this interview about a cat had suddenly swung back in my direction.

Everyone looked intrigued. Well, all but Ms. Peach, who looked a bit miffed that I'd somehow stolen Hector's limelight.

We somehow managed to transition back to the cat, thank goodness. I'd already overstepped.

Before Mollie left, I pulled her to the side and asked her not to publish anything in the paper about Joey Hansen.

"I think his wife would be very upset if she knew I told anyone," I said. "It honestly just slipped out."

"I won't." Mollie gave me a compassionate look. "You've been through a lot over the past few days. I wouldn't do that to you."

"Yeah, I have. And that photographer was already on my radar. He followed me out to Mari's place last Saturday."

"He did?" Mollie's brow wrinkled. "Do you think he's up to trouble?"

"Don't know," I said. "But it was scary."

"I'm sure. Well, I promise not to write anything about him," Mollie said.

I followed her to the front door of the clinic, where she turned to face me.

"Hey, I totally forgot to tell you something. I got on the Internet and did a little browsing to see if I could find out anything about La Palencia and that theater troupe."

"Oh?" This caught my attention, for sure.

"I found pictures of a production they did. You'll be excited to hear that our door blocker is a leading lady in a show called *The Purple Tomato*."

"Never heard of it."

"Yeah, no one has. According to a reviewer from the *Houston Chronicle*, her performance in *The Purple Tomato* was, well, Rotten Tomatoes."

"I daresay she pulled off a better performance sprawled out right here in front of our door."

"Yep. She was almost believable. If that Ray Haas fella wasn't whispering in her ear."

"Right. Ray Haas." Hmm.

Mollie offered me a warm smile. "I guess we'll hang out at Mari's wedding next Saturday? I'm looking forward to it."

Should I tell her that I would be there with a date? Nah, I didn't want to give her any reasons not to come. She looked like she could use a friend, and I knew exactly what that felt like. We would pull Mollie into the fold—Lone Star employee or not.

CHAPTER THIRTY-TWO

A little sleuthing on Corey's part turned up an explanation for the warrant. Turned out Mr. Hansen was wanted on drug-related charges and failure to pay child support. Not exactly a traffic violation. The assault and battery charge had nothing to do with his ex-wife. Apparently, Joey frequented bars and liked to scuffle. A lot.

On Thursday afternoon, we got word that he had been arrested. I placed a call to his wife and asked if she could inquire about Ginger. I was still hopeful Joey might have some clue as to her whereabouts. If he'd taken her hoping to get the reward money—something that now made perfect sense, understanding his financial woes—I needed to find her. And quickly.

Unfortunately, I didn't hear anything that proved helpful, but Sabrina promised to be in touch if she heard anything.

On Friday, we somehow made it through our day at the clinic but closed a little early in preparation for the wedding rehearsal at the ranch.

Trina and Wyatt were still putting the finishing decorative touches on the ceremony area in the field, as well as the reception area in the barn.

Peach fussed around with a team of Presbyterian ladies, who had returned with the finished quilts, which they spread over the bales of hay.

I couldn't help but gasp when I saw how gorgeous it all looked. I could never have envisioned a field looking this lovely, but all those handmade quilts spread over bales of hay? They were remarkable.

"Mama and the ladies have been sewing for weeks to cover all this hay." Trina laughed. "I think they've run the local fabric store out of quilt fabric."

"No doubt."

"Actually, she got all of the Presbyterians to work in tandem, which is how and why you see the color scheme that you do."

It was lovely. And so was the reception area. Somehow Trina had turned an ordinary barn into a high-end wedding reception. The tablecloths and chair covers were the prettiest shade of blush. And the centerpieces? Regal! I could almost envision what those elegant vases would look like filled with blush-pink roses tomorrow evening.

Before the rehearsal began, I checked the weather report to make sure we didn't have any incoming storms. The weather app predicted clear skies through the night and bright sunny skies all day tomorrow.

Mari and Parker totally deserved it. After all they'd done—for us and for Brenham's dog community—they had earned bright, sunny skies.

We had such a good time at the rehearsal that we couldn't stop laughing, especially when Grandma Peach stepped in for Mari, playing the role of the bride. This was a tradition I knew well. Rarely did both the bride and groom play their own roles at southern wedding rehearsals.

Still, when Reverend Nelson almost put the couple through their actual vows, we thought we might end up with Peach and Parker married that same night.

Thank goodness Mari stopped him in time.

After the rehearsal, we shared an amazing meal in the big house, catered by our favorite Mexican restaurant, Mario's. I loved their fajitas—we all did—but they didn't hold a candle to Carmela's. I wouldn't tell Mari that, however. She looked far too happy for any critique.

I noticed that Trina was in whirlwind mode, scurrying around like a proper wedding coordinator.

"I think she's finally getting her chance to pull off a big wedding," Mari whispered in my ear as she slid into the seat next to mine.

"What do you mean?"

"She and Wyatt did a quiet little ceremony on the beach in Hawaii, remember? They didn't do a big wedding."

"And she's living vicariously through you?" I asked.

Mari smiled. "Well, let's just say she's enjoying this experience. And I'm so glad. I thought I could do all of this on my own without a wedding planner, and Trina has been a godsend." She paused. "Then again, she's always been a godsend. Ever since Mama died. . ." Her words trailed off.

I rested my hand on hers. "Your mama would've been so proud of you, Mari. I know you're really missing her this weekend."

"I am." Her gaze shifted downward. "And my dad. . ."

I waited for her to finish the sentence.

"He's never going to know all that he's missed by not being a part of my life."

"Definitely his loss," I said. "But don't focus on that today. Look at what you do have. Look at *who* you do have."

Her gaze shifted from table to table at all of her friends and family members. Then she looked at me and squeezed my hand. "Thank you. I needed to hear that. And in case I haven't said this before, I'm so glad you're in my inner circle."

"And vice versa." Tears flooded my eyes. "God never gave me real sisters, but I feel like He has through you and the rest of the Lone Star Ladies."

"What's this about the Lone Star Ladies?" Cassidy approached and slipped into the seat to Mari's right.

Mari turned to face her with a smile. "We're just talking about how good God is to give us each other."

"You're the sisters I never had," I said.

"Aw, man. Are we getting emotional over here?" Cassidy put her hands up. "I promised myself I wouldn't cry tonight. I'm saving all of my tears for tomorrow."

"Why tomorrow?" Mari asked. "Don't cry because I'm getting married."

"I'm an emotional sap. You know that." Cassidy laughed. "I can assure you I'll cry."

I thought about her words as I climbed into bed that night. The dynamics were about to change, now that Mari and Parker were getting married. But our relationships would stand the test of time. I knew it.

Before dozing off, my phone dinged. I looked down to find a text from Corey that read, Bought my boots and hat. Hope I can play the part to your satisfaction.

You won't have to play the part, I responded. You're the real deal, an honest-to-goodness Texan.

Good one, he said. Very witty. I like a witty girl.

I had to laugh at my cleverness. But he really *was* a Texan now, and not just the team. He'd settled in and made himself at home—in our state and in my heart.

CHAPTER THIRTY-THREE

Saturday, September 30

I awoke Saturday morning so excited I could hardly think straight. I still had to work a half day, but once we closed at noon, all eyes—and attention—would turn to Mari and Parker.

And what a glorious day it turned out to be! Saturday morning dawned bright and clear with temperatures in the high seventies. It was as if the heavens had opened up and rained down sunshine and warmer weather, just for them.

Mari and Parker were off this morning, thanks to Tyler, but the rest of us managed to tend to our clients in the usual way. I could hardly keep my clients straight, though, as I pondered the afternoon ahead.

I had promised to be at the ranch at two with my bridesmaid's dress neatly pressed. Once there, we would do our hair and makeup and get ready for the big event. If I could remember what needed to be done with this bichon, anyway. I finally managed to refer to my notes. A bath and a clip.

Just before we closed at noon, Parker randomly showed up. He caught us in the reception area closing up for the day. One look at him, and I knew something was wrong.

"Dude." Tyler gave him an inquisitive look. "What are you doing here?"

"I know." Parker groaned. "Please don't tell Mari, but I got a call late last night about a pregnant dog living on the streets near Blinn College."

"Tell me you didn't." Cassidy smacked herself on the forehead.

"I had no choice. The older woman who called it in was so worked up. So, I drove out there and picked the dog up."

"Why do I get the feeling this story is about to take a twist?" Brianna asked.

"Because it did." Parker yawned. "I was up all night."

"You're kidding." Cassidy planted her hands on her hips.

"She delivered nine puppies in the first couple hours after I got her to my place."

"Heavens to Betsy," Cassidy said.

"Why your place?" Tyler asked. "Why not take them to the rescue?"

"Because it happens to be on the same property where I'm about to get married. I knew Mari would see me."

"True." Tyler shrugged. "Didn't think of that. So, what are you doing with all of those puppies?"

"Eventually we'll be looking for a foster who's willing to commit for the full eight weeks until the pups are weaned and the mama can be spayed. Let me know if you think of anyone."

"I will."

"So, why are you here?" Tyler asked.

"Mama dog needs some flea killer, and we're out. I was hoping you would—"

"Of course. Go and get it." Tyler groaned as Parker left the room, headed for the supply cabinet. "He's never going to change, is he?"

"No," Kristin said. "And we wouldn't want him to. Neither would Mari."

Parker got the meds and headed back to his place after assuring us that he would have Maggie take over with the puppies, secretly transporting them to the rescue within the hour. That way he could focus on his big day.

"She's already there taking care of the dogs today," he said. "Mari worked out all of that in advance so that we could relax and enjoy the whole day."

"Mm-hmm." Tyler gave him a knowing look. "You look really relaxed to me."

"You look like you need a cup of coffee," I said.

"And a nap," Cassidy threw in.

"I've got time for the coffee but not the nap."

Cassidy pointed him in the direction of the coffee maker, and a few minutes later he headed back our way, cup in hand.

"Okay, I'm out of here." He lifted his hand to prove that he had the meds for the mama dog. "I just want to say how grateful I am to all of you for all you've done for us."

"This, from the man who was up all night saving lives," Kristin said.

"No, I mean it. Mari and I are really blessed to have you in our lives."

"Don't go getting emotional on us this early in the day, Parker," Cassidy said. "You're going to wreck my mascara."

"Waterproof," Brianna said. "Don't forget to wear your waterproof mascara at the wedding."

I had a feeling we were going to need it.

We closed up shop, and I headed home to take a quick shower and grab my things. By one forty-five I was at the ranch, arms loaded down with curling iron, makeup bag, dress, and shoes.

I made it past the security guards—four, to be exact—and found Mari in the big house, peering out the window.

"Come look!" She pointed to the field, and I squinted to take it all in.

"Oh, Mari, it's lovely." I looked out over the whole area. The bales of hay looked amazing from this angle. "Those Presbyterians outdid themselves."

"Turns out they're a whiz behind a wheel of a Singer sewing machine."

"We're pretty good at performing nuptials too." These words came from Reverend Nelson, who stepped into place beside Mari.

"I wouldn't have it any other way," she said.

"I've been speaking to your pastor," Reverend Nelson said. "I've asked him to take care of the opening prayer. How would you feel about that?"

"I think it's perfect." Mari beamed. "And I know Parker would agree. We love our pastor. Love our church." She turned to face us. "Love our friends. Love my family. . ." Her eyes flooded with tears.

"And love dogs!" I said with as much enthusiasm as I could muster.

"Yes, and speaking of which. . ." She turned to look around. "Has anyone seen Maggie? She's going to help me with the dogs."

"Help you. . .what?" I asked.

She just smiled and said nothing. I had a feeling I was about to find out for myself.

The next few hours were a blur. We laughed. We nibbled on sweets. We did our hair and makeup and eventually put on those beautiful blush bridesmaid dresses. I took a look at my reflection and smiled as I tried to envision what Corey would think.

Turned out, I was so distracted by how he looked that I completely forgot about my own attire. He arrived nearly an hour before the ceremony was set to begin and texted me from the sixth bale of hay on the left-hand side of the makeshift aisle. I looked down from the bedroom window on the second floor, smiling as I got a glimpse of him from a distance.

I slipped away from the bridesmaids long enough to meet Corey on the field.

Wedding field, not football field.

I took one look at him and my breath caught in my throat.

Jeans. Check.

Button-up. Check.

Boots. Check.

Hat. Check.

Handsome as all get-out. Check.

"Oh my." I stared at him in disbelief.

"Howdy, little lady." He tipped his hat. "I've come to fetch you fer the big shindig out in this-here field. Would've brought my horse and buggy, but the horse threw a shoe." He stuck a piece of straw in his mouth and struck a pose, nearly falling over in the process.

I laughed like a hyena.

"Too much?" he said.

"Um, yeah. But I have to give you an E for effort. If your skills on the football field don't pan out, you can always go into acting."

"Maybe I will. I might just hit the big screen in my boots and hat and two-step my way to stardom."

"Is that right?" I asked.

"Yep, little lady. Sure as shootin'."

"Well, that's interesting. Guess I'll look for you on the big screen."

"Want me to see if I can get you a gig as a model, 'cause you sure look purty in that lovely bridesmaid's dress. Pink is yer color."

I spun in a circle to show off the soft pink dress. "Thanks. Bridesmaid 101. Wear whatever the bride likes. She likes pastels."

"Lucky for you. That color really suits you."

I could tell he wasn't teasing now. His eyes never left mine. He pulled me close, and I gazed into his eyes.

"So, how's it going in there?" He gestured to the house, and I smiled.

"Pretty good, actually. The photographer has been taking spontaneous pictures for the past couple hours, but we're about to do some posed shots. I can't wait for you to see Mari."

"Already saw the groom."

"Oh?"

"Yep. I accidentally wandered into the barn, where the guys were just wrapping up their photo shoot. That was fun to watch. Trina put them to work adding flowers to the centerpieces. I skedaddled out of there as quick as I could."

"No doubt. Speaking of which, I'd better get back in the house so I don't hold things up for the photographer."

"Sure you don't need my help?" he asked. "It's kind of awkward, sitting here all by my lonesome."

I pointed to the incoming crowd. "Looks like you won't be alone out here for long."

He gave a sweeping bow, and I had to smile when the hat fell off. Corey reached down and grabbed it. "How am I ever going to win over the locals if I can't even keep my hat on?"

"Impress them on the field, my friend," I said. "Impress them on the field."

CHAPTER THIRTY-FOUR

I headed back to the house to join Mari and the other bridesmaids. Along the way, I found Maggie with Beau Jangles and Parker's dog, Baxter. The dogs were dressed in bride and groom costumes. I couldn't help but laugh—and sigh—when I saw them.

Clearly, Ms. Peach had been sewing more than just quilts.

Maggie was beside herself, very worked up about something as she tried to control the two rambunctious dogs. A gentleman I'd never met before took a few steps in our direction and smiled at me. She introduced him as Chuck Davenport.

Chuck extended his hand. I shook it and introduced myself as well. These two looked perfect together. Almost beaming, in fact. Or maybe that was the bright afternoon sun, doing its work.

Maggie almost lost her hold on the dogs as she reached to grab my hand. "Isabel! We're going to Honduras."

"Wait. . .what?"

"Yes, I've been feeling so bad for little Juanita since her mama died. I decided a trip to visit might lift her spirits."

"What a lovely idea! I'm sure you'll have a lovely time."

"Not just me. *We*." She slipped her arm through the crook of Chuck's.

"Maggie?" I looked back and forth between them. "Is there something you want to tell me?"

"Well, shucks." She kicked the toe of her boot against the dirt. "I was kind of hoping to wait until after the wedding was over to tell y'all. We didn't want to horn in on Mari and Parker's big day."

"Wait to tell us what?"

"All that stuff I said about being so set in my ways?" She sighed. "It's true. But something you said the other night convinced me I was overthinking it. When God opens a door to love someone, you need to walk through it, even if it's scary."

Her words were speaking to my very soul.

God had opened a door in my own heart...was it time to walk through?

"What she's trying to tell you," Chuck interjected, "is that we went off to the justice of the peace a couple days back and got hitched."

"Are you serious?"

I was about to let out a loud Texas whoop when Maggie put her fingers to her lips.

"Shh! Don't breathe a word until the happy couple is off on their honeymoon."

"Which happy couple?" I asked. "Because it sounds like you two are headed to Honduras for a honeymoon of your own."

"Yep." She grinned.

I hugged them both, overcome with emotion. "Look what God did!" I said.

"And He used you to prompt me," Maggie said. "I'm not sure I would have had the courage if someone hadn't suggested it."

"Mighty grateful to you," Chuck said with tears in his eyes.

"Happy to be of service." I glanced at my watch and gasped. The photographer would be looking for me. I promised Maggie and Chuck not to breathe a word about their nuptials then bounded toward the big house.

Twenty minutes after that, we were having our photos done.

And twenty minutes after that, we were lined up, ready to head out to the field.

My mind should have been solely on the bride and groom. But for some reason, that Pittsburgh cowboy really had my full attention now.

Until the music started. When we made it to the field, I was blown away by how perfect everything was. All the guests were seated and ready. The music played from nearby speakers, and the participants took their places.

I watched as Mari's grandmother walked down the aisle, escorted by Reverend Nelson. She was seated in the front row in a special chair, set just for her. He then took his place in front of the beautiful decorated arbor Parker had built, alongside the pastor from Grace Fellowship.

Parker came next, stepping out from behind a makeshift wall to our right. He took his spot next to Reverend Nelson. Then his groomsmen lined up beside him—Wyatt, his younger brother James, Cameron, a college friend named Murphy, and Tyler.

I could tell, even from the back of the field, that Parker was a nervous wreck. Who could blame him?

I shot a glance over at Corey, who had somehow ended up on the other side of the aisle closer to the back. He flashed me a winning smile and a thumbs-up.

Maggie made her way up the aisle with the dogs serving as ring bearer and flower girl. The crowd *oohed* and *aahed* as the canines made their way to the front and then took their places next to the pastors.

The pups were followed by Kristin.

Then Brianna.

Then me. My heart was in my throat as I took those first steps down the aisle between the rectangular bales of hay. I kept my focus on the bridal party.

Cassidy followed me, pacing herself.

Then came Trina, the matron of honor.

Just as we all got into position, the music stopped, and the most gorgeous sunset I'd ever seen in my life flooded the west side of the expansive field with light—brilliant golden hues that shimmered down in perfect display for the most precious couple ever. I would have spent more time gazing at it if the bride hadn't erupted in tears, right then and there.

The wedding ceremony was a blur. I remembered the tears. I had a few of my own. And I remembered the song Trina sang, one she had written just for the ceremony. Mostly I remembered it because Mari was sobbing by the time she reached the final verse.

Okay, most of us were.

Reverend Nelson and our pastor from Grace Fellowship did a lovely job of sharing the microphone to bring the happy couple to the "you may now kiss the bride" part at the end.

And when they kissed, Parker dipped Mari in dramatic fashion, and the crowd went wild. Absolutely wild.

We then proceeded to the back of the field once more, where we celebrated with the new bride and groom, everyone talking at once.

The guests made their way to the barn with Trina leading the way. I watched Corey pass by. He offered me a shy smile and then kept going.

The photographer got some great shots of the wedding party with the sunset providing just the right lighting. Then it was time to be introduced to the guests, who were enjoying appetizers in the beautifully decorated reception area.

I was never much for attention, so when my name was called, I felt my face turning hot. I went inside and made my way to the table at the front to be seated with the wedding party.

I'm not sure how they managed it, but Corey was seated at the table directly to my left, within just a couple of feet of me.

Sly one, Mari. Sly one.

Mollie Kensington came up behind me a few minutes later. I turned and let out a whistle when I saw her in a fabulous blue dress.

"Mollie, you look great."

"Thanks." Her cheeks flushed the prettiest shade of pink as she stared at Corey.

"You know Corey Wallis, right?" I said after a moment of awkward silence.

"Well, we haven't met in person." She extended her hand. "Mollie Kensington."

"Nice to meet you." He flashed a welcoming smile as he shook her hand. "Corey Wallis."

"I was in the crowd when you came to the clinic to get your dog." She paused. "I mean, when you came to get her but. . ." Her gaze traveled to me, and I glared at her. "You know."

"Understood."

Mollie turned her attention to me. "Hey, I promised Mari I would do a little research into that theater troupe."

"Right."

"She's a little busy today, obviously, but I have learned something, and I think it's pretty important, so I need to tell someone while it's on my mind."

"Oh?" I asked. "What's that?"

"It's run by a guy named Peter Channing."

I offered a shrug as the name rolled around in my mind. "Never heard of him."

"I hadn't either," Mollie said. "But no doubt you've heard of his brother-in-law. . .Ray Haas."

CHAPTER THIRTY-FIVE

Ray Haas' brother-in-law runs the theater troupe that sent fake protesters to our clinic?" My breath caught in my throat. "Are you serious?"

"Yep." She paused. "Do I run with the story or leave it there?"

"Wait." Corey put his hand up. "You're telling me that my manager had something to do with that protest?"

"We knew the protesters were from a theater company," she said. "But we didn't have anything to link them to the instigator until now."

A memory flooded over me. "My mother said my cousin Luis was close to a guy named Peter from that theater troupe, but I never would have pieced this together if not for you, Mollie. Thank you so much."

"You're welcome. I still haven't published that article. I was looking for more evidence. Guess I've found it now." She turned to face Corey. "Sorry to have to give you such bad news on a happy night like this."

Corey shook his head. "I'm still so confused. You're sure Ray is behind this?"

"Yeah." She sighed. "It didn't take much of an effort on my part to locate one of the troupe members willing to talk. The general complaint is that he didn't follow up with the promised payment, so they're none too happy with him."

Corey's jaw flinched. "Why would he do that?"

"Attention?" I suggested. "He's trying to get the public on your side."

"At what cost?"

"One hundred dollars a head," Molly responded. "That's what he promised the actors. But like I said, he never paid up."

Corey's expressions tightened. "Excuse me. I've got to make a call."

He took off in the direction of the field. I turned back to face Mollie.

"I'm sorry, Isabel," she said. "I should have just told Mari directly instead of letting the cat out of the bag in front of Corey. But this isn't the day to tell her anything like this. And I had to let you know because it's going to be the lead story in tomorrow's paper."

"It's better that Corey heard it from you, trust me. Hard as it might be to face news like that, he's got to know. And I suspect he's already on the call with Ray now."

"Ray, who would do anything to win public support for his client." Mollie shrugged.

"He went too far this time, and it's definitely going to backfire."

I just hoped it didn't backfire on Corey too. No telling how the public would respond if they thought he was tied to this prank.

Mari walked up, all smiles, and Mollie plastered on a smile as well. We shifted gears to talk at length with the bride about how beautiful the ceremony had been and how great the barn looked.

I took my seat at the head table again but kept a watchful eye out for Corey. He returned a few minutes later.

"You okay?" I asked.

He nodded. "Yeah. I'm sorry I left in such a hurry, but I had to call Ray to see if. . ." He paused. "He admitted it. Told me he cooked up the whole protest thing to make me look good to the press."

"If he's willing to do something like that, do you think he. . ." I shook my head as I thought about that precious little dog we were still missing.

"Surely not. He's an opportunist, but he's not really a bad guy."

"I'm not sure the people in the theater troupe would agree with you. Apparently, he still owes them a lot of money."

"And if he pays it, then what?" Corey sighed. "Then he'll really be complicit."

"Well, just so you're aware, the story is going to break in the Brenham newspaper in the morning. And you can bet your bottom dollar that if the local story breaks, you-know-who-at-channel-2 is going to run with it as well."

"Ugh. I hope people don't think I had anything to do with this."

"They might." I felt awful saying it aloud, but some folks might think he put Ray up to it as some sort of publicity stunt.

I hated that this news had come out tonight, in the middle of what should have been a blissful evening. Thank goodness no one besides Corey and Mollie and I knew, and we weren't breathing a word.

We settled down at our respective tables and had dinner, and I did my best to put all of this out of my mind. I was disappointed, but I wouldn't let it ruin my night.

After eating, the real party began. The bride and groom had their first dance. Then Mari danced with Reverend Nelson. All over the room, phones were lifted as photos were taken. After that, Parker danced with his mother. Then the floor was opened so that anyone could dance.

Cassidy came my way with Jason on her arm. "Isabel, check it out." She gestured across the dance floor to Cameron and Brianna, who were slow dancing.

"Oh, wow." I didn't know which intrigued me more, that Cameron knew how to dance or that Brianna looked so natural in his arms.

"I think it's about time Cameron settled down," Cassidy said. "And Brianna's just the one to settle him."

"She's certainly won him over with her snickerdoodles," I countered.

"Just like this sweet gal won me over with her strawberry-rhubarb pie." I turned to discover Chuck and Maggie standing behind me.

He gestured to where the barn doors were open to reveal the night sky, directly behind where we were standing. "That, and all of these wide-open spaces. There's something to be said for a night sky so uncluttered that you can actually see the stars."

Chuck sighed, and we all turned to face the great outdoors, just beyond where we now stood.

"Check that out," he said. "Have you ever seen anything more beautiful?"

We took a few steps forward to get a better look at the night sky. Then all of us gazed up at once. The sky was brilliantly splattered with shimmering stars, each one on full display. Perfect for Mari and Parker's celebration.

"I'm so glad God brought me to Brenham, Texas." I sighed.

"Me too." Corey slipped his arms around my waist, and we stood in silence, gazing upward.

My gaze traveled back up to the stars. I could almost envision Little Lita up there, shining brightly, lighting my way. She had made a home for me. Now it was time for me to make a home for myself.

I cradled myself into Corey's embrace, ready to forget our troubles and enjoy our time together. It all seemed so easy, out here under the stars.

Maggie and Chuck went back inside. We heard the band start to play a new song, and Corey extended his hand. "Could I have this dance?"

"Out here? In the dark?" I asked.

"Mm-hmm."

I took his hand and he pulled me close. Then, with the stars twinkling overhead, we shared a private dance for two. I couldn't remember a moment when I'd ever felt so happy. . .or peaceful.

When the dance ended, we headed back inside the barn to join the others. The party carried on, and we had a wonderful time, until just after the bride and groom left, headed to a beautiful hotel in Houston. From there, they planned to board a plane for Grand Cayman in the morning, Trina's gift to the happy couple.

The whole thing happened in whirlwind fashion. One moment they were there; the next they were gone.

All my coworkers gathered at the back of the barn to gaze up at the stars once more. I finally had a moment to catch my breath.

Until Trina approached, worry lines creasing her brow. "Houston, we have a problem."

"What's that?" I asked.

"I've heard there are reporters here, just outside the gate."

"What reporters?" These words came from Corey.

I knew before she even responded with, "Lance. . ."

"The Legend," we all chimed in together.

"Why is he here?" Kristin asked. "Because the niece of a country star is getting married or because the new quarterback for the Houston Texans is attending?"

"Yes," Trina said. "Both. And I have a feeling he's going to make it hard for you to get back home, Corey. He knows your car, so I'm guessing he's going to tail you."

"Well, he doesn't know mine," Maggie said. "I drive a ranch truck, and I'm pretty sure he wouldn't recognize it. So Chuck and I will take you back home, cowboy."

"You're going to drive me all the way to Houston?" Corey asked.

"Why not?" Maggie shrugged. "Better yet, you drive my truck back to your place, and we'll drive your car back to mine. They can follow us and think it's you. I'll lead that newshound on a wild goose chase through the backwoods of Washington County. It'll be a lot of fun." She nudged Chuck in the ribs. "We'll get that reporter good and lost. What do you think, Chuck?"

"Sounds like fun." He planted a kiss in her hair. "I'd go anywhere with you, Maggie."

I could see the panic in Corey's eyes. No doubt the idea of letting a stranger drive his BMW convertible on country roads wasn't high on his to-do list, especially on a wild goose chase.

"I'm an excellent driver," Maggie said, as if picking up on his concerns.

"But what if they follow Isabel's car when she leaves instead of mine?" he said. "I don't trust Lance as far as I can throw him."

I didn't either, especially when he voiced those concerns aloud.

Corey looked my way and reached for my hand. "I don't want you going home alone."

"Then you two can leave together," Maggie said. "In my truck. You two just head on over to my place. It's not far from here anyway. No one will ever suspect you're in my vehicle. We're going to stay here and help Trina and Wyatt clean up, and then we'll come home in the rescue van when we're done. We'll leave both of your cars right here at the rescue overnight, locked up in Mari's garage."

"Now, *that* I can live with," Corey said.

I offered to help stay and clean up, but Maggie wouldn't hear of it. This scheme of hers was too complicated.

Corey and I put both our vehicles side by side in Mari's fancy garage, then Trina locked the doors. Afterward, I changed back into the clothes I'd started in—before putting on the bridesmaid dress—and we climbed into Maggie's truck and headed to her place. I was grateful for the tinted windows as we pulled out onto the main road and passed Lance's car, which was pulled off the side of the road.

Thank goodness, he didn't even glance our way.

"Maggie was right," I said. "He never suspected a thing."

I guided Corey down the road to Maggie's property. We pulled in her long driveway and parked the truck, then made our way to the front porch. With keys in hand, Corey managed to get the front door open. Then we stepped inside the spacious house and turned on the lights.

"Now what?" Corey asked.

I set my things down and then turned to face him. "Want to sit on the front porch? I noticed some great rocking chairs out there."

"Sure."

We went back out and settled into chairs. Moments later, I was rocking back and forth, gazing up at the sky overhead.

"So, this is what living on a ranch is like," Corey said. . .and then sighed.

"Yep." I glanced his way. "What do you think?"

"I think I could get used to this, honestly."

"You'd give up football for a few acres?"

"Maybe eventually. Right now, I'm pretty much committed, at least for this year." He paused. "What about you? Are you settled on Brenham forever?"

I paused to think that through. "I'm from Houston, actually. My family is there, as you saw. I'm here because Lita brought me here. I think she wanted me to be here so that I could experience life apart from everything I'd known."

"And have you?"

"I have. I had to come all the way to Brenham to find myself." I glanced his way. "And you."

He chuckled. "If anyone had ever said they had to come to Brenham, Texas, to find me I would have laughed. Funny how that worked out."

"Isn't it, though?"

He rose and took me by the hand. I stood and leaned into him as he slipped his arms around my waist. He gave me a tender kiss. Afterward, we both stood quietly gazing up at the night sky.

"When I'm with you, I see stars," he said after a moment of stillness.

"Like, literally?" I asked.

"Yes," he responded. "The sky is brilliant out here. So dark and clear. And the stars are so obvious. I've never noticed them so distinctly before."

"In the city there are too many lights," I explained. "You can't see the forest for the trees."

"I think there's more to it than that." He planted a tiny kiss on my nose. "I think it's you."

"Being with me makes you see stars?"

"Yes. That's it."

"Well, hopefully they won't blind you." I offered a nervous laugh.

"Hopefully they will." He gave me a kiss so sweet, so intense, that I didn't care if we were both blinded for life.

And in that moment, as he held me close, I had to admit. . .I saw stars too.

I peeked back up at the sky again, wondering, if Lita could hear this conversation, what she would say.

Unfortunately—or fortunately—I didn't have time to think about it for long, because Corey's lips got in the way.

CHAPTER THIRTY-SIX

Maggie and Chuck arrived home less than an hour after we got there. We had a lovely visit with the two of them. Then she got me settled in one guest room and Corey in another. She loaned me a nightgown that was a couple of sizes too big, but I didn't even care, I was so worn out.

By midnight I was fast asleep. And when I awoke at eight on Sunday morning, the smell of bacon drew me out of bed and into the kitchen. I wrapped myself in a lightweight blanket and followed my nose to the breakfast table, where I found the three of them deep in conversation about child sponsorship in Third World countries.

They looked up as I entered the room.

"Hey, sleepyhead," Corey said.

I had to laugh when I saw his hair sticking up on top of his head.

"Have you guys been up for long?" I yawned.

"Only three hours," Maggie said, followed by, "just kidding. Woke up thirty minutes ago. Fix yourself a cup of coffee and join us, kiddo."

I did just that, and before long I was seated across from Corey eating bacon, eggs, and homemade biscuits. Were all the other women in my world great cooks, or what?

I glanced at the clock a while later and tried to figure out a plan. This was Sunday, after all, and I usually went to church. But I didn't have a car. Or the right clothes. And then there was the issue of Corey.

Before I could give it any more thought, my cell phone rang. I answered it to find Kristin's name on the screen. Weird.

"Hey, I just heard something you might find interesting," she said.

"What's that?"

"Mama called. She said the Haas family has a new little dog."

"What?" I put the phone on speaker. "Say that again, Kristin. I want Corey to hear."

"You're with Corey?"

"We stayed at Maggie's place last night. Long story. But say it again."

"Mama called to say that the Haas family came into our family's antique store in Navasota yesterday with a new little dog. Mama called it a wiener dog. Said it was dressed in a cute little dress. She told me they tried to pass her off as a service dog."

"Was she red?" Corey asked.

"Mama said she was the color of cinnamon with a white patch on her right front paw."

Corey bounded to his feet.

The phone trembled in my hand, and I almost dropped it. "Kristin, we owe you. Big-time."

"Thank my mama," she said. "Oh, and by the way. I've got the Haas' address. I'll text it to you when we hang up."

"Thanks, girl," I said.

We ended the call, and everyone scrambled to come up with a plan.

"Let's all go together," Maggie said. "We'll take the rescue van. I'm used to driving it."

"And you know how to get to Navasota from here?" Corey asked.

"Honey, I've lived in this area my whole life. Of course I do."

I slipped back into my casual clothes from the day before and quickly shot off a text to Mollie, offering her the scoop. I also sent her the address of the Haas family in Navasota. She responded with three words: MEET YOU THERE.

We headed out to Navasota with Maggie behind the wheel and Chuck in the passenger seat. Corey and I found ourselves seated on a bench seat behind them, with several dog crates in the empty space behind us. They rattled and clanged with every bump we hit.

"How far is Navasota?" Corey asked me as Maggie hightailed it down the road.

"Maybe half an hour, but at the rate of speed she's driving, twenty minutes."

"What if it's not Ginger?" His eyes met mine. "I'm scared to get my hopes up."

"Me too," I countered. "But what if it is?"

"Then I have a much bigger problem than just a missing dog. I have a manager who has betrayed me, stolen from me, and risked my reputation just to gain a little publicity."

"In a weird and twisted way, he was doing his job."

"Hardly." Corey's jaw flinched. "But trust me when I say he's going to be fired the minute I get that dog back in my arms, whether he's the one who took her or not. I heard enough last night to break off that relationship for good."

Just outside of Navasota, I made a call to the local police. A few minutes later, we pulled into a driveway of a run-down house with broken shutters. Maggie came squealing to a stop in the driveway.

A woman with messy hair came out of her house wearing a bathrobe. She stared at our vehicle from a distance, then rushed back inside.

A few seconds later, an older man came out. He took one look at us and came barreling our way. Maggie bolted from the front seat with Chuck beside her.

"Should we get out?" Corey asked.

"Yeah, let's." I knew Maggie well enough to know she was probably armed. And gauging from the way Chuck carried himself, he was too. So I felt safe.

Until the heated argument began. Mr. Haas insisted that he didn't own a dog.

Which made things really awkward when the yapping started in his backyard.

I was tempted to head that way, but Maggie stopped me. "Police are on their way," she said. "Let them handle it."

Right on cue, Mollie pulled into the driveway.

Unfortunately, a familiar vehicle pulled in behind her.

I squinted to make sure I was seeing correctly. "Is that Lance?"

"Ugh." Corey groaned.

Mollie got out of her car and headed straight for me. "I'm sorry, Isabel. He was on my tail the whole way."

"But how did he know we were headed here?" I asked. "Lance is all the way in Houston."

"He's been following me since last night," Mollie explained. "I tried to ditch him back in Brenham, but I couldn't shake him."

Lance bounded from his vehicle with a young man that I didn't recognize behind him. Carrying a camera. They headed our way. Lance flashed a bright smile as he grabbed his microphone and gestured for his new camera guy to start filming.

Moments later, a police car pulled into the driveway. . .and it was on.

Mr. Haas finally came down off the porch, arms flailing, carrying on about how his brother-in-law had made him do it. Then Mrs. Haas stepped out onto the porch holding a dog.

A tiny little red dog with a white patch on her front paw.

I let out a cry and started running toward Ginger. The police officer stopped me before I got there.

"Let me handle this," he said.

Only Ginger didn't want to be handled. She wanted me. And nothing—it would seem—was going to stop her.

She made a flying leap out of Mrs. Haas' arms and came bounding my way, tail wagging. She passed right by Corey and started jumping up and down like a yo-yo at my feet.

I reached down and scooped her up and let her kisses distract me for a good minute as I carried on and on about how much I'd missed her. And in that moment, I was awfully glad that Lance the Legend was catching the whole story so that I could watch it again and again when this was over.

Corey reached over and scratched Ginger behind the ears. "I'm so glad you're okay, little girl."

I passed her into his waiting arms. She allowed him to cuddle her but kept a watchful gaze on me.

Then, as the officer passed by us with Mr. Haas, Ginger growled.

"Easy, girl," I whispered. "Everything's okay now."

And I knew it would be. I knew this story would end well—for all of us.

Off in the distance I heard Lance speaking to the camera: "All's well that ends well in the dognapping caper that started in Houston, led us to Brenham, and ended in the tiny town of Navasota."

"Hey, Navasota's not that small!" These words came from Mrs. Haas. "I'll have you know we have a McDonald's and even a Walmart!"

"The story of the MIA dachshund has twisted and turned," Lance continued, flashing a cheesy smile. "And we at KBRT have been with you every step of the way. We're happy to report that famed quarterback Corey Wallis is now holding the dog in his arms."

He took a few steps in our direction and frowned when he realized that Corey was not, in fact, holding the dog in his arms.

I was. Again.

And the dog wasn't going anywhere anytime soon.

"What's the plan for little Ginger, Corey?" Lance thrust the microphone into his face.

"Well, I'd have to say she's already celebrating her recovery."

"Is she headed back to your place in Houston?" Lance asked.

Corey looked my way, his eyes soft with compassion as I placed a tiny kiss on the pup's head. "I believe, Mr. Henderson, that you're looking at a potential opportunity for shared custody."

"With the woman you once suspected of stealing your dog?"

"I never for a minute thought Isabel took my dog," he countered. "And I'm grateful to Second Chance Ranch for the role they played in helping with her care. As you can see, Ginger is very happy with her foster mom."

I smiled as I heard the words *foster mom.*

And smiled even more when Ginger gave me a couple of sweet kisses on the cheek just as the cameras started clicking.

Mama would read all about this in the paper, no doubt.

Or see it on the evening news.

She would comment on my wrinkled blouse and my runny mascara caused from the tears that now tumbled down my cheeks. But right now, I simply couldn't help myself. This little doll was home where she belonged.

CHAPTER THIRTY-SEVEN

Sunday, October 1

That night, after Ginger's rescue, I gathered with my parents, Carmela, and Curtis at NRG Stadium in the seats Corey had acquired for us. We had the time of our lives watching the game. Corey led his team to victory that night. It was an evening none of us would forget.

The week that followed was quite a ride as well. Corey and I found ourselves featured on dozens of local and national news shows and not just the sports-themed ones.

Mari and Parker returned from their honeymoon to discover hundreds and hundreds of donations to their rescue, which we mentioned on every single show.

Mari was beside herself with joy over all of it. So was I. To be honest, I loved every moment with Corey and Ginger.

Okay, so the pup was spending more time with me than him. But Corey didn't seem to mind.

On the second Saturday in October, we all gathered at Mari and Parker's ranch for a BBQ dinner together to celebrate. I was tickled pink that Peach and Reverend Nelson joined us. And a little surprised when Mollie showed up. . .with Lance Henderson.

"I'm just here on personal business." He put his hands up. "See? No camera."

"Mm-hmm." Corey didn't look very convinced.

Mollie, on the other hand, looked deliriously happy. Go figure.

I pulled her to the side of the room, ready to get to the bottom of this. "Mollie!"

"What?" She turned my way, a hand-in-the-cookie-jar look on her face.

"Are you seeing Lance Henderson?"

"I, well..." She paused. "We're in the same line of work, as you know. We have a lot in common."

"Mm-hmm."

"And, well, I was working on a story that I thought might be of interest to him."

"About?"

"About, well..." She paused and appeared to be thinking. "Actually, it's a feel-good story about Maggie and that beautiful little girl she and Chuck visited in Honduras. Did you hear they're talking about adopting her?"

"Yes, she told me they've already started the paperwork."

"I'm planning to cover the story for the local paper, you see."

"Oh yes. I see very clearly." I did my best to force back the smile that threatened to erupt.

It looked like the single ladies in our little text group were dropping like flies.

About halfway into the meal, Peach rose and clapped her hands together. "Folks, could I have your attention? I have an announcement to make." She reached under her chair and came out with a beautifully wrapped package, which she passed my way.

"What's this?" I asked.

"Open it and see, honey. I made it special, just for your little Ginger."

I carefully unwrapped the beautiful gift and gasped when I saw the costume inside.

A Texans uniform.

"Oh. My. Stars!" I threw my arms around the woman's neck and gave her the tightest hug possible. "This is pure perfection."

"Isn't it, though?" She beamed. "I've done a lot of sports uniforms in the past but never anything this special."

Everyone insisted I put it on Ginger at once, and she pranced around in it, showing off.

Right before piddling on Mari's rug.

My friend didn't seem to mind. In fact, she beat me to the punch with the cleanup. "This is my life," she said. "Remember? Besides, it's the least I can do after all you and Corey have done for me."

"You're welcome," I said. Then I turned my attention back to her grandmother. "Ms. Peach, how was your trip to the capital?"

"It was magnificent." She giggled. "Hector wasn't on his best behavior, but I'm sure the governor's arm will be fine with just a few days of rest and a good round of antibiotics."

Mari's eyes widened. "Hector attacked the governor?"

"Attacked is such a strong word. I prefer to think of it as a difference of opinion. The governor wanted to cuddle, and Hector didn't."

Hector had never been the cuddly sort. That was sure.

"That's a little more than a difference of opinion, Grandma," Mari said.

"Pshaw." Peach waved a hand in the air. "So much good came out of that visit. We were the headline story in the Austin paper that night."

"Hopefully with no photos of the injury," Trina interjected.

"Of course not. Just a lovely photo of the governor and First Lady sitting next to me on the veranda of their mansion."

"They have a veranda?" I asked.

Trina laughed. "That's very Southern of them."

"A lovely one," Peach explained. "But anyway, Hector was in my lap looking like the sweet, good boy he is. The photographers got the loveliest shot of the four of us."

"Five," Reverend Nelson said. "I was there too."

"Oh, right." Peach flashed him a playful smile. "You were, weren't you?"

He quirked a brow.

"Did anything else happen that we need to be made aware of?" Trina asked.

"Well, there was that moment when they brought out Jax, their cocker spaniel." Ms. Peach shivered. "In all fairness, I did warn them that Hector has never been much for canines."

"That's true. It took months for him to acclimate to Beau Jangles," Mari said.

"Thank God our governor has a sense of humor," Reverend Nelson said. "He just took to singing 'Who Let the Dogs Out,' and it turned into a concert."

"Yes, and by the end of our visit, he said he fully understood the lyrics of Trina's song," Peach added.

"No doubt." Trina erupted in laughter.

"And the First Lady promised she'd come visit Brenham," Peach added. "I'm taking her to the Blue Bell factory for a tour. I promised them both that Hector would stay at home in his catio. They seemed intrigued that he has his own space in my house."

"Join the crowd," Mari said and then laughed.

"Anyway, it was a wonderful visit." Peach beamed with obvious joy. "If anyone had told me I'd one day sit in the governor's mansion because of my cat, I wouldn't have believed it."

"Well, it's not really because of Hector, Mama," Trina said. "I'd like to think I had a little something to do with it."

"Right, right." Peach shrugged. "You've somehow managed to take pieces of my life and set them to music."

"You're welcome."

"Maybe the president will call next," Wyatt suggested.

"Oh my goodness." Peach clutched her pearls. "I just can't even imagine going all the way to the White House with Hector."

"I can't either." Trina's brows elevated. "Should we call ahead and ask for the medical team to be on standby, just in case?"

"Goofy girl." Peach jabbed Trina with her elbow. "Hector's not that bad."

"He's not that good either," Trina muttered under her breath.

Peach glanced at her husband, then back at her daughter and grand-daughter. "Truth is, we're already planning our next trip in the fifth wheel, a few weeks out. Howard's got a hankerin' to see the changing of the leaves, so we're headed east to Tennessee. We're leaving the last week in October. If the president does call, I won't be far away."

Trina looked stunned by this news. "Mama, you're going to Tennessee?"

"Sure, honey. But it's a couple weeks from now, so don't you fret."

"That's not my point. I lived in Nashville for years. You hardly ever came to see me there."

"Sure I did."

"Once."

"Well, I hear the leaves are beautiful in the fall."

"Yes," Trina said. "You heard that from me. Dozens of times, as I tried to talk you into coming for a visit. But you were always too tied to Brenham because of Hector."

"You have to admit, he has been an integral part of my life. And what a life it's been." Her face lit up. "I have you to thank for my recent blessings, Trina." Peach slipped her arm around Trina's waist. "You made this silly old woman proud."

"Proud of me or proud of Hector?" Trina asked.

"Of you, of course." She paused and a thoughtful look came over her. "I was always proud of Hector."

Trina slapped herself on the forehead. "Um, thanks? I think?"

"Well, I didn't put that right, I suppose." Peach's eyes filled with tears. "You know I'm proud of you, honey. I'm proud of both my girls." She looked back and forth between Mari and Trina.

"Your mama would've been so proud of you, Mari." Peach's eyes filled with tears. "And even though she wasn't able to be here with you on your wedding day, I can't help but think she was watching over you, offering her love and well-wishes."

Mari's eyes flooded with tears, and she threw her arms around her grandmother's neck. "I love you, Grandma Peach!"

"If you get too mushy on me, you're just going to give Trina more fodder for songs," Peach said. "Not that I really mind being the center of attention where her songs are concerned."

"Where *anything* is concerned," Trina said. "Oh, but you've reminded me of something, Mama! Hang on a minute. I'll be right back."

She took off out the door, and we watched through the glass as she headed to her truck. A couple minutes later, Trina came back in with her guitar case.

"Are we about to have a concert?" Reverend Nelson asked.

"We are. I think y'all are gonna like this one." Trina pulled the guitar out of the case, her face bright with excitement. "I'm pretty sure I really did it this time."

"What?" Mari asked. "What did you do, Aunt Trina?"

"I wrote a new song you're all going to love. Well, I hope you are. Want to hear a few bars?"

We all responded with a resounding yes.

Trina took a seat in a chair at the end of the table, strummed a few chords, and then started singing her new song.

About Mane and Tail horse shampoo.

At first I thought it was a joke, but by the time she came back around to the chorus for the second time, most of the ladies in the room were tapping their toes and attempting to sing along with her.

"Is this some kind of a joke?" Corey whispered in my ear.

"Nope. Country songs are sacred around here."

"Well, yeah. . .but she's singing about shampoo." He slipped his arm over my shoulder and leaned in close so I could hear his hushed words.

Or maybe he leaned in close because he wanted to lean in close.

Either way, I didn't mind it one little bit.

"You might *think* she's singing about shampoo," I said. "That would be a logical conclusion to draw. But, as with any country song, there's always some sort of story buried deep within the lyrics if one is paying attention."

He quirked a brow. "Are you calling these lyrics deep? 'Cause all I heard was something about Bubba's Weed & Feed and two-stepping shampoo bubbles."

"That's what you heard with your ears," I said. "But it's what you hear with your heart that matters."

"Um, my heart heard a song about swapping out fancy salons for ordinary shampoo."

I turned and gave him an encouraging smile. "That's it! You've just proven my point. There's always a deeper story if you're willing to open your heart to it."

"Whelp, if horse shampoo is deep, then I must be pretty shallow."

I couldn't help but laugh at that. He hadn't figured out the gist of Trina's tune just yet. She'd turned in her fancy Nashville life—with all of its glitz and glam—for the simple life on a ranch in Brenham.

Sure, the horse shampoo angle was a little hokey. In fact, Mane and Tail was pretty much the goofiest country song I'd ever heard in my life.

Which, of course, led me to believe it would be a terrific success, possibly even hitting #1 on the country charts. . .right behind Trina's best-selling single about a now-infamous cat named Hector who had won the hearts of millions, not just here in Brenham, but all the way to the governor's mansion and beyond.

CHAPTER THIRTY-EIGHT

January

On the second Sunday in January, I traveled with Carmela and her fiancé, Curtis Elban, to Houston for a much-awaited playoff game. My parents met me there.

We made our way through the crowd to our seats, which were as close to the fifty-yard line as anyone dared dream.

You could feel the excitement in the air. Everyone was buzzing with excitement, especially my father, who couldn't keep still. Corey had done it. He'd turned Pop into a football fan. I wasn't sure when it had happened...but it had happened.

My father finally took his seat and turned my way. "I can't believe we're sitting here at the playoffs." He unfolded a Texans blanket and placed it over his knees.

"It was so good of Corey to get us the tickets." Mama beamed as she turned her attention to the field. "Not every mother can say that her daughter's boyfriend is the star quarterback for the Houston Texans and led them all the way to the playoffs."

No, they couldn't. But Corey had done exactly that, and I had enjoyed every single minute of the journey with him. It didn't hurt that I was able to see most of the games in person these days. I couldn't help but think that Little Lita would have been giddy over all this.

"Not every father can say his daughter's fella bought him a top-of-the-line riding lawn mower for Christmas." My father beamed as he adjusted the blanket. "But I can!"

Pop had paid him back in more ways than Corey could have imagined. His carpentry skills had really been put to work on that River Oaks mansion, turning it into more of a home and less of a show piece.

"Who wants a soda?" my father asked. "I'm so thirsty I feel like I'm walking across the Sahara. Corey gave me some concession stand vouchers, and I want to use them."

"Root beer for me," Mama said.

"Just a bottle of water for me, Pop," I said. "Thanks."

Carmela and Elban both asked for Dr Pepper, and I quickly changed my order to Dr Pepper too. Sounded good.

Then I turned my attention back to the field. "These are the best seats we've had yet." I couldn't get over the fact that Corey had managed to get us so close to the field. I loved a good game on any day, but watching my beloved Texans in the playoffs? I really was living the dream.

About fifteen minutes later, my father returned with the drink holder, looking a bit frazzled. "I don't think I'll do that again. It's a mob scene out there."

"Well, these are the playoffs," I said. NRG Stadium felt a lot fuller than usual. Hopefully, today's game would go well and Corey would lead the team all the way to the Super Bowl. I was praying to that end. So was he. But if it didn't happen, I knew he would still be okay. He had fallen in love with Texas. . .and with me.

"How's Ginger doing?" Pop asked as he took a seat and passed our drinks over.

"She loves my house, and she loves Corey's house. She's a happy girl."

I was a happy girl too. These past several months had been a whirlwind. Corey and I bounced back and forth between Houston and Brenham, spending as many hours together as our crazy schedules would allow. And Ginger—God bless her—had acclimated beautifully.

"Did I show you the costume Ms. Peach made her?" I pulled up a picture of a Texans costume.

Pop laughed as he saw it. "Now *that's* a dog costume I can get on board with."

"I want some for my pups," Mama said. "Do you think she'll make some for us?"

"Maybe when she gets back in town. Ms. Peach and her husband are off to see the president."

"Of the United States?" Mama's eyes widened.

"No, of the Country Music Association. But it might as well be the president of the United States. She's so excited. But when she gets back in town, I'll ask if she can whip up a couple of costumes for your babies."

I didn't have time to say much more. The Texans entered the field with fans screaming their welcome. Corey sought me out through the crowd. I caught his eye and gave him a little wave. He returned it with a smile and a wave of his own.

And then the game began.

The Texans played an amazing first quarter, and the second was even better. I'd never seen my father so hyped.

Okay, scratch that. Astros. World Series.

Still, Pop was all in on this game, and that did my heart proud. Curtis and Carmela had lost their voices by the end of the second quarter. Mine was rapidly going too. Only Mama seemed unfazed by all of this. A little distracted, even.

When the halftime show started, I decided I'd better make a quick trip to the bathroom. I rose and said, "I'll be right back."

Only, Mama wouldn't let me leave.

"Wait till this is over, honey," she said. "You don't want to miss anything. It's supposed to be a really good show this time."

"I'm deliberately going during halftime," I explained. "So I don't miss any of the game."

Only, she wouldn't take no for an answer, so I plopped back down in my seat. I reached for my phone, realizing I had a string of messages coming through, most from my friends at the clinic. They were all pretty jealous that I was here and they weren't.

There was a cute picture of Ginger dressed in her Texans ensemble. Corey must've sent it. But. . .when? Judging from the background, it wasn't sent from his house. Weird. Looked like the message had just come through.

Before I could give it any more thought, the SkyCam traveled the crowd and homed in on this person and that. Folks waved at the camera, and some of the couples even kissed. Cute.

I nearly lost my breath when the camera landed on me. And stayed there.

"What in the world?" I shoved my phone in my purse.

Then, over the booming loudspeaker, I heard a voice. A familiar voice. Calling my name.

I glanced down onto the field and gasped as I saw Corey walking to the center of the fifty-yard line dressed not in a uniform but in a tuxedo.

Walking alongside him, fastened to a leash, was Ginger. In her Texans getup.

I couldn't wrap my head around this. Everything faded to a blur.

"See?!" Mama said. "I told you that you couldn't leave!"

I glanced her way, stunned. "Mama, what's going on?"

"Keep your eye on the prize, honey," Pop said. "This is the playoffs."

So I did. I kept my eye on the man—and the dog—on the field.

And when Corey instructed me to join him, I almost felt my knees give out from under me.

"You can do this, sweet girl," Carmela said. "Go get him."

I rose and somehow made my way through the throng of people to the small opening leading to the field where one of the coaches awaited me. He led me to the center of the field and placed my hand in Corey's.

The roar of the crowd was deafening. I could barely hear myself think. So, instead of thinking, I just focused on those eyes. Those brilliant, loving, compassionate blue eyes.

Until Ginger started doing that yo-yo thing and ended up in my arms. I cuddled her close, tears springing to my eyes as Corey—my wonderful, gentle Corey—dropped to one knee.

Which only served to activate the crowd even more.

He asked the question.

I responded with a tearful, "Yes!"

He reached for a ring.

And Ginger bounded out of my arms and tried to snag the box from him.

Which only got the crowd more worked up than ever.

Corey wrangled the box back from the ornery pooch, who took to rolling around on the field in playful fashion. Then he somehow managed to get that ring on my finger before sweeping me in his arms.

The kiss that followed was memorable, but what really stood out was what flashed through my mind as the cameras all went off and "Here Comes the Bride" began to play loudly overhead— I could almost hear Little Lita's voice above all the chaos and confusion as she hollered out the most heavenly word of all: *Touchdown!*

JANICE THOMPSON, who lives in the Houston area, writes novels, nonfiction, magazine articles, and musical comedies for the stage. The mother of four married daughters, she is quickly adding grandchildren to the family mix.

GONE *to the* DOGS *Series*

Grab a lapdog to cuddle and relax into a
fun small-town Texas mystery series.

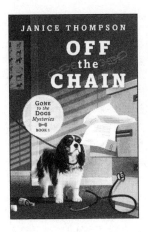

OFF THE CHAIN
(Book 1)

BY JANICE THOMPSON

Marigold and her coworkers at Lone Star Vet
Clinic only want to help animals, but someone
is determined to see them put out of business.

Paperback / 978-1-63609-313-0

DOG DAYS OF SUMMER
(Book 2)

BY KATHLEEN Y'BARBO

Country music star Trina Potter is back in
town to help her niece start a dog rescue,
but more than one person wants to send her
packing back to Nashville.

Paperback / 978-1-63609-394-9

BARKING UP THE WRONG TREE
(Book 3)

BY JANICE THOMPSON

Veterinarian Kristin Keller is determined to figure out why her star patient is suddenly acting like a very different dog just days before his next big agility competition.

Paperback / 978-1-63609-451-9

THE BARK OF ZORRO
(Book 4)

BY KATHLEEN Y'BARBO

Someone is spray-painting local dogs with the letter Z. The cops blame pranksters while pet owners are blaming each other.

Paperback / 978-1-63609-517-2

Find this series and more great fiction wherever books are sold and at www.barbourbooks.com

BARBOUR
PUBLISHING